HIDE
IN
PLACE

HIDE IN PLACE

A NOVEL

EMILYA NAYMARK

CROOKED
LANE

NEW YORK

Published in the United States by Crooked Lane Books, an imprint of The Quick Brown Fox & Company LLC.

Crooked Lane Books and its logo are trademarks of The Quick Brown Fox & Company LLC.

Library of Congress Catalog-in-Publication data available upon request.

ISBN (hardcover): 978-1-64385-637-7
ISBN (ebook): 978-1-64385-638-4

Cover design by Kara Klontz

Printed in the United States.

www.crookedlanebooks.com

Crooked Lane Books
34 West 27th St., 10th Floor
New York, NY 10001

First Edition: February 2021

10 9 8 7 6 5 4 3 2 1

For Keith and Ian.
My heart and soul.

PART ONE

CHAPTER

1

Laney Bird's son vanished the night she drove a busload of high school seniors to see *Wicked* on Broadway. He left home before she did, loping down their driveway toward marching band practice, his saxophone case swinging in his hand.

"Stew in the Crock-Pot!" she yelled at his retreating back. "I'll be home by eleven!"

He waved without turning around, a shimmy of raised fingers in the raw February wind.

The bus smelled like bologna sandwiches, fruity body sprays, and old soda and sounded like a monkey house. But she was used to it. And she needed the extra money.

Once the students erupted into the glittery Manhattan night, she parked and texted him but heard nothing back. This concerned her, though not overwhelmingly so. She figured he'd stayed late for practice or left his phone in his backpack on vibrate. She tried to nap. Listened to the radio. Played a game on her phone.

As icy rain turned to snow, the students clambered back on the bus, collapsing against green seats and smudged windows, and she carted them homeward through tortuous, storm-soured traffic toward upstate New York and their waiting families.

She wasn't home by eleven.

Laney walked into her empty, dark house a few minutes past midnight and dumped her keys onto the key dish by the front door. Alfie's saxophone did not trip her as it usually did, but she barely noticed, the long day hitting her hard.

After wriggling out of her bra (through her sleeves, blessed relief) and toeing off her shoes, she tipped the lid from the Crock-Pot and paused, unease needling her.

The beef and potatoes had gone cold, congealed. Untouched. She dropped her bra to a chair and walked over to Alfie's room. His door was open and, when she flipped the light switch, his bed neat, empty.

With shaking fingers, she called his phone, then again, and again. Again. The line rang through to voice mail every time. The GPS Phone Tracker showed him a block from school at five PM, then nothing. He had either disabled the app or powered off his phone, both of which she had forbidden him to ever do.

Between the frantic phone calls, she glanced in every room and closet, climbed into the drafty attic, then into the dank basement, calling his name as if he were a toddler playing hide-and-seek and not a mercurial thirteen-year-old.

He was still not home by one AM, when Laney rang and woke the few parents whose sons bothered with Alfie. They answered their phones with voices groggy or scared, turning quickly to irritation. He wasn't with any of them. But she'd known that before she called and made the calls anyway out of some dim, crazed hope. He never visited other kids, never texted, wasn't, as far as she knew, active on any social media.

At one thirty AM she screeched into the Sylvan PD's parking lot, knocking over a garbage can as she slammed on the brakes. Sylvan, a sedate hamlet in Rockland County, population less than nine thousand, slumbered under a cloud-swept sky, and the station house in the middle of the night on a Tuesday was quiet.

Laney burst into the building, then hesitated as the doors clanged shut behind her. Ed Boswell was the desk officer on duty, and if he was not exactly the last person she wanted to see, he was right up there in the top five candidates.

"Laney," said Ed, turning his eyes from the screen, where, no doubt, he'd been watching the latest episode of *CSI*. He'd told Laney once it was his favorite show, and the midnight shift in Sylvan was so slow he usually spent at least half of it bingeing on some TV series or other.

It's not that she thought he was a bad police officer. He was all right, calm and steady, with a slow way of looking at every problem even when the problem required immediate, ten-alarm action. Laney had been a cop herself before her personal life imploded. In her deplorably short career with the NYPD, Laney had risen to detective and worked three years as an undercover, first in the Bronx, then in Brighton Beach.

As Ed Boswell clicked something on his computer, *tsk*ed in irritation, clicked again, then looked at her, she wished, not for the first time, she could call her ex-partner. But he didn't work in Sylvan. Ed did. Ed, who knew nothing of her past, nothing of the shield she'd earned by doing countless buy-and-busts, of her skills, her extensive knowledge of police procedures. Ed, who saw only what everyone else in Sylvan saw when they looked at her—a bus-driving single mom of an odd boy—and treated her problems with her child accordingly.

"It's Alfie," she said, her voice coming shrill and taut from her throat, hurting her. "He's not home. Hasn't come home."

"Again?" asked Ed.

His eyes settled on her (with pity? condescension?), and she realized she'd run out of the house in her slippers, her coat still hanging on its hook in the hall and her bra on a kitchen chair.

Ed glanced at the window, where a wet sleet had started to slap against the glass. The storm had traveled north and was just beginning to hit their town.

"Did you check the high school?" he asked, just as Laney knew he would, because he'd been on desk duty the last time Alfie decided to disappear.

"The school is locked," Laney said, thinking this should have been obvious, schools were like fortresses nowadays, hermetically sealed after hours. But she was not the cop, she reminded herself. Not anymore.

She said, "He's not answering phone calls or texts. He's disabled the phone tracker. I called three families who have sons he's friends with"—to describe them as friends was a stretch, and she knew Ed knew this and her face colored—"and he's with none of them. I left a message for his band teacher. Alfie was scheduled for band practice this afternoon. Prior to that he came home from school as usual at two fifteen, had a snack"—she paused, swallowed; that was the last time she'd spoken with him—"a PBJ sandwich, did his homework, then left for practice at four fifty. He was supposed to be home before seven."

She closed her eyes, running through anything else she might have done, anything else she should say, but all she could envision was Alfie's back in his maroon parka as he strode down the slippery driveway, saxophone case in hand, blond hair escaping from under his black knit cap. She hadn't even hugged him, just waved as he stepped past her for the three-block walk to the high school.

Ed sighed and typed something. "I'm sure he's fine, Laney. He's done this before. We'll have a patrol car out to the school."

But it wasn't the same, Laney wanted to scream. That last time, a month ago, she and Alfie had had an argument—a real, honest-to-God shouting and crying fest. She had (had she really?) slapped him and ransacked his room for the drugs she was sure he'd hidden there. His blown-out pupils, his clammy skin, his overly cautious movements, as if he didn't trust his own limbs, terrified her, reminded her of the lost souls she'd had to lock up in the past. He cried, bawled, his face red and swollen, a child, even though he was thirteen and would be fourteen soon, in two more months. He denied everything, and by morning she had to admit she might have overreacted—the years buying drugs on the street as an undercover had skewed her vision, darkened her interpretations of the most normal behaviors. He might have simply been fighting off a cold. Mightn't he?

By morning it was too late to make amends. Alfie had left and didn't come home until the next day. Afterward, after the missing-child reports had been filed and alerts issued to local police, after hours of searching, Alfie simply walked up the driveway and into their living room. He'd spent the night in the school theater's backstage, among the dress forms and discarded curtains. In the morning he'd washed in the gym locker room, ate in the cafeteria, and walked to the frozen lake a mile away, where he spent a few hours sliding along the thick ice until he grew cold and hungry, at which point he came home.

Laney wanted to ground him, punish him, take away screen privileges for running away, because didn't he know what he meant to her, didn't he know he was all the family she had in the world? But the sight of him, tall, pale, thin, worried about her reaction, destroyed any disciplinarian instincts, and she clung to him wordlessly. She then cooked them a big pasta dinner.

And after she put away the dishes and Tupperwared the leftovers, she installed the GPS Phone Tracker on his phone.

"Look," Ed said, "I'm sending the patrol car out now. We'll start at the school. How about you go home and get warm. We'll call you as soon as we find him. What's the band teacher's name? Is that Mr. Andersen?"

So placid. So sure. Laney ground the heels of her hands into her eyes. It's possible she was overreacting again. But what did Ed know of her and Alfie? Certainly she hadn't told him—or anybody—the reason Alfie skedaddled the last time, of that god-awful argument. Most depressingly, nobody who knew her had asked why he might have disappeared then, not even Ed Boswell, who had taken the report and should have.

Alfie was strange, a loner, prone to both inappropriate outbursts and intense shyness, and never mind his near expulsion following the fall talent show. Consequently, any strange behavior from him was not surprising. Certainly not to Ed, whose son was also a Boy Scout in Alfie's troop. That's how Laney and Ed knew each other, through their children, even though Ed's son ignored Alfie at best and sometimes, when he thought no parents were in hearing distance, ridiculed him with the sharp, callous cleverness of the smart and popular.

"So," she said, trying to keep her voice neutral, "should I tell you what he was wearing?"

"Oh." Ed peered at the paperwork in front of him. "Yes, let's do that. What was he wearing?"

She pictured Alfie, her stomach clenching with fear. Where was he? Things had improved lately. A lot. He'd been sweet, even-tempered, talkative with her, had even been mentioning a friend.

"Blue-and-gray-striped sweater, horizontal stripes. Dark-blue jeans"—skinny cut, Christmas present and already floods on him two months later—"white socks, black sneakers, maroon parka, black watch cap. He had his sax with him when he left."

Ed sat back and sighed. "Got it. He's fine, Laney, really. It's Sylvan, not the inner city. Go home. I'll call you as soon as we find him."

She nodded, her eyes welling, then gestured to the hallway. "Gonna use the ladies'," she said, already walking toward the bathroom.

It wasn't so much that she minded crying in front of people—she really didn't. Feelings were feelings and everyone had them. But being inside the station brought back her old ways. Cops didn't blubber, and if you were a female cop, you better keep yourself zipped shut or you'd never hear the end of it. She splashed cold water on her face and dried off with a paper towel, kneading it into a tight, brown ball before shoving it into the metal bin.

A little of Ed's sureness had penetrated her swooping panic, and she felt a touch easier now. He was right about one thing—Sylvan was not the inner city. The nearly nonexistent crime rate and country setting were why she had moved here in the first place. Alfie was being his difficult self. That was all.

She walked out of the bathroom tired but composed, willing to let the situation take its course, if only until morning.

On her way out, she passed an office and would have kept walking except she heard Alfie's name. She stopped just behind the doorway, keeping out of sight.

"That kid's got problems," said a man's voice. "Listen, I had to come out five times last fall to the high school because of him. Five times! What's he even doing in a normal school? Shouldn't he be up in Pinelane?"

"Apparently not," another man answered. "I know what you mean, though." He sighed. "That boy is overtime waiting to happen. And it doesn't make me happy to say it."

"What? You not happy about overtime?" the first man said.

"You know what I mean. What if your kid was like that?"

"Nope, not me. That's why I ain't having kids. I got snipped."

Laney looked up to see Ed coming toward her, his lips a line across his face. Without saying anything to her, he marched into the office and said, "I'm happy to hear you won't be reproducing, Raguzzi. Now get the hell to work and shut the fuck up."

She turned and ran out into the spewing snow, her slippers instantly soaked and her face burning with shame and guilt and worry.

2

Laney's alarm bellowed dutifully at four thirty AM, as if it were to be any normal day. She hadn't gone to bed after reporting Alfie missing, instead dropping into a restive unconscious state on the couch, the woolen throw bunched under her knees.

Yesterday at this time she'd risen from bed, showered and dressed (no makeup, quick comb through short hair), cooked a cheese omelet for Alfie, left it covered in the skillet, grabbed a bagel from the fridge, and drove to work.

Driving for the school district paid the bills (allowed her to scrape by) and provided desperately needed health insurance. Most crucially, it meant she was home after school, during vacations, snow days. When her life upheaved three years ago and left her a single parent of an anxious, tantrum-prone, school-hating ten-year-old boy with a stutter, being his protector and companion became her top priority. God knew he had no one else.

She loved being home for him, loved the movie nights, the pizza nights, loved sitting cross-legged in the armchair as he practiced the saxophone or the piano or did his speech exercises. As the years passed, her presence grew less important to him (she felt), and this was okay, was as it should be. Was, if anything, proof that he was maturing, that she was doing a good job.

Wasn't she?

Laney checked her phone, plugged it in to make sure it was charged. It was. She opened her laptop and checked her email. Nothing from the police, nothing from Alfie.

She dialed his number again, and again, and again. Ten times, then another ten times. Texted him. Tried the phone tracker once more. Nothing, nothing, nothing. Silence.

Her eyes burned and she was both exhausted and wired, her worry a bitterness in her throat. She started coffee, dropped bread into the toaster.

As a cop, she'd handled a few missing-child cases. Most had turned out fine. With hope, she remembered an eight-year-old girl who'd decided to visit a cousin across town without telling anyone and had spent a comfortable afternoon YouTubing and Minecraft-ing before Laney pinned her location using "some class A detective skills," as her sergeant put it. But it wasn't that case that made acid wash up her gullet as she took a bite of buttered toast.

It was a boy—Alfie's age exactly at the time, nine—who'd begged and begged his parents to let him walk alone the one block from the bus stop to his apartment. He never made it home. Three days later Laney's team broke down the door of the neighborhood drunkard and found the boy's cut-up legs in the man's freezer.

She spit the toast into a napkin and covered her face. That's the thing about being a cop, even when your cop days were behind you—you think you can beat the bad guys. You train and prac-tice. You walk around with twenty pounds of equipment strapped to your hips. And the bad guys do what they will anyway. If you're lucky, you get them. If you're very, very, very lucky, you get them before they cut a nine-year-old boy into foot-long pieces.

Her cell rang, and she jumped, spilling coffee over the table, dropped the phone, grabbed it with slippery-wet fingers, jabbed at it until it finally answered the call.

"Hello?" She was breathless, her voice strangled, thin.

"Laney? You weren't sleeping, were you?"

Goddammit, it was her supervisor, Janine. Laney'd forgotten to call in sick. She should have been at the garage fifteen minutes ago.

"Janine, no, sorry, no, I wasn't sleeping." Then, quickly, to fill the silence, "Listen, I can't come in today. I'm sorry, I can't."

Janine sighed. Laney pictured her eyebrows rising, her mouth pursing, her manicured fingers tapping her desk. "Laney, you're putting me in a difficult spot. There are other people to consider. Children will be waiting. I know you know this, and I know you're not a fuck-up, but what am I supposed to do?"

Laney couldn't imagine going to work, driving for hours while Alfie was who knows where. But she needed this job. She barely made the rent every month as it was, and who would pay for Alfie's speech therapy if she lost her insurance? The therapy had been helping. His stutter had all but disappeared in the past six months.

"You're right," she said, her tone all wrong—resigned instead of remorseful, sad instead of diplomatic. "I'll be there in ten minutes. I'll work an extra shift if you need me to make up for it. Okay?"

"Laney, I don't know what's going on with you, but this is your job. If you can't be professional, you might need to start looking for something else."

She pressed her fingers into her eyes. She'd have to beg. "It's Alfie. He's gone." Beg, yet reassure. "But the police are on it. They're looking for him. So, I can come in. Just give me ten minutes."

Usually that's all it took, showing Janine how much of a mess she, Laney, was, so that Janine could feel safe and secure in her universe by comparison. But now a tense silence stretched between them.

Laney couldn't count how many times she'd called in sick or taken personal days. For two years she'd had to take personal days without pay, since she would usually burn through all her allotted time off by May or June—Alfie's meltdowns, the anxiety attacks, and once, the suicide threat.

Not that she'd ever told anyone about that. She'd barely even processed it herself. When he said it, she had grabbed his shoulders, knelt before him, and told him that if he killed himself, she'd die too, so unless he wanted to be responsible for killing his mother, he better eject that thought right out. She stared into his eyes until she saw the agony in them transform to garden-variety sadness, at which point she pressed him to her chest so tight she felt his heart rat-a-tat-tatting. He never said it again, and she would not think of it now. She would go insane if she did, and then she'd be no use to him at all when he came back.

"Janine, are we good? I'm on my way." And yet she didn't hang up, wasn't on her way. This silence was different than usual.

"I'm so sorry, Laney. I hope your son is okay." More silence. More sighing. "Look, every time you don't come in like this, I get dozens of calls from pissed-off parents. I don't want to sound like I don't care about your situation, because I do. I feel for you." The next silence was brief. "But I just can't keep doing this. I need drivers I can rely on. I'm going to give your route to another driver for now. Call me after the February break, and we'll see if there's something else for you here. Okay?"

Laney nodded at the phone. "Okay."

That was that, and she couldn't think about it now. Later. Later, when Alfie came home, she'd let him have it, show him how his selfishness was destroying them.

She cursed, grabbed her parka, shoved her feet into her boots and barreled outside. The night's storm had expended itself, and the roads were slick, slushy, ugly. She'd walk. She'd go to the lake. Alfie liked the lake, loved the woods surrounding their tiny house. Maybe he was camping out. Though why he'd do that in the middle of a sleet storm, she didn't know. But then again, there were many things Alfie did that she couldn't understand.

She checked her phone. And almost walked into Holly.

CHAPTER

3

HOLLY, MIDTHIRTIES, PETITE, girly in a pink knit hat and a fitted pink puffy jacket, gently touched Laney's shoulder. Laney had never had a friend like Holly; as a teenager she had found girls like Holly silly, even pointless. Coming from a family both strict and overprotective, Laney had been athletic, no-nonsense, the NYPD her goal from toddlerhood. She'd never had a mani-pedi, despised high heels, owned just one dress.

And yet, over the three years she'd lived on this woody, lovely street, Holly, who'd die before leaving her house without lipstick (was even at this unholy hour wearing a soft-pink gloss) had become her best friend. Funny, sociable, genteel in an almost old-fashioned way, Holly never judged, never gave Laney advice, laughed at her jokes. Hell, laughed at Alfie's jokes.

"I saw all the lights on," Holly said. "What's going on?"

Laney's supervisor wasn't the only person overly familiar with Laney's sudden schedule changes.

"Is Alfie all right?"

"He's gone!" Laney said, then shook her head to forestall questions. "I don't know where. I've been to the police." She peered at the snowy path winding into the woods from her house. It was still dark, the streetlight a stark yellow cone through the shadows. "Why are you up?"

"Oh, Buster was asking for a pee." Buster was Holly's tiny shih tzu—a grayish-white bundle snuggled in the crook of her arm. "Then I saw you, and I know you're usually gone by now." She shrugged. "Thought I'd see what's up." She took in Laney's face. "Let me get Buster home, and then I'll come and help you. Okay?"

"I was going to walk to the lake," Laney said.

"I'll walk with you. Just give me a minute."

As she waited for Holly to come back, Laney called the station house. Ed picked up the phone.

"No," he said when she asked. "Alfie's not at the school. Yes, we checked the basement. Yes, the kitchen too. And the locker rooms. Yes, the auditorium. No, there's nobody in the building now, and it doesn't look like he was there overnight. He's not at the lake. Yes, we sent a description of him to all local patrol cars and to the nearest towns too. Everyone's aware, yes. We're looking for him, Laney. We'll find him. Aha. Yes. Oh, and be sure to call us when he comes home, okay? Yes, I know you know to do that. Okay. Got it. We're on it. Good-bye. Yes. Okay."

By the time she hung up, she'd started sweating. She knew the cops were going by the book, following the patrol guide. She knew they'd filed all the right papers, filled out all the necessary forms online. And yet. She could hear in Ed's voice that he thought Alfie was just being Alfie. Not knowing where her son was or the reasons for his absence oppressed her, and she tried to find comfort in Ed's evident confidence. She should refrain from imagining the worst. Her child was not an infant, was taller than she, could hold his own if cornered.

God! Had he been cornered?

She turned to the road he'd taken to walk to school yesterday afternoon. Surely the weather had destroyed any evidence by now, washed away shoe prints, car tracks. But she walked down the slippery path anyway, head down, feet toeing debris for anything out of the ordinary. She glanced at Holly as the woman joined her.

"I just spoke to Ed Boswell. Alfie's not at the lake," she said, and her friend changed direction, matched her pace to Laney's.

Tall, shaggy pines shook with icy drops overhead as she and Holly made their way slowly toward the school, the frozen ground crunching under their boots. Having grown up and lived most of her life in Long Island in an overcrowded colonial on a lot just big enough for a carpet-sized front lawn and a patio-sized backyard, Laney invariably marveled at the violent and wild beauty of her new hometown.

"I started a Facebook post for you," Holly said.

Laney squinted at her friend. "For me?"

"You know, have you seen this boy, share it." Holly looked ahead. "It helps. Kids have been found this way."

"Isn't that what you did when Buster ran off?"

"Yes. Anyway, it just proves my point. People will see the post."

Laney sighed. "Okay. Why not." They walked for a few minutes in silence. "Thank you. I should have thought of that."

"Hmm . . . You would have. How's he been? I mean lately?"

She'd been asking herself the same question over and over for the past five hours, barring the hour or two when she dozed fitfully on her couch. "Good. Weird, right? I can't think of a single bad day in the past month." Not since that last time. He'd been golden. "He's sweet. He did great on his geometry test. Last week he did my laundry as well as his. He even talked about school. A bit. But still." She raised her eyes to the lightening sky. "I thought he made a leap, you know? Progress."

They slid on the hard snow but caught each other, hands on forearms, knees against thighs. A crow cawed above them, pushed away from a bough, and flapped into the forest, sending white flurries onto their heads.

Holly opened her mouth, closed it. Took a breath, opened her mouth again, closed it again.

"Go on," said Laney. "Out with it." She had an inkling what her friend would say.

"Do you think he was covering something? You know, something was going on and he was being good so you wouldn't get suspicious?"

Yep, it was what she thought Holly would say. "Tell you what," Laney said. "If he developed that kind of self-control, my job here is done. But it's not impossible. He's bright enough."

"No one says he's not bright. Or that he has to playact to pretend being sweet. He's a very sweet boy."

A part of Laney was so ridiculously grateful to Holly for her words that she had to fight the urge to grab her friend and hug the crap out of that pink puffy jacket. She couldn't afford getting emotional right now. If she did, she'd be no use to her son or anyone.

They started to walk again, carefully. "What would you do if you were the detective on the case?" Holly asked.

Laney kicked a fallen branch out of the way. "I'd start by talking with everyone who saw him yesterday."

"Well, it's early. Nobody's up yet. I'm sure the police will do that."

"Yes."

"What?"

"What do you mean, what?"

"Your voice. You don't think the police will do that?"

"I don't know, Holly. Will they? I would if I were investigating a missing child in the city, sure. But here in *Country Home and Gardens* Sylvan? I get the feeling they're just waiting for Alfie to mosey on out of the woods all on his own." There was a time she'd been a damn good detective. Even better than she'd been an undercover, and she'd been excellent at that. Maybe Ed's colleagues would do everything they had to. But would the kids talk to them? Would the teachers?

While still on the job, Laney learned that people got all weird around a uniform. They held their bodies differently. They used big words inaccurately. They wouldn't volunteer information. When she interviewed witnesses or suspects wearing a suit, she'd get slightly more cooperation. As an undercover, in shorts and tees, her hair mussed, she could get anybody to tell her anything.

"What?" Holly had stopped with her. "What? What are you thinking?"

"You're right," Laney said.

"I am?"

"I need to go home. I've got people to interview."

4

D URING ALFIE'S THREE years' enrollment in the Sylvan school district, Laney had been called to see the principal fifty-four times. She knew exactly how many because starting with the thirteenth visit—"Lucky thirteen, eh?"—the principal made it a point to give her the count every time she walked through the door. On her twenty-fifth visit, after Alfie had collapsed in stutter-fueled agony in French class, he'd said, "What, no silver anniversary present?"

Sometimes she tried to remember what she'd fantasized her child would be, before she had him, when Alfie was only a teeny bean inside her uterus and every possibility seemed magic. She was certain she'd never envisioned fifty-four visits to the principal.

Her pregnancy had been miraculous to her, a gift from an otherwise greedy God who had taken her entire family before she'd turned eighteen—parents by a his-and-hers calamity of cancers, brother following shortly by suicide.

She was in her first year at John Jay College of Criminal Justice when she met Theo and a year out of the police academy when she fell pregnant. And just like that, at twenty-two, she was part of a family again.

Theo moved his easels and paints and brushes and took over her brother's bedroom as his studio, and the little colonial on

Long Island ten minutes from the beach where she'd grown up was once again full of chatter and love and family dinners. And wine. Bottles upon bottles upon bottles of it, rubied or golden, refracting warm light throughout the rooms.

The division of labor had been an easy decision. She worked; Theo painted and, when he wasn't painting, cared for little Alfie.

As far as Laney saw it, she had a perfect life. She worked the only job she'd ever wanted, and she was good at it. Her husband was a breathtakingly beautiful man who loved her and loved their equally exquisite son. Sure, Alfie was not an easy child, and together they had already accumulated plenty of hours with principals and therapists. But he was hers, molded and baked inside her body, knit from Theo's artistic compulsions and her need to instill order on a chaotic world. No wonder he had difficulties adjusting to changes, following commands, making friends. She accepted him and his troubles, accepted Theo and his moods. They were her family and she was devoted to them.

It was all peaches and kittens until the day (a brutally cold, bleak November day) when she came home from a thirty-six-hour shift, bleary and shaking with sleeplessness, to find Theo sitting at the dining room table, an empty bottle of Pinot Noir by his elbow and a half-empty glass in his hand. Three suitcases crowded his feet, and the way he looked at her woke her real fast.

It's your turn, Theo had told her, then called the cab that would take him to the airport. You deal with him, he'd said. You cook the three things he will consent to eat. You placate the principal, the other parents. You deal with the kids who beat him, who tease him, who hate him. Your turn. It's my turn to focus on me.

And then, before she could ask her question, before she absorbed his announcement, he said, "I don't love you. I don't want this. I don't want you. I don't want him."

He blew away on the wind, scraping aside twelve years of marriage like dung on his shoes. It wasn't until two weeks later that she found out about the credit cards he'd used to buy canvases and paints and brushes and all those bottles upon bottles of (apparently very good) wine, somehow accumulating over eighty thousand dollars' worth of debt.

Although Alfie was ten at the time and much too old for such things, he wore Theo's sweatshirt (old, ratty, stinking of turpentine) every day and night for one month after his father left. He slept in it, crying when Laney tried to take it off. He asked to speak with his dad every day. But when Theo left, he didn't say where he was going, and he didn't answer calls, and he never called back.

"It's my fault," Alfie whispered to her one night, his voice clogged with tears. "Dad's gone because of me."

"No, honey." She gathered him into her arms, even though they were already almost the same size—she'd always been tiny; it was why she was an ideal undercover. "It's his fault. You're awesome."

She watched her son at the bus stop, alone while the other children huddled and laughed and talked. She came to get him when the principal called, when the nurse called, when the school psychologist called. At home, he clung to her like a monkey while she lurched from room to room, his hot face pressed into her neck, his feet hooked around her calves, his chest heaving with suppressed sobs.

In January, as she was back to buy-and-busts in the aftermath of a disastrous Russian mob racketeering case, Alfie broke.

He'd gone to school as usual, silent, eyes downcast, gait slowing as he approached the giant metal doors, led by Laney's occasional babysitter. When a young, male teacher reached for him, intending to help him with his bag, his saxophone case, whatever it was he felt was too much for the little boy, Alfie began to scream. He opened his mouth and shut his eyes and bellowed, howled, shrieked, the startled teacher stepping back with his hands raised and helpless. Alfie fell to the black mud, bucked his legs, his tongue bulging inside his open red mouth.

Blindly, he kicked the teachers who tried to calm him, he punched the frigid, viscous earth, he bathed his bright hair in it. He yelled until his vocal cords broke and he could do nothing but lie in the dirt and heave, shaking.

It took Laney two hours to make her way to the school from Brighton Beach. She'd been assigned to a location far from her last case, but it was clear to her she was already burned. Everyone seemed to know who she was and stayed clear. She had requested a transfer, but who knew how long that would take.

She was still in her undercover makeup and clothes (leather miniskirt, bare legs, low-heeled booties, and a white leather jacket crunkly with zippers). As soon as Alfie saw her, he closed his mouth, got to his knees, then to his feet, then plastered his muddy little body against her. And she held him, rocked him, smoothed his filthy hair, kissed his feverish skin.

Her boy was grieving. She was as well. The way she saw it, the only difference between them was she could control herself and Alfie couldn't.

The school had grown tired of them, no longer knew what to do with Alfie and no longer wanted to know. She understood that too.

She had to choose. She couldn't manage the hours and days that police work demanded and be there for her child. Sure, others did it, but they had a support system—spouses, parents, in-laws, siblings, friends who would step in and watch the children. Who did she have? Only Alfie.

And although she loved her job, adored being an undercover, treasured her alter egos, the trickery, the hunt, she cherished her son above all. And anyway, nothing felt right anymore at work. Nothing felt right anywhere. Moving away seemed the most logical step.

The next day, she put in her resignation. She'd be father, mother, protector, and friend to Alfie. He needed her, and nobody ever again would need her this way.

She sold her parents' house, paid off the credit cards, and rented a three-bedroom colonial in Sylvan—a place she selected precisely for its schools, negative crime rate, and wild, soul-soothing beauty.

But the past lodged inside her, a splinter in her view of the world, shading her interactions with everyone, including her son.

She'd let it come between them the last time he ran away, but God help her, she had no idea what she did wrong this time.

This morning after her walk with Holly, she showered, rubbed a little pomade into her dark curls, made sure her blouse and slacks were without stains and relatively wrinkle-free. She tried to remember what it was like to be on a case, where you had to focus on the details but not miss the big picture, hear everything, write everything down, cast a wide net and then see what got snagged.

As she paced outside Principal Gavin's office, her eyes slid past the familiar display cases of sports awards, academic achievement awards, terrible high school art, a shelf of cockeyed ceramics made in pottery class.

"Mrs. Bird." Principal Gavin opened his door and motioned her in. By the cautious way he assessed her, she knew the police had already spoken to him. "Have you heard anything more?" he asked after she sat down.

By unlucky coincidence, he'd been principal at Alfie's middle school, then took the job as the high school principal just when Alfie entered ninth grade. Laney felt she'd been sitting across from this man way more times than she cared to. Which was about fifty-four times too many.

He'd started out kind and patient but over the years progressed to bewildered, then frustrated; settled for a while on resigned; and now was giving her the kind of look she'd only seen bestowed by judges upon hapless perps at arraignments. Unexpectedly, the fact that he didn't greet her with the visit's number rattled her, under-scoring that everything was different today.

"No, Gerry, I haven't heard anything else," she said. At this point, not only were they on a first-name basis, but she'd made sure to send him, his staff, and his wife holiday baskets before every winter and spring break as appeasements. "I was wondering if you could shed light on some things for me, though."

"Oh? You know, Laney, the police were already here. They're doing a good job." He spread his hands as if to say he was done, had nothing else to say.

"I know. They're awesome." She smiled, a quick flash of teeth. "I was just wondering if maybe I could talk to the people who saw Alfie last." She shrugged. "Just, you know. Talk."

"Well." He folded his hands in front of him on his desk. "How do you mean exactly? You want to talk to his teachers?"

"Yeah. Starting with his band teacher." Laney smiled again, but he didn't. He wrinkled his brows and sighed.

"Laney, the police are already doing that. I can't disrupt everyone's day."

But my son is missing, she wanted to scream.

"I know." She leaned forward, gripped the armrests. "Well, doesn't he have group therapy on Tuesdays? Did he go to that?"

Gerry Gavin looked at his laptop, nodded. "Let me check. Yes, he did. That would be Ms. MacDonnell in room two-oh-eight. I'll ask her to come to the office next period, if you would wait outside."

"Oh." She stood up. "Okay. Thank you."

"Laney. Is everything okay at home? Did you have a fight or something?" It was a natural question, and the implication that Alfie left on his own because of something she'd done or said was a gut punch, not least because it mirrored her own worries. She thought she detected the same condescension in his voice, the same glint of pity in his eyes she'd seen in Ed Boswell's last night.

She looked away. Had they had a fight? Alfie had been taciturn for weeks. Calm, though, and quiet, and sweet. He'd set the table every night and washed the dishes. He did his laundry and his homework. When asked about his day, he said fine, good, no problems, no troubles. When asked about therapy, he said fine, good, we just talked about TV shows and school and music. He'd done well on his last few tests, handed in his projects on time.

She thought he'd been happy. She'd been happy. The night before he disappeared, they watched an episode of *The Walking Dead*, his lanky body draped along the length of the couch, his legs thrown carelessly, companionably over her lap, his stockinged feet dank but not so much that she kicked him off.

"No," she said. "We didn't fight. He seemed good."

5

WAITING FOR THE therapist in the school's hallway gave Laney a chance to observe. Somebody in this school must know something. She was sure of it. She'd find out. Eyes narrowed, arms crossed, she tried to see these children the way her son saw them. She immediately dismissed the expensively dressed and coiffed, the overly beautiful, the cocky, the pushy, the loud. Certainly she didn't know a lot about her son's habits nowadays, but she knew his reticent nature.

A movement caught her eye and she tensed, her body responding to familiar signals before her brain had a chance to process. A skinny boy in a black sweatshirt had swiped his hand across the palm of a bulky jock wearing school colors as they walked past each other. A second, two, and then she was no longer sure if she'd seen what she thought. A hand-to-hand? What were the chances? Here? Illuminated by the pale, clear winter sunlight, in this middle-class school, in a hallway stuffed to the rafters with honor students and overachievers? She looked down the corridor at the skinny boy, who was now turning into a classroom, his head down and his fists stuffed into his jeans pockets. Her heart thumped a faster beat in reaction to what she'd seen, and for the second time in the past twenty-four hours she remembered her argument with Alfie and his dilated pupils, his sickly sheen.

She peeled away from the wall, all senses sharp and on alert, when the school's counselor-in-training, Ann MacDonnell, trotted out of the therapist's office. She had led Alfie's group therapy this past year, presumably overseen by the school psychologist. Laney realized she didn't know for sure. She had never seen a single document written by this woman, and Alfie's own reports on his sessions consisted of generalities, grunts, and shrugs.

Ann was short, plump, dimpled, and looked like a high schooler herself in black stretchy leggings and a ruby-red sweater dress. Her nail polish was a sparkly purple (chipped), and her mascaraed lashes were thick and spiky over green eyes. Laney wondered what Alfie thought of this cream puff of a woman. He'd always been dismissive of trend chasers. But then again, she had no idea what he thought of women at all, or girls. For all she knew, he'd run off with a girl.

"Mrs. Bird," said Ann, "you wanted to see me?"

She didn't invite Laney into her office, didn't offer a private place to talk. They stood by those absurd ceramics as the decreasing flow of students eddied past them. The bell rang again.

There was a time, her gun in her holster, her badge in her wallet, Laney would have insisted on privacy, but what gave her authority now? She was just another parent of a troublesome teen.

Nevertheless, she had some tricks she could deploy. Use the other person's first name to put yourself on an even field, never apologize, don't ask, make (polite) demands. Act like you know what you're doing. "I did want to see you, Ann. Did Alfie meet with you yesterday?"

"Yes, he did. We meet every Tuesday."

"Just the two of you, or are there other kids?" She affected a cool professionalism, as if she were simply collecting data instead of desperately scrabbling for information she should have known. But she could beat herself up about this lack of knowledge later.

"There is one other boy."

"I see. Did Alfie say anything to you about—" Laney paused. About what? Running away? Alfie loved being home. He loved his blue-walled room, and his oak desk, and his shelves stacked high with completed Lego sets. He loved the predictability, the safety of home. How could he have run away? A night, a few hours on his own, maybe, but nothing more. Her stomach churned. The alternative scenario was much more terrifying. "—how he was feeling?"

Ann put her hand lightly on Laney's forearm. "He didn't say anything that might lead me to believe he wanted to run away. Or harm himself. I'd tell you if that was the case."

Useless. What did this woman do with him if he could take off and she wouldn't know why? "Can I speak with the other boy?"

"I can't tell you who it is. That would be breaking his confidence. But I can ask him if he'd speak with you, and I'll give you a call if he says yes. I'd have to be in the room."

"Right." Laney nodded. "Of course. Well. Call me then."

"Mrs. Bird?"

"Yes?"

"I was wondering if you're familiar with the Pinelane school?"

Laney took a step back, shaking the woman's hand from her arm. "What about it?"

"I think that when Alfie comes back, we should consider a transfer." She smiled, all benevolence and compassion.

"What? Why? No! No way. No." Laney had to clench her jaw or she would have screamed that last *no*. As it was, it came out muffled, spluttered between her teeth.

"It's a very good school. And I think Alfie would be happy there." Another commiserating smile, a sincere nod. "I mean, happier. Than here. We can talk more tomorrow after he's returned home."

"Pinelane doesn't offer a proper high school diploma," Laney finally managed to say.

The therapist's smile wobbled, her eyes hardening slightly. "Mrs. Bird, it's my professional opinion that Alfie may be a threat to this school. In this day and age, we need to consider all the children's safety first, and particular children's well-being second. I was going to speak with you about this anyway, and now that you're here"—she spread her hands—"we might as well face it. I don't think we can meet all of Alfie's needs."

This conversation had veered way off track. Laney's hand felt weird, and she realized she'd been pressing it against her hip, looking for the gun she used to carry. For a second, she wondered what she would do with that gun if it miraculously coalesced in her pocket. Arrest this woman in front of her for expressing opinions dangerous to Alfie?

"Ms. MacDonnell. Ann. Must I remind you that my son is missing. In fact, from what I know, he went missing while on school premises. So, if we are to have any discussion about what we will be doing after he comes back, that discussion involves lawyers. And investigators. And a lawsuit." Although somewhat shorter than the other woman, Laney managed to look down on her. "Are we absolutely clear on where we stand?"

The therapist stopped smiling, paled, and squared her shoulders and legs.

"Mrs. Bird. Let's not forget the events of the fall semester. Your son set fire to the building. How do you think that went down at the PTA meeting?"

Laney didn't need to think; she knew all about how it went down, seeing as she'd been there, sitting in the back, biting her lips bloody.

"It was a talent show," Laney said. "It was an accident. And he did not set fire to the building. The stage curtains are not, the last time I checked, an entire building. That it was an accident was fully explained and proven beyond doubt to everyone."

"And what I'm saying," the woman barked back, "is that the kind of kid who thinks tricks with fire and blowtorches are acceptable for a school talent show belongs at Pinelane."

"He didn't have blowtorches!" Laney shouted, startling a student into dropping her bag.

They stood, facing each other, mirrored poses with arms akimbo, hands on hips, legs firmly planted and toes pointing at each other.

"Go to . . ." Laney stopped herself. Cleared her throat. Counted to ten. Rearranged her body. "Well, let's do this. Let's leave planning my son's educational future for when he, as you say, comes back. Until then, I would very much appreciate your help with any insight you might have. And please do pass my request on to the other boy. I would really like to speak with him."

Ann MacDonnell looked at the floor, color high in her cheeks. She seemed even more childlike now, almost sulky. "I will ask him," she said. Then, in a conciliatory tone, "Do you have any sense where Alfie might have gone?"

Laney shook her head, her rage spent and a deep weariness taking its place. "I really don't. I don't think he likes being anywhere more than he likes being home. He likes camping, but it's twenty degrees out."

It was time to leave, the next bell was about to ring, and she wanted out of the school, away from this woman, away from the warm, living bodies of her son's peers. She considered leaving through the side doors down the hall, which would take her past the classroom the skinny boy had entered earlier, but the therapist was staring at her, wouldn't go back to her office, and Laney spun on her heel and left through the nearest exit.

As she walked the glacial expanse of the school's white lawn, she wondered if Alfie'd really go camping in the winter. In the snow? He'd done winter backpacking trips with the Boy Scouts, and he enjoyed them, but.

Just in case though, once home, she called the police station and, after being transferred to Ed Boswell's extension, told him about Alfie's affinity for camping and listed the campsites he'd been to with the Scouts.

She did this while standing in front of his open closet, every bit of his camping gear accounted for and dry, stacked neatly on his two bottom shelves.

6

IMPOSSIBLY, HER PHONE insisted it was only eleven AM when she finished speaking with Ed. She'd been aware of Alfie's disappearance for almost twelve hours, and he'd been gone for anytime between that and twenty hours.

A lot can happen to a missing child in twenty hours. She paced the hallway, came down the stairs, stopped and listened to the absolute emptiness of the house. How could she live without her son? Was it possible that everyone would be taken from her? Parents, brother, husband, and now her boy? There'd be no way to go on living then.

And yet, somehow, when she had been a detective herself, she went days without seeing Alfie and was all right with it. She had trusted Theo—had loved her husband so intensely, so completely, that she felt his presence would make up for her absence, since surely her own love would flow through him to their child.

Those were days when she arose at four AM to get into the office by six, made an arrest in the afternoon, and rolled over into the next shift to process the perp and finish the paperwork. She missed Alfie, sure, but she knew Theo had him, cared for him, fed him, and played with him between bouts of painting.

Except, of course, Theo complained he had no time to paint. Couldn't, he said, not after a day of hide-and-seek and story time and naps not taken.

Screw Theo.

Laney warmed another cup of coffee, opened her laptop, and found the Facebook page Holly started. It had already been shared 322 times (Holly was popular). Somehow Holly found a recent picture of Alfie, and he stared out from the page, a smile dimpling one cheek. He was a beautiful boy by any standard, Theo's blinding good looks made delicate through Laney's pixie bone structure and coloring—a sweet, heart-shaped face, small, neat nose, full lips and dark-blue eyes, all of it framed by soft, blond curls. There was something antique about him, as if he'd been molded from a nineteenth-century cookie tin illustration.

She scrolled through the comments, most of them generic, benign—*hope he's found okay!*; *Godspeed!*; *What a beautiful angel!*; *I'll be praying!* And then she paused, her fingers hovering over a comment from JP Spankthemonkey—*yo, that kids a weeerdo*. And another one from Bondage Balls—*I bet he joined isis hes a freak*.

Laney shut the laptop lid.

Then opened it and made herself read every comment. Five times in her career she'd caught criminals by following their posts on Facebook or Instagram or—on one whirlwind afternoon—Snapchat. People were stupid. She had one case where a kid posted a video of himself with the car he'd stolen two hours earlier. His handle was carfreak2000, and he continued to post updates with his location right up until Laney's team knocked on his front door.

Fourteen comments caught her attention, and she clicked on each author, inspecting everything from the handle to the number of friends to the photographs associated with the profiles.

Then she signed into her undercover Facebook account.

She wasn't supposed to still use it, of course. The NYPD had given her a set of ID cards when she became an undercover: a driver's license, a social security card. On her own initiative, she'd obtained an AA card, an NA card, a key card for a rehab in upstate New York, and social media accounts. Kendra Wilkes, her alter ego, was a recovering alcoholic and heavy drug user, lived in a Coney Island housing project, and loved tweeting about her troubles. Laney had felt a weird sort of freedom when she became the wrecking ball that was Kendra Wilkes and had amassed hundreds of friends and followers in the online world.

When she resigned, she'd also quit Kendra. For a while, anyway. Then, in the midst of selling her house, divorcing, and packing, she had the sort of day where the only thing she wanted was to be someone else, if only for a few hours. Kendra had come to mind—angry, funny, say-anything-and-don't-care Kendra—and Laney had signed in as her and spent a few hours venting about a fucked made-up life, which, paradoxically, made her feel much better about her fucked real life.

Since then, she'd periodically checked in as the other woman, letting loose pent-up frustrations.

Kendra had 543 friends on Facebook, over a thousand followers on Twitter, and used as her profile a photo of Laney so old and blurry she could easily have passed for a teenager.

A quick Google search and Laney changed it to a picture of a random pouty teen with blonde hair and long eyelashes. Back on Facebook, she scrolled through the comments under the missing-child post and sent friend requests to the six commenters who, based on their profiles, appeared to be Alfie's schoolmates: JP Spankthemonkey, Bondage Balls, Allison Marie, Madison Addison, Tom Riddle2002, and Frankie Furter.

She knew with near certainty that her son was not on any social media. Laney had given Alfie a phone for his thirteenth birthday, not because he asked but because it seemed odd for him not to have one, not when six-year-olds texted at the school bus stop next to their simultaneously texting mothers. Despite this, she had no evidence he ever used his phone or laptop for anything other than taking pictures of furtive wildlife, watching videos of musicians he admired, or researching fire breathing. She forbade him to practice anything fire related, but she couldn't bring herself to stop his Googling, or whatever it was he did when he spent hours watching men and women play with fire.

Because of her upbringing, she'd always been respectful of her son's privacy. Even the occasional peeks at his phone were done in his presence and with his (indifferent) permission, the exception being that horrendous argument last month when she tore his room apart. A rancid heat surged up her throat as she realized she had probably been on the right track back then. But yet somehow not. He had been so forceful in his denials, so hurt at her refusal to believe him.

Her own parents had been both strict and intrusive, instituting surprise searches of her and her brother's rooms, forbidding locks on their bedroom doors, interrogating their friends on the few occasions the friends stopped by. Her father, a thirty-year NYPD veteran, had risen to captain before retiring, and Laney held the job responsible for his distrust of everyone, his own children included. The job affected everyone differently. Some, like her father, became cynical, seeing criminal tendencies everywhere. Others, like her old partner, Harry Burroughs, fell in love with the authority that came with the badge, relished both helping people and bringing them to justice. For Laney it was about setting the world to order. The bad guys arrested, the good guys safeguarded, the missing found, the victims avenged.

But world saving comes at a price. Harry used to call it shit-colored glasses: spend six months looking at people being their absolute worst to each other, and pretty soon even your nearest and dearest will acquire a craptastic gloss.

Laney closed the laptop again. She'd check the page later, see if the Facebook users she suspected were students had accepted her friend requests. Maybe it was time for her to don her shit-colored glasses and go through Alfie's room again. That search a month ago produced nothing, but she'd been wild with suspicion, angry, unable to think clearly.

Although she always thought of Alfie as being almost pathologically honest, she was no longer sure of anything. What does a person really know of another? How honest had Alfie really been with her?

CHAPTER

7

ALFIE LOVED ORDER in his room as much as Laney craved order in the universe. Even as a little boy he'd never gone to sleep without putting away his Legos, stacking the stuffed animals around his bed (where they either guarded or spied on him— Laney had never been quite sure which; he seemed wary of them if he woke in the night).

His bookshelves were neat, his bed made, his dirty clothes inside the hamper, his mechanical pencils poised at attention in a clay cup he'd made at camp one summer. Laney stood in the middle of the room and rotated, focusing on one quadrant at a time. She breathed in deeply, her son's boyish smell all around, a mix of shampoo, fabric softener, Old Spice deodorant, sweat, and grape-flavored gum.

She started with his books, taking down every chapter book and graphic novel from the lower shelves, moving to histories and biographies he favored lately, interspersed with the occasional dystopian YA. She shook each one, slid her palm across the exposed smooth wood of the shelves, checked for anything that might clue her to Alfie's whereabouts (papers, glassine envelopes, pipes, pills, weapons, letters, postcards, cash, credit cards, bank cards).

His shelves were innocent.

His closet volunteered even less evidence. She checked every pocket, felt along every seam and cuff.

When she sat at his desk, the sense of his unexplained absence overwhelmed her and she had to grip the edge for a few seconds, her eyes shut, her breathing raw. But she couldn't afford self-indulgence.

She had to stop thinking like a mom and think like a detective. Nobody can live without leaving crumbs of their existence littering their environment. The universe did not open its maw and swallow her son into nothingness. He was somewhere, and got to that somewhere somehow—and quite possibly of his own volition.

She opened his top desk drawer and started removing his papers. Geometry homework, Global History, a paper on *Romeo and Juliet*.

When she pulled out the chart, she thought it was some kind of science project, boxes filled with numbers and seemingly random letters. She had already opened another drawer and taken out his calculator and index cards when her hand froze, fingers bent midair, and her eyes turned back to the chart and the letters in the third box from the top. *JP*, underlined three times.

She grabbed the paper. JP? A name? She scanned along the row belonging to JP, but the letters in the corresponding boxes didn't make sense to her. It was some kind of code that only Alfie understood.

Over and over she looked at the chart. There were seven boxes that belonged to JP, and in order, their contents were: *Wd, DS, Ho, ND, YM, YS, Ma*.

Some of those acronyms had been entered in the others' boxes as well, but made just as little sense there.

Laney jumped when her phone rang, and she grabbed it, answering on the second ring.

It was Detective Boswell, Ed, calling to ask if Alfie had come home.

"No," Laney said. "I'd let you know if he did."

"Oh, I'm sure, Laney. I was just checking. Sometimes the parents forget."

She cleared her throat to keep from saying something sharp. He was right, of course. Parents often did forget to let the cops know their kid had come home. Sometimes they were too busy being relieved, sometimes too busy beating their child for causing trouble.

"Listen," she said, "have you spoken to any of his classmates? To his band teacher? He was coming home from band when—"

"Laney, he never went to rehearsal yesterday."

Blood rushed to her head. He said something else, but she didn't hear.

"I'm sorry," she said after a moment. "Can you repeat that?"

"I said that you were the last person to see him, as far as we can tell. Laney, he didn't go to rehearsal. He left school; we have corroboration on that. But he never returned for band practice. His music teacher never marked him as absent, so we thought he'd been at school until late, but no. There's a two-hour window between him leaving his last class and when he should have come back. This means the last person he was with was you."

"But . . ." She looked around her son's room, frantic. Wasn't there anything to give her an idea of what happened? "But he took his saxophone with him. And he didn't . . . Look, all his clothes are here. His backpack is here."

"I'm not far from your house right now. Are you home?"

"Yes, but—"

"I'll be over in a few minutes."

She ended the call and sat back, a cold shock rolling over her. The image of him walking away, holding his saxophone, played over and over in her mind. Alfie was terrible at deception, and if he'd intended to run, she'd have known it. No, he'd meant to go to practice. So what happened?

A weird little whine escaped her throat, and she swallowed it down. Once again she reminded herself she couldn't afford to think like a mother. She was a detective. Probably better trained than anybody in this town, if only due to the sheer number of crimes she'd worked in the city.

Her eyes settled on that chart. The *JP* snagged her attention once more.

She grabbed the paper and went to get her laptop. It could be a coincidence. It could stand for *June Prom* (as if). She opened her alter ego's Facebook page, and there under notifications she saw she was now friends with JP Spankthemonkey.

JP Spankthemonkey used a crying-clown oil painting as his profile picture. He had shared the Alfie missing-person page with an accompanying comment—*this is serios shit hes weird but still a reelygud guy hes my friend if you see him call the police.*

Laney frowned. JP was Alfie's friend? She clicked on JP's photo album, but most of the pictures were of body parts: expressive fingers, studded tongues, pierced nipples, a tattoo of a pug with a halo on a forearm. She clicked on his friends and checked whatever photos they had made public (apparently most of them, including videos of themselves smoking joints, vaping, and flashing even more body parts). She then searched for anything tagged with JP Spankthemonkey. This produced a number of photographs. She bent so close to the laptop that she was almost pressing her nose to the screen. Who was this boy? He looked to be the same age as Alfie, barely into his teens, no longer childish, not yet manly. He had angular, pockmarked cheeks, clear, light-blue eyes, and shaggy, copper-red hair down to his shoulders. In one picture she saw he wore braces. And in another, she saw Alfie.

JP was in the foreground, grinning at the camera, a can of Red Bull in his hand, and next to him, in the process of turning away from the lens, was her son. They sat on the bleachers by the football field, Alfie in his marching band uniform, his sax across his lap. She squinted at the date—October of last year. Had Alfie been friends with this boy since the fall and she not known it?

Something else snagged her attention. She peered at the picture, trying to figure out what was bothering her, then sat back with a gasp. It was JP she'd seen this morning doing what she was convinced was a hand-to-hand. She was sure of it, the image of the boy's hand sliding over the jock's fingers, a baggie slipping in one direction and a rolled-up bill in another. She'd seen this done hundreds, thousands of times on the job. She had no doubt she'd seen it this morning. Well. Almost no doubt.

The doorbell ringing sent her scrambling to close the laptop and tuck the chart into her pocket. It was only after she opened the door and let Ed in that she realized she meant to keep this new information to herself. She wasn't sure why. But she'd share it as soon as she understood it. Of course she would. Why wouldn't she?

The detective accepted the cup of coffee she offered (two sugars, black), and opened his notepad.

"Laney, what was your son's behavior like when he left yesterday?"

Her face burned as she thought of that moment again. She'd been so comfortable in the armchair, so safe in her assumptions about her world, too lazy to stand and hug him good-bye, to ask him if he was all right.

She shrugged. "He was okay. Same as always."

"Uh-huh." He wrote in his book. "So, you wouldn't say he was planning to go away?"

"All his clothes are home."

"Uh-huh." More scribbling. "And do you think he might have stashed some other clothes at school?"

Could he have? No. None of this made sense. Alfie was a homebody if anybody was.

"He was happy at home," she said.

"Yes, of course. But"—he shrugged—"teenagers." Smiled. "I have two myself. As you know. They drive me nuts." The fact that his well-adjusted, popular, industrious children most likely did not give him the kind of grief Alfie gave her was not lost on either of them, and they dropped their eyes to the floor, Laney's old analog clock ticking, ticking in the silence.

He closed his notepad, tucked his pen inside, sipped the coffee. "I'm sorry, I need to ask—have you been in touch with Mr. Bird?"

Laney tried to keep her feelings out of her voice. "No."

"No?" He waited, but when she said nothing, asked, "Okay. Well, I would like to reach out to him. Do you have a contact number?"

This time her denial came quick.

Ed lowered his cup, raised an eyebrow.

"Alfie's father and I are divorced. Almost three years."

Ed nodded. This was not news to him. In tiny Sylvan everyone knew at least that about her. He said, "My sister has been divorced for ten years, and she still has her ex over for barbecues every summer. But you're saying you don't know where he lives?"

"I know the general vicinity. Somewhere in New Mexico. Near Santa Fe, I believe." She didn't want to think what this made Alfie's life sound like. That his own father (damn his eyes) would keep himself apart like that. She brought her coffee cup to her lips but didn't drink. She didn't think she could swallow right now.

"I see." The detective sat back, held her gaze just long enough to make her even more uncomfortable. "Is it possible your ex-husband had something to do with Alfie's disappearance?"

Laney placed her cup on the table. "Like what? Like his father kidnapped him?" It happened. She'd worked at least two cases where the fathers had maintained secret communications with their children and used friends or relatives to pass along cash, arrange for flights. In one of those cases the kidnapped daughter had refused to come home to her mother, said her father lived in a bigger house and bought her better things.

But Theo? I-don't-want-to-do-this-anymore Theo?

"I need to ask these things," Ed said, and she recognized his guardedness. He was observing her, her reactions, cataloging her answers. She thought of another case, one of her first as a detective, where the mother had poisoned her adolescent daughter because she believed the daughter was having sex with the mother's boyfriend. The mother had dumped the body in an elevator shaft and then reported her child missing, going on to suggest her ex responsible for the disappearance.

Laney nodded. "I know. But Alfie's father, Theo, abandoned us. He"—even all these years later she couldn't give voice to how that abandonment made her feel (enraged, betrayed, bereaved)—"he thought he needed to pursue his art career, and he couldn't do it while taking care of a child." At the detective's inquisitive stare, she clarified, "I had the full-time job."

"So you don't think it's possible there was communication between them?"

Well, anything was possible. Her son had a friend he'd never talked about. A friend who appeared to be the school drug dealer.

"I guess I don't know," she said, the truth of this a needle in her heart.

Keeping his face and voice neutral, his body so stiff he seemed mechanized, he said, "It must be hard to do all this on your own."

She knew from conducting these kinds of interviews herself that this was not sympathy talk. He was giving her an opening, an invitation to admit something he could use. And he was right, it was his job to ask, and even though she approved of his thoroughness, she also resented it, if only because she already felt responsible for every bad thing that happened to her son.

"I love Alfie," she said, her voice hoarse. "It being hard is simply part of the package." She rose to her feet, hoping to end the interview.

He stood up. "Do you think it would be all right if I took a look at Alfie's room?"

Laney thought of all the books now on the floor, the clothes in a heap, the desk turned inside out. The only place she hadn't searched yet was the bed and the spaces around it.

"Okay." She pointed up the stairs. "It's the room on the left that looks like a twister went through it." She shrugged, hoping her laugh was not as hideously nervous as it felt. "I've been search-ing through his things."

Ed paused. "For something in particular?"

"No. I don't know. I guess I figured I'd know if I saw it." The chart folded in her pocket.

He studied her for a few seconds, then disappeared down the hall.

8

THE SILENCE IN the house after Ed left ate at her. It was only one PM but already gloomy, the sky hanging low and metallic above the pines. She grabbed the remote and turned on the television for background noise, then flipped to the news. Nothing held her attention.

After a moment's indecision, Laney punched in the number for Ann MacDonnell, the school counselor-in-training she'd argued with that morning, and left a message asking her to call back.

A half hour later Ann did, and Laney asked, "Does the name *JP* mean anything to you?"

The surprised silence on the other end elated Laney. Please, please, please, let that name mean something.

"Mrs. Bird, I can't betray another student's confidence," Ann said, her voice cool.

God, this woman was inexperienced. All students were assigned a counselor automatically. Many (most) of the kids never visited them to discuss personal problems. Ann could simply have said that yes, JP was one of the students on her list, but she hadn't. What she said was about as good as saying JP had also sought out or been assigned therapy with her. This in turn was an insight into the other boy's life and possibly into Alfie's.

"I understand," Laney said. "You said you'd ask the boy who had group therapy with Alfie if he'd speak with me. Have you had a chance to do that?"

Another pause. Not a good one. "I did, as a matter of fact. I'm afraid the boy doesn't want to."

Laney looked up at the ceiling, wondered if there was anything she could say.

"Can you call his parents, please? Explain to them this is important? Maybe they can ask him to speak with me. They can be present, of course."

"Mrs. Bird, I can ask, but that's all. It's up to them." And then, just as Laney was about to hang up, she said, "Besides, the police already spoke to them."

Not just inexperienced, but a sieve. If Laney had been the detective on the case, she'd be fuming at this bit of information passed on to a potential suspect. (Yes, she knew she was on the suspect list. Parents were always on that list, and she had no alibi.)

She had to talk to that boy. She just had to.

"Okay," Laney said. "Keep me posted."

She hung up without thanking the woman, which she knew was a mistake, but she was having difficulties being professional and polite today.

This boy, this JP, knew Alfie. What did he know about her son that she didn't know?

She doubled back into Alfie's room and sat down at his desk again. His laptop was closed but warm to the touch. Ed must have looked through it, something she would have done if she'd had the time.

She flipped it open. The wallpaper was a watercolor of a winter scene, all pearly grays and cool whites. But something about it wasn't right. What she'd first thought was a shadow turned out to be a gray wolf. She peered closer. No, not a real wolf—a robot wolf, steely, sharp, with glowing slits for eyes. And in its jaws a limp (human?) thing, bleeding bright red onto that ashen snow.

The picture was unsettling, but Laney wondered if she'd be bothered by it if Alfie had been sitting next to her. Warm, alive, he'd explain how it was a representation of the abnormal in a seemingly normal world, of the artificial within the natural, of the inscrutable aspect of the universe. She could almost hear his hesitant voice, the tortured consonants breaking through his teeth. In so many ways, this choice of wallpaper was exactly him.

Holding her breath, she clicked on his Gmail.

Let him be signed in.

He wasn't.

She then typed in the address for his school's website. She knew Alfie's password for the student portal, and in seconds she was in. A few clicks and she was scrolling through his homework assignments, class chats, and project outlines. She focused on the class chats. Then pulled the chart out of her pocket and smoothed it on the desk.

If the JP in Alfie's chart was a boy, then the other letters were likely initials as well. There were five rows of them, two above *JP* and two below: *HH, KJ, CF, MF*. She matched these initials to a total of fifteen students. But none of them seemed to have any particular interest in Alfie. None of them used the chats to talk with him. The four JPs she found were just as indifferent toward her son as his other schoolmates were. Exasperated and in need of caffeine, she closed the laptop.

What was happening?

Even on her worst day—when she resigned from the only job she'd ever wanted, divorce papers waiting for her signature at home and a freaked-out, heartsick little boy clinging to her jacket (she'd had to bring him along; he wouldn't go to school that day)—even then she had not felt her life to be so utterly out of control.

Her phone vibrated, a message from Holly. *R U ok?*

Do you know a JP who goes to the high school? Laney texted back.

Why? Who's JP?

Maybe Alfie's friend?

Give me five mins

Holly, Laney reflected, was better than a Google search. She, her parents, and her grandparents had all grown up in Sylvan. Streets and buildings bore her relatives' names. She either knew or was kin to everyone, as evidenced by her family Sundays—sometimes as many as fifty people stuffed into her four-bedroom Cape, spilling onto the deck even in winter. The few times Laney accepted the standing invitation, she'd felt so lonely, had missed what used to be her family so much, that she had to leave.

Laney was barely thirty-five, and already everyone she ever loved was gone. If Alfie disappeared as well, what would be left of her? Every person who exited her life took a tiny bit of her with them. An entire life full of memories was contained only in her head now. And who's to say if the memories were accurate? Who's to say if her memories were dreams or had really happened?

No, without Alfie, she would cease to exist. She would pare down to nothing, to the basics. And something else would grow in its place, but whatever grew would no longer be Laney Bird.

Johnny Pallisser? came the text from Holly. *Freshman?*

Maybe, Laney texted. *What do you know about him?*

My cousin Marcy's boy is friends with him. What do you need to know?

Any idea if he knew Alfie?

Hold on, I'll ask.

What would I do without you, hon? Laney texted.

While waiting, she made toast and filled the kettle with water. The answering text came as she was stirring a teaspoon of honey into her tea.

He knows Alfie. They all have classes together.

Laney dropped her spoon and opened her phone's browser. Within seconds she had Johnny Pallisser's address, and within minutes she was warming up her car.

9

SHE KNEW THE moment she clapped eyes on the boy that he wasn't the right one. Not the one in the pictures with Alfie, not the one at school this morning. This boy was small for a freshman, with a childish haircut and pronounced overbite. But what if she was wrong in her sureness? God knew she kept being wrong about all kinds of things, constantly.

Maybe he *was* the one.

His mother stood over the boy's shoulder, staring at Laney with an expression both confused and polite.

"J.P.," Laney said, after she'd come in, introduced herself as Holly's friend, and accepted a glass of water. "Do you know a boy named Alfie?"

J.P. shook his head slowly, his eyes made larger by his glasses. "Not really," he said. "We're in English together, but he never speaks."

"Are you sure you're not friends?" She took a step forward.

J.P. nodded and stepped back, thumping into his mother.

"Because it's wrong to lie," Laney said.

"Excuse me?" the mother said.

"I'm just saying it's wrong to lie," Laney said. What was she doing? Her mind felt fragmented and soft. She couldn't focus. "I mean, if you lie, someone could die as a result." It happened. She'd seen it happen. Though truthfully, she'd seen it happen between junkies and criminals, not so much suburban schoolchildren.

"Mom?" The boy turned his supersized eyes to his mother.

"I don't know what your problem is," the mother said, "but you need to leave now." Her arms went around her son's shoulders, drawing him against her.

Of all the things Laney could have experienced then, the feeling seething inside was envy. Her arms ached with it. Her head pounded with it.

A half hour later, Laney sat slumped on her front steps in spite of the cold wind blowing residual snow sideways and the firs bending and shaking above her head. She needed the fresh air.

When the police car pulled into her driveway and Ed stepped out, she was not surprised. In fact, after the interaction she'd just had with little Johnny Pallisser and his mother, she was surprised the detective hadn't arrived sooner. Like when she was still at the Pallissers'. Did she really tell the boy he could go to prison if he lied to her? She did. And did she really ask him if he was JP Spankthemonkey? She did. She really, really did.

"Laney." Ed walked toward her and planted himself squarely in the middle of the front path. "I was wondering if you would explain the phone call I just received from the Pallisser family."

Laney sighed and staggered to her feet. Other than a few pieces of toast and the three hours' fitful dozing on the couch, she hadn't eaten in over thirty hours, her sleep cycle upside-down. She wasn't hungry so much as woozy. Not sleepy so much as floaty.

Woozy and floaty. The Seven Dwarves' long-lost cousins. She stumbled over her threshold, leading the detective into her dark, cold living room, then fumbled with the light switches.

"Have a seat," she said, waving at the couch, then folded into the armchair. Her eyes felt grainy, inflamed. "Please extend my apologies to the Pallisser family."

"Laney, did you tell them you were a detective?"

The only person who really knew the details of her past was Holly. She hadn't wanted to discuss it with anybody else since she'd moved to Sylvan.

Laney sighed again. She wasn't even drunk! She would have liked to use that as an excuse. When faced with a stupefied Johnny Pallisser, frustrated with her inability to extract a confession from someone, anyone who knew her son, Laney, to her own surprise as much as the Pallissers', had claimed she was police.

"Yes, I'm afraid I did."

"You know that it's against the law to do that?"

She stood again, opened a drawer in the side table, rooted around, and withdrew her shield. She looked at it, ran her finger over the numbers—*6996*. She'd loved that number, the beautifully vulgar symmetry of it.

"Retired." She handed the shield to Ed.

He turned it toward the light, then put it down on the coffee table. Squinted at her, his mouth a skeptical line.

"Retired?" he asked. Nobody retired at her age. They quit or were fired.

"Resigned," she said. "So I could care for Alfie."

He blinked, his face softening slightly, looked away, then back at her.

"I know this is difficult for you. But you can't harass other people's children. I will extend a professional courtesy this time and forget it happened. But you must let us do our job."

"Ed." Laney drummed her fingers on her thighs, then shoved them into her jeans pockets. She had to at least try for composure. "Have you spoken with Alfie's friends?"

He frowned. "We have a process for these cases. We've interviewed a number of the students, yes."

"Who?"

"I can provide you with a list. I don't have it on me right now. But you can't interrogate them yourself, you know that, right?"

"Anybody whose initials are *JP*?"

Boswell gave her a hard look, then stood up. "We spoke with over thirty students whose schedules intersect with Alfie's. A few of them have initials *JP*. Can you tell me the significance of this person?"

"I just think he might be Alfie's friend." And maybe a drug dealer. Who maybe gave Alfie drugs. Which she couldn't find. But still.

"You think? But you don't know who it is? Laney, is there something you're not telling me?"

She pulled Alfie's weird chart out of her pocket and handed it over.

Ed studied it, then glanced at her. "What do you think it means?"

She shrugged. "I think they're initials. In the first column. But I can't figure out what the rest of the letters mean. And JP is the only one that's underlined. That's why I thought . . ."

Boswell raised his hands. "Okay. I need you to stop right now. I appreciate that you used to be on the job. And like I said, I'll extend the professional courtesy to you and let your behavior of this afternoon go. But this is not your case. Please, let us do our job. If you find anything, anything at all, you must bring it to us. Do not, I repeat, do not sit on it, do not act on it on your own."

He glared down at her. She noticed, for the first time, the dark smudges under his eyes, the grayish tint to his skin. He'd been on this case since last night, which meant he'd slept even less than she had. A vertical wrinkle deepened between his eyebrows. He asked, "Are we clear?"

She nodded.

"We will find your boy. Now try to get some rest."

She watched him get into his car and slam the door. He sat in his car for several minutes before starting it, his dark silhouette immobile, his head lowered.

She never liked considering the role her gender played in her career, but it was unavoidable. The cop world is a man's world, even in the twenty-first century. The detective bureau even more so. The bosses had been ecstatic when she asked to be an undercover—her ability to seem harmless, flaky, was a rarity in the field, and she knew how to charm information, introductions, drugs out of anybody. There had been plenty of cops who distrusted her, who insulted her to her face and behind her back. She'd been called ugly, asked if she was PMSing, scheduled for the worst shifts. When she made arrests, some of the other detectives sneered, made it clear they thought her partner had done all the work.

So now, when Ed rebuked her, she, strangely, felt better. She knew he was right, of course. She'd had no business troubling the little Pallisser boy. Ironically, her interaction with Ed reminded her of her old self—the self who took the ribbing, the put-downs, the pettiness, the orders to back down, and understood it to mean that she was doing good. Her successes had annoyed some of her colleagues. Not all, of course. Certainly not her old partner, Harry. He made her feel like the saltiest pretzel in the box.

Too tired to do anything and too worried to sleep, she sat by her window and watched the road until even the snow grew shadowed, blended with the twilight. Then she locked the doors, checked the windows, drew the shades, and took off her clothes. She ran herself a bath. Afterward, clean, hollow, light-headed, snug in her thermal pajamas, she climbed into bed and piled Alfie's blankets over hers, then placed her phone on the bed stand.

Just as sleep finally began its pull, she lifted her phone and texted Harry, her ex-partner and, despite everything that had happened three years ago, the one person she knew who could find anyone, anywhere, even if it meant bending (or smashing) the rules.

The answering text lit her face shortly after, but she was already dreaming, and so very, very tired.

"Five more minutes," she mumbled into her pillow, and turned her back to the phone as it vibrated again, illuminating the damp cowlick at the back of her head.

CHAPTER

10

SHE WOKE AT three AM, thirsty and hot, tangled in all those
blankets. It wasn't until she came back to bed with a glass of
water that she noticed the text on her phone.

At first, the text didn't make sense. It said, *Harry is dead.
Overdose.*

Laney thought very hard whether she had any other contacts
in her phone named Harry whom she might have messaged by
mistake. No. She had not. Then she wondered if maybe it wasn't
her phone. It was.

She typed, *Harry, not funny.*

The answer came back immediately. *No not funny. Not Harry.
Harry is dead.*

She blinked. Then typed. *Who the fuck is this?*

The answer came right away: *Cynthia.*

Harry's girlfriend. Laney winced.

With shaking fingers, she pressed the call button and waited.
Harry's phone rang and rang, then went to voice mail. She listened to his familiar, jokey voice, did not leave a message, hung
up. Dialed the number again.

This time Cynthia picked up. "What." Not even a question.

"Cynthia, are you serious?"

"Why are you texting Harry at night?"

"Where is he? What happened?"

"He's dead, Elaine."

Elaine! Laney hated that name. Nobody, not even her parents, had called her that. Except Cynthia. She pressed her hand over her mouth. Harry dead?

"Oh God. What happened?" she asked.

"Looks like he overdosed. On heroin, the son of a bitch."

"That's not possible."

"Do you want the autopsy report?"

"Jesus, Cynthia. No, I don't want the autopsy report. It's just . . ." Harry had been rabidly anti-drug. It was the biggest reason he'd joined the Street Narcotics Enforcement Unit (SNEU). His father had been a vicious addict, had contracted HIV in the eighties, early enough in the epidemic for it to have been a death sentence. He died skeletal, shivering, covered in sores, and left Harry and his seven siblings to fend for themselves.

No, she could imagine Harry driving drunk into the Harlem River. She could imagine him jumping from a bridge, hell, even shooting himself dead. She could never imagine him overdosing on heroin, his father's drug of choice.

"Cynthia, I'm so sorry. I'm just so sorry. When did this happen?"

Not that he didn't have reasons lately. She should have called him months ago; it's not like she wasn't aware of what was happening in his life. Guilt heated her face. Could she have helped him?

A whimper reached her through the phone, and for the first time since she'd known the other woman, Laney felt sorry for her. Cynthia had loved Harry. More than he'd loved her, Laney knew, remembered their rambling talks at the ends of shifts.

"Last week. The funeral was four days ago."

She hadn't called Laney. Nobody had. Not even the other guys she'd worked with.

That hurt.

"It was just the family," Cynthia said, a wet, sad whisper. "They didn't want anybody from the job there."

They sat in silence, Laney's missing son's blanket twisted around her shoulders, the cold dark pressing on her chest, on her face. She imagined Cynthia in a similar darkness, their pain over this man uniting them for once.

"But you knew how he felt about drugs, right?" Laney asked.

"I know."

"So something is not right. Something is wrong."

The silence this time was electric, taut. "Please don't call this number again," said Cynthia. "I'm going to hang up now."

Laney gripped her phone harder, as if by doing that she could keep the woman from leaving. "Wait," she said. She didn't know how to phrase what she was feeling, the shame and regret knuckling into a tightness in her throat. She should have been nicer to Harry's girlfriend.

"Elaine?" Cynthia breathed out, then said, enunciating every word, "He didn't hate you." And with that, she hung up.

Laney stared at her phone. He didn't hate her? Harry? Harry didn't hate her? Well, why would he? It never even crossed her mind that he might.

She extricated herself from her bed and threw on Alfie's sweats, his socks, his thick bathrobe. She couldn't stop wrapping herself in him, and she wasn't going to analyze it or even think about it. Obviously she'd stop all deranged behaviors the minute he came home.

CHAPTER

11

IT WAS TOO late/early to contact anybody else, so she put the coffeepot on and opened her laptop.

A quick search turned up a small news article in a local Long Island paper confirming that, yes, Harry Burroughs of Mineola had been found dead a week before. The paper sidestepped the details of the death itself, instead devoting a short but lurid column to Harry's (and Laney's) last big case.

She poured the coffee and tried unsuccessfully to focus on something other than that case. Nothing good came of remembering it.

Once settled back at the table, she checked Alfie's missing-child Facebook page. The shares numbered 463 now, the comments being mostly of the *I hope he comes home soon* variety.

A sip of hot beverage, a second of vacillation, and she signed in as Kendra Wilkes, then sent a message to all six of her new high school Facebook friends. She'd sign into Snapchat in the morning and try there as well.

At just past four AM, she figured she'd be in for many hours of nothing when Bondage Balls pinged her back.

Hey, he said. Bondage Balls' profile picture was an orange dildo.

Hey, Kendra replied.

Wassup

First things first.

So, she typed. *Did you know this Alph guy?*

Alph?

Laney took another sip of coffee. *Alfie. That guy whose missing. Yous all shared his page?*

Hahah, yous. What r u, a jersey girl?

Yup. So, you know him?

Hes cringy. Hes friends with my cousin.

Oh yeah? Whose your cousin?

Jordan. You know Jordan? Looks like yur friends with him.

Not really. I'm new around here.

Cool. So, new girl, what r u doing up in the middle of the night?

Can't sleep.

Come by and I'll help you. If you know what I mean.

I keep thinking about this Alfie guy. He's from around here, right? In Sylvan?

Yeah, he goes to my school.

So what do you think happened? You think he got kidnapped?

Don't know. Maybe. Jordan says he was talking to some old guy after school on Tuesday.

Laney swallowed hard, every brain cell at attention. She had to go gently now, not sound like a cop. She wrote, *Creepy! So you think some old guy kidnapped him? And here I was thinking we just moved to some boring ass place.*

Well you got that right tho its batshit boring here. Jordan says he thinks Alfie went with the old guy cause the old guy is like some kind of drug dealer.

Laney's stomach clenched, and a sour swell of coffee rose up her gullet.

Coolz! There's drug dealers in this town? Doesn't sound so boring. You know the old guy?

Jordan knows him. He said they been hanging out with him for weeks and hes been all over Alfie. So maybe hes really into him.

The old guy is into Alfie? Is Alfie gay?

Who knows. I always thought he was weird anyway. I didnt think he wuz gay, but weird. Like maybe he likes weird shit.

Says Bondage Balls

Oh yeah, hahah. Hey, u wanna come over? I'm just off Dyad street. Where r u?

Callisto street.

Hey, thats real close. Ill come by.

No, god no. My dad will kill me either way. Tell me more about the deep dark secrets of Sylvan. So far I got a creepy old man drug dealer kidnapper, insomniac bondage aficionados, and runaway weirdos. I might just like living here.

Haha, insomniac bondage aficionados! Good one. So when can I see you?

Ugh, stop it. So pushy!

Sorry, sorry. But you look hot in that picture.

So can Jordan get us some drugs from the creepy old man drug czar?

What r u, some kind of addict?

I'm bored!

Okay, okay, I'll ask him. What's yr number? I'll text u tomorrow when I have some.

Laney texted her number and sat back. Then, in a fit of desperation, *Wait, is your cousin Jordan Perino? He lives around the corner from me!* The only thing around the corner from Laney's house was a patch of birches on one side and the path leading to the lake on the other.

What? No, Jordan Rogers. Hes on Selkie rd. By the shoprite?

Oh, okay. Shit gotta go.

She closed the message window and logged out, then immediately Googled the Rogers family on Selkie Road. Their house was much like hers, an economically sized colonial with a ramshackle porch and a roof that would need replacing soon.

Unable to sit still, or, worse, to stay in the silent house alone, she slipped her feet into boots, grabbed her parka and hat, and drove the three miles to the police station.

Ed was at the front desk again, wiling away the wee hours toward his shift's end.

"Laney," he said, his face cautious, neutral. "Do you have news? Has Alfie been in touch?"

She shook her head. "No, but I found out something."

He nodded. "Oh yeah? Do you know where he is?"

"No, Ed, I don't. But I found out there's an older man that's been hanging out outside the school and he might be dealing drugs to the students."

Ed's eyebrows rose halfway up his forehead. "Do you have a name for this person?"

"No. But I know that a Jordan Rogers, a student, I think a freshman, knows him." She cleared her throat. "I think Alfie also knows him."

Ed sat forward and laced his fingers together. "Really?" He jutted his lower lip, looked at his hands, then back at her. "I know Matt Rogers, Jordan's dad. I've known Jordan since he was in grade school. Who told you this thing about the drug dealing?"

Laney always found the best way to be dishonest was to be mostly honest. "Looks like Alfie might have been friends with Jordan. You know, I just wanted to know if you all talked to him. To Jordan. About the drug dealer." Never mind about Jordan dealing those drugs himself.

Ed typed something on his keyboard. "We are absolutely going to look into that. Soon. It's another four hours before school starts. Right? Laney, we're on this. Go home and I'll call you. Okay?"

It wasn't okay, not by a long shot. Three years ago, she would have been running checks on Jordan, his parents, all the drug arrests and petty thefts reported in the area, all the break-ins. She would have been working this case, not sitting on her hands. Not waiting four hours for school to start. Using all her strength to hide her exasperation (and desperation), she went back out into the raw night.

At home, the lights on, the television a murmur in the living room and bedroom, she waited until six AM before going outside and texting her and Harry's old sergeant.

Huddled inside her parka on her front steps, watching the weak sun struggle upward through the iron-hued clouds, she squeezed her eyes shut and tried to pray, but couldn't remember how.

Holly materialized out of the gloom, her sniffly dog mincing delicately ahead through icy patches, its tail up and alert, its little gray face curious.

"No news?" Holly asked. One of the many things Laney liked about Holly was her directness. She might be frivolous sometimes, but she wasn't dull, and being with her never felt like a waste of time, no matter what they were doing.

"Do you know Jordan Rogers?"

Holly smiled. She really did know everyone in town. "Sure, he's my friend Diane's oldest. A bit of a problem child, if you ask me." Then, concerned, "Why? What did you hear?"

"I think someone's been dealing to the kids. And Jordan and Alfie are mixed up in it, but I can't quite put my finger on how." She cocked her head at Holly. "Do you think your friend will let me talk to her son?"

"I'll ask. I would think so, though." She glanced at her phone. "It's too early. Give me a couple of hours." Then back at Laney. "You look like . . . well, you don't look that great. Not that you don't have reason to—I didn't mean that."

Laney shook her head. "No, that's fine. I know what you're saying." She took off her hat (fake fur with floppy ears—Alfie's hat) and rubbed her fingertips along her scalp. She told Holly about Harry and then about her chat with Bondage Balls and then about what she thought she'd seen happen in the hallway at school. And about how the house, so quiet and dark and empty, was impossible.

"Never in my life," Laney said, "did I think things would be this horrible." She rubbed her eyes and her cheeks, raking her fingernails over her skin. "If Alfie's gone, that's the end of me."

Holly sat down next to her and drew her close. Even this early she smelled of strawberry body spray and freshly washed clothes. "Laney," she said, quietly, her cheek pressed against Laney's shoulder, "you are one strong motherfucker. You know that?"

12

THAT AFTERNOON, LANEY rang the doorbell of 15 Selkie Road. She'd deliberated the tone to take—grief-stricken mother (would appeal to Jordan's mom, not so much to the boy), detective (she would get in trouble, but it would be worth it if she got something useful out of him), forlorn lost soul (as an undercover, acting helpless often induced even the most cagey to cooperate).

When Diane Rogers opened the door, her face guarded, an undercurrent of irritation and displeasure in the set of her mouth, Laney settled on detective. If Jordan really was a problem child as Holly had said, then no amount of empathy could overrule his mother's instinct to protect him, whereas a subtle threat in the form of law enforcement might work in Laney's favor.

As they settled on the beige couch in the living room, Diane Rogers crossed her arms and said, "I'm sorry about your son."

"Thank you." Laney opened her wallet and showed her shield. "I'm not here in an official capacity. But in the interest of full disclosure . . ." She let the shield speak for her. At least this way nobody could accuse her of impersonating something she wasn't.

Diane shifted, placing both her feet squarely on the floor. Her eyes flicked upstairs, then back at Laney. She said, "Holly said you had questions?"

"I was wondering if I could speak with Jordan?"

"What about?"

Laney moved her legs so that her position mirrored Diane's. "I believe your son knew my son. I believe he might have some information about what happened."

"He said the school already spoke with him and he told them everything."

Laney shook her head slightly. "I doubt it. I don't think he would have told them about the fact that he's been associating with a drug dealer. Or that he saw Alfie talking to that individual on the afternoon he disappeared."

In the ensuing silence, Laney heard a creak on the stairs, and a quick glance in that direction revealed a foot just at the top of the landing, the rest of the body hidden. Diane heard it too but didn't move, kept her eyes glued to Laney's, her face closing.

"Elaine, right?"

"Laney, please."

"Erm. Okay. I'm not sure I understand. Are you with the police?"

"No. Well, I am a detective. But as I said, I'm not here in any official capacity."

"Then I'm sorry. I need to ask you to leave now." Diane stood, gesturing toward the front door.

Laney looked up at that stealthy foot in its dingy white sock. "Jordan," she called out, "Alfie is in trouble. I promise nothing will happen to you if you help me. Who was that man you saw him with?"

"No, no." Diane, still too nice to lay hands on Laney, managed to shepherd her toward the front door. "You can't talk to my son. You need to leave."

"Or what?" Laney said. "You'll call the police?"

The other woman blanched and flattened her lips, her eyes dancing in her face. She pointed at the door, her entire body tense and forward leaning, blocking any movement on Laney's part other than out.

Laney drove home with her windows wide open, wanting the stinging, numbing cold to go through her.

When she checked her phone a short time later, she had three texts from Holly, a missed call and voice mail from Ed Boswell, and a response from her old sergeant to the message she'd sent in the morning. She tapped that one first. It said, *Can you meet me tonight?*

She frowned. *Why? Where?* she typed.

Noonan's. Near me.

So up in the Bronx. Not that far.

She texted, *Do you know about Harry?"*

The answer, right away: *Meet me. 6:30.*

She stared at her phone. She started typing a response, then deleted it. Started a second one, deleted it as well.

Finally, aware of both the inadequacy of her answer and the risk of writing what she really wanted to, she typed, *Okay.* She didn't think she could take one more crisis in her life, but she couldn't ignore whatever this conversation was going to be either. Mike would not have asked this of her if he felt they could have a chat over the phone.

More worrisome, would he have asked her if she hadn't texted him this morning? Unease squeezed her rib cage, and she closed her eyes. One clusterfuck at a time, as Harry used to say.

The voice mail from Boswell was next. She wouldn't have needed to be a former detective to predict the tone or content of that voice mail, all of which had to do with her visit to the Rogerses and nothing to do with her missing son.

13

TRYING TO PARK anywhere in the city, even in the Bronx, at dinnertime is an exercise in futility. Laney paid for a garage and walked the five blocks to Noonan's, stepping through its darkly polished doors at six forty-five.

Being a cop was hard on the body—the enforced immobility for desk jobs, the long hours, the bad food. If you didn't watch it, you could end up with a heart attack by fifty. Mike Stegner, six foot three and a fan of all food, good and bad, had fought this with all his might. He joined a gym near the precinct, worked out at home. His plan, as he never failed to tell Laney and Harry, was to retire after twenty years and live a fuck-long life doing fuck all. The last time she saw him, he'd been fit, energetically muscled, and tan, his brown hair combed back, sideburns regulation short but defiantly visible, tattoos on both arms ending above the wrists, also per regulations.

He was waiting for her at a table, his back against the wall. His skin, even in the pub's flattering dim lighting, was raw, unhealthy. His hair was too long above the ears and stuck out as if he'd not combed it for days. Most disturbingly, he had a doughy, bloated look about him, and his forearms, previously as firm and thick as a boxer's, were now flaccid with loose skin.

Out of habit, Laney cataloged all this, plus the missing wedding ring. She hugged him, pecked his stubbly cheek, and sat across from him.

Seeing him filled her with a lonesomeness she thought she'd left behind years ago. She'd resigned with a clear head and a sure heart. Nothing was more important than giving Alfie a proper life. A steady life with a parent who would be there. But she missed her friends, missed the person she used to be when work was good. Sure, there was plenty she didn't miss, but that's not what tugged at her now as she settled across from her old friend.

"You look awful," Mike said to her. "What happened?"

And just like that, the distance the years had put between them vanished, and her face crumpled. She picked up a paper napkin and blew her nose. Said, "Alfie's missing. He disappeared two days ago."

He paled. "Jesus, Laney, why didn't you call me?"

"Well, what can you do about it? The police by me are handling it." She wiped her face with another napkin. "I hope."

Mike shook his head. "How old is he now?"

"Almost fourteen." She swallowed, shook her head to indicate she wouldn't talk about her son right at that moment. Mike had asked her here for a reason, and that reason had to do with Harry, which ultimately had to do with all of them. She couldn't afford to ignore that, especially now that Alfie needed her. "What's going on? What happened with Harry?" she asked.

He looked around, his shoulders hunched, as if he didn't want to be overheard. He started saying something just as the barmaid came over, then changed his mind. They shooed her away.

"What the hell, Mike? What's with the secrecy?" she asked.

The waitress circled back and they gave in, ordered two drafts.

When he was sure they couldn't be overheard, he said, "Remember Owen Hopper?"

Laney dropped the coaster she'd been bending this way and that, a coldness expanding inside her. She nodded.

"He's out."

"What?" She'd stopped following the case in the news, but she was sure he had at least four years to go. Her neck and shoulders stiffened, sending a lancing pain zigzagging up her spine. "That's . . . are you sure?"

Mike nodded. "Out. Back in November."

Hopper. There was only one reason Hopper would be out—the evidence that put him behind bars was suspect, enough to overturn the conviction—and her feelings about both the reason for his release and the fact of it were so muddy she felt a headache starting. She'd put the case behind her, walked away from it. Thinking of it now gave her a dark, greasy feeling.

Mike leaned forward just as the barmaid came back with their beers, and they waited for her to set them down, never taking their eyes from each other. When she left, Mike said, "I think Harry? I think that was . . ."

Laney turned her head to hear him better over the din. "Was what? Harry was what?"

"I think Owen Hopper did Harry."

She was about to scoff, was about to ask him where he'd gotten that crazy idea, but the words dried in her mouth. Because what Mike just said made absolute sense.

Owen Hopper, a pharmacist with a good job, a wild streak, and an even wilder wife, had gotten himself in trouble, then got himself into more trouble, then became a confidential informant for Harry, which, as it turned out, was his worst trouble of all.

Hopper was Laney's (that is, Kendra's) guide into the lunatic world of Russian mobsters. Minor Russian mobsters, nothing huge, nothing international. It should have been a straightforward case—he was to help Kendra get in with his boss in exchange for complete immunity.

Except that's not how it went. Not how it went at all.

Mike gulped a third of his pint in one go. After putting his glass down, he said, "Who knows your new address?"

The cold feeling inside Laney bloomed and spread until it numbed her arms, chilled her legs. "I didn't tell anyone. But it's not like I'm in hiding. Why? Why are you asking? Hopper thinks the woman he worked with was Kendra. He never knew who I really was, did he? Mike? Does he know my real name?"

Mike frowned. "He might."

"Are you fucking with me right now?"

As an undercover, her real identity had been so erased by the NYPD that for the time period she was Kendra, Elaine Bird wasn't even listed in the database except for payroll.

"I'm not certain. I know he asked a lot of questions in prison and then he stopped asking questions and started with the threats."

"Mike, what the hell. Does. He. Know. My. Real. Fucking. Name?"

He downed the rest of his beer. "Probably."

Her words snapped out of her mouth. "Are you sure?"

Mike shook his head. "No. If I were sure, he'd be handcuffed to a hospital bed with his legs broken and his face beat in." He swigged the rest of his beer. "Apparently he spoke of us extensively while he was away."

"What do you mean, us?" She sat forward so that their faces were inches apart. "What do you mean? And how do you know what he talked about while he was away?"

"I know." He gave her a hard stare. "I just know." He sat back, the space between them open and stark. "I meant he spoke about me and Harry. Not you."

The hesitation in his voice set her teeth on edge.

He said, "But after he got out, I heard he was asking around about you. A lot. And it's possible someone told him. That's it. That's all." He lifted his hands, palms out. "I don't know who told him, so don't ask. I don't know. Really." He squirmed. "I'm leaving. I have thirty days' vacation saved and I'm going away. I'll figure out what to do about him before I come back." Rolled his shoulders. "Or who knows. I might put my papers in and never come back. Maybe you should go someplace else too."

The coldness seeped into her throat and into her brain.

"I can't, Mike, because my son is missing." She took a minute to control herself. "Were you going to tell me?" she asked. "If I hadn't texted you this morning?"

He looked at the table, at her hands shredding her damp coaster.

"Mike? Were you going to tell me?"

Color rose in his cheeks and his eyes slid to the side, away from her. "I didn't know where you moved to. I heard you got divorced, so I figured maybe you changed your name."

She walked to the bar, asked for a double vodka, then swallowed the whole thing in one big, needy gulp. There was a time she'd thought of Harry as her best friend, of Mike as a brother. Betraying them, keeping anything dangerous from them, was just as unthinkable to her as betraying her own family. Now she couldn't understand the person she used to be. It was almost as if losing her parents and brother had done something to her brain and she'd latched on to the first set of people who were good to her.

And yet it was more than that. She'd trusted her colleagues with her life; she had to, because she wouldn't have been able to do her job otherwise. After the Russian case fell apart, the thought of trusting anyone like that again induced a breathless panic.

For as long as it took the vodka to hit, she allowed herself the luxury of outrage. For her ex-sergeant to know what he knew, suspect worse, and not reach out to her was devastating, slicing open old scars she'd thought had toughened if not healed.

Then she put her shot glass on the counter, scraped a napkin across her eyes, and shoved it into the glass along with her self-pity.

Her skin a splotchy red, she sat back down at the little table. In a tone that invited zero objection, she said, "Mike, while you're gone, I need your passcodes. And your laptop. I'm going to VPN in."

PART TWO

CHAPTER

14

ALFIE JIGGLED THE doorknob again, with the same result as the last two or three hundred times he'd jiggled it over the past two days. A big, fat, dick's worth of nothing. This predicament was his fault. He owned it. Nobody had forced him into the man's car. Nobody told him to accept the things the man offered him. That was all on him.

The man had taken his phone from him. Yes, he knew he should have fought for it. But he didn't. That was on him too. He'd been surprised was all, thinking the man only wanted to check the weather or something. He didn't expect his phone to go into the man's inside jacket pocket and be zippered away. And even after the hours-long drive, it seemed rude to demand it back.

Once again, he began pacing, nervous energy burning through his legs, his belly, warming his face to a fevered, blotchy pink. Wood paneling (dark, dull) covered the walls and ceiling. The coffee table, couch, and love seat were also made of wood, stained the same brown as the walls and ceiling. The cushions, upholstered in a monumentally horrendous red-plaid wool, were abusively scratchy to boot—something he'd discovered last night when he finally collapsed on top of them in exhaustion.

The room lacked windows, a television, a phone, or any electronics. No bathroom either. A Spackle bucket had been planted in the corner, where it fumed quietly with Alfie's emissions. Alfie hated that bucket more than anything he'd ever hated in his entire life. Granted, he'd been okay enough with relieving himself against a tree when camping, but that was different. He didn't then have to sleep next to said tree in a locked room.

He flopped onto the couch and threw his head back. As far as basements went, this one was at least dry, though cold enough for him to see his breath. He opened his mouth into an O and blew a puff. When was the man coming back? He needed to pee, and today, his second day with the bucket, he awoke determined that if he couldn't use a bathroom like a proper, civilized human being, he'd rather go the way of Tycho Brahe, whose bladder had burst after he drank too much and refused to leave the banquet table. Alfie'd demanded access to the upstairs bathroom twice already and been denied, but he was resolute. No more bucket.

When the man first approached Jordan and him, he'd said they should call him Mr. Blue. Alfie liked that, despite the name being glaringly false, because who has names like that? He liked other things about Mr. Blue, though they were not the obvious things. Not the things Jordan liked, for example. Jordan sought Mr. Blue for the beer he bought them, and the weed he gave them for almost no money at all, for the pills. For letting them haunt his ratty, weird apartment that always smelled like something done crawled in and died in the basement, which rather than turning them off added a touch of bizarre recklessness to the whole deal. For introducing them to porn.

Alfie liked him for the way he talked, as if they were equals, and for all the different kinds of music he knew about and played for them, and the way he'd put his large hand on the back of Alfie's neck when showing him things. It was something his dad used to do, and nobody had ever done it since he left. Not until Mr. Blue.

Once, after Alfie declined to visit because he had a chemistry test (he'd been borderline failing chemistry), Mr. Blue said come over anyway, I'll help you study. And Alfie came over. Mr. Blue made the subject vibrant, describing reactive and stable elements as if they were characters in a play: Fluorine, the crazy hellcat demanding union with everything she touched, toxic on her own, often explosive in her coupling; Iron, stable and independent, needing nothing, strong and popular.

So when he offered the boys weed that first time (fat little blunts nestled inside a tin box), Alfie accepted. And why not? Mr. Blue was playing dancehall reggae on an old-fashioned turntable (Jordan later said that was so hipster it was practically Brooklyn), and he gave them beers and packets of salt-and-vinegar chips. Alfie couldn't remember ever feeling as content as he felt that afternoon. Whatever Mr. Blue offered him, he would have taken, no hesitation, no questions.

The pot made him feel odd in his head, like nothing really fit, not words, not meanings. Panic flooded him, and he couldn't speak, his jaw immobilized as if wired shut. And even worse than that, he couldn't stop the feeling. In retrospect, he suspected Mr. Blue had added something to the pungent leaves that heightened the effect. Jordan loved it. He lolled on Mr. Blue's couch, drooling and laughing until (he said) his stomach hurt.

Alfie, on the other hand, coughed, threw up the beers and chips, then left, stumbling along Route 35, the trees lurching toward him. He came home late, dying to collapse quietly in his room, but of course his mother clocked how blitzed he was and they had that terrible fight. He'd been furious with her. She should have understood how horrified the pot made him feel—the panic, the nausea, the crazy fear that he'd never be himself again. His stutter had locked his throat, twisted his jaw, and all he could do was beg her from inside his mind, and she didn't hear him.

For years she'd told him he needed friends. What's a life without a friend, she'd say. It's sad. It's empty. You need to find a way to get along, to be a friend to someone. If you don't know what to do, watch what the others do and do the same thing.

And when he finally snagged Jordan, following months of preparation, investigation, and calculation, he'd done what Jordan did.

His mother always told him she loved him and understood him. But the day he got stoned and hated it and came home seeking comfort (or at least peace), he saw the lie in her words. He was just as alien to her as she was to him. As everyone was to him.

He hadn't smoked pot or taken pills since that day, though he'd pretended to. He watched Jordan and mimicked him, doing what his mother had told him to do after all. Subsequently, Jordan started spending more time with him at school, had introduced him to his cousin, his other friends.

Oh, he knew where he stood in the social pecking order of high school life—all the way at the bottom, even below Oscar, who had Down's syndrome and always smiled at everyone as he waddled down the hallway. That's why Alfie started his chart, and the chart led to Jordan, and Jordan led to Mr. Blue, and Mr. Blue had one day up and kidnapped him to this dank, piss-fumed, scratchy-wooled basement. So there you go. All his fault.

Alfie got up off the couch and fiddled with the doorknob again. Then knocked.

"Hey!" he yelled at the door (brown paint, chipped). "I need to puh . . . puh . . . puh-ee!" Fuck the stutter. He couldn't even act outraged without sounding ridiculous. He kicked the paneling.

A few minutes later the door opened, and Mr. Blue blocked the doorway, his face backlit.

"Let me up!" Alfie shouted. He took one step forward, then faltered, unsure of the man's response, dogged in his intent. "P . . . lease," he said.

Mr. Blue swayed slightly, his head dipping. His voice was hoarse as he said, "Fuck sake, you have the bladder of an infant. Didn't I just empty that bucket an hour ago? There's no way you need to pee again." But he held the door open and stepped aside. "Whatever. I'm not the chambermaid."

Alfie climbed the stairs two at a time, wanting to stretch his legs. He paused in the narrow hallway, taking in the cracked walls and the burnt-orange carpeting that was so matted and old, bits of linoleum it had originally covered showed through the bald spots.

"I thought you had to pee," said Mr. Blue.

"Yeah." He wanted to say *sorry*, but the *s* would have given him so much trouble that he swallowed the word, ducked into the bathroom, and tried without success to close the door—Mr. Blue had shoved his foot between the door and the frame. The bathroom had a tiny window, and he guessed Mr. Blue thought he'd try to escape through it, a feat only a very small child could realistically achieve.

Mr. Blue was definitely not firing on all cylinders.

Alfie didn't mind. As the resident weirdo in his old school and the new one, it only made sense he'd attract weirdos. They were reactive compounds, he and Mr. Blue, one needing something the other had. He knew he should be afraid. But like everything else about Alfie, the things that scared him were not things that scared others. He was scared of butterflies, for example. Hated the way they flitted out of nowhere and invaded his space. He felt the same about bicycles, skateboards, scooters—much for the same reasons.

He should have hated Mr. Blue for commandeering his life. But he didn't hate him. He didn't understand why Mr. Blue had taken him, and not understanding made it hard to hate. Did Mr. Blue like him? Did he want him for his own? He always acted happy to have Jordan and him around. Perhaps he wanted to make the situation permanent. Alfie wouldn't have minded having Mr. Blue in his life more permanently, just not in this terrible house. Certainly not in that insufferable basement.

Alfie turned his back on Mr. Blue and peed into the bowl, flushed, washed his hands. Luxuries, one and all. A quick glance in the mirror showed Mr. Blue's attention elsewhere—looking at something down the hallway. Alfie dropped the towel and bent quickly to retrieve it, nudging the vanity door open a smidge and cataloging everything inside. He neatened and hung the towel. He'd seen what he hoped he would.

As Mr. Blue led him back to the basement, Alfie paused and placed both hands on the doorjamb. " 'an I 'tay upstairs?" he asked. His speech coach had told him he shouldn't avoid sounds, but sometimes he just had to.

"No, I told you, you can't." Mr. Blue sounded tired, as if he'd been the one who spent the night on an impossibly scratchy couch, not Alfie.

"Why?"

"Fuck sake, boy! Get in there!"

But Alfie bridled, wouldn't move. A dread stirred within him. Over the past few years, after his father left him, he'd begun a quiet campaign of self-discipline. He'd learned, slowly, to swallow his terrors, to clam up on his frustrations. He'd transformed himself, without any outside guidance, from a tantrum-prone, willful child to an eerily reserved, watchful teenager.

It wasn't a perfect metamorphosis. Not by a long shot. Faced with another night in that silent, scratchy, fetid, empty room, Alfie's old worries scurried headward, waiting for him to surrender all that willpower, waiting to spread darkly inside his chest, fill his eyes with night, his ears with rushing water.

"Can I stay upstairs, please?" he whispered. He'd broken out in a cold sweat and the doorjamb grew slick under his hands, but the words came out smooth, as if spoken by someone else.

Mr. Blue glared at him, then shook his head and went down the hallway, leaving Alfie to do as he would, and Alfie followed, grateful to the point of faintness. Behind him was the front door, and he knew it was bolted on the inside with a heavy lock, having seen Mr. Blue fasten it when they first arrived, the key going on a chain around the man's neck.

The living room, dim except for one flickering lamp, seemed almost as much a cave as the basement. Forest-green blinds blocked any remaining daylight, and from the stuffy, stale smell, Alfie guessed the windows were shut tight. As he passed one, he drew an exploratory finger along the sill, only to have his thumb snag painfully on something sharp. The window was nailed shut.

A quick glance at the others showed him they all were, the nails like thorns scarring the sills and frames.

A doorway led to a kitchen, and a damp, moldy odor shimmered in the air, as of a fridge that had never been cleaned out. The fluorescent in the kitchen flickered as well, and Alfie had to squint against the light's vibration. It bothered him, the way a toothache might.

Then a shape in a corner caught his eye. An old upright piano! He glanced at Mr. Blue, who was scraping a malodorous mass out of a pot into two plastic bowls.

"Mr. Blue?"

The man worried at a blackened lump in the pot, poking it with a fork.

"Mr. Blue? Would you"—Alfie paused, got his breath, relaxed his throat—"mind if I play the piano?" He drew the words out slowly, in a slightly singsong fashion, the way he'd been taught.

Mr. Blue cocked an eyebrow at him, then shrugged.

Alfie sidled into the kitchen to grab a chair and did a quick study of the kitchen windows. Nails all around the sills there too.

He brought his chair to the piano, raised the lid. The keys were, unsurprisingly, discolored, webbed with fine cracks like roadways on a map. He positioned his hands—gently rounded, as if each cupped a sleeping hamster—and played a chord. The sound was thin, plinky, but amazingly, in tune. He closed his eyes and played. Chopin's Nocturne No. 20 in C-sharp minor—not a very original choice, but it seemed apt for the situation.

As a child, he'd started playing before he even knew how to read, or, for that matter, before he could speak properly. He was nearly four before he spoke in complete sentences, and three and a half when he first figured out how to play the *Sesame Street* song on his toy keyboard. His father had lifted him in the air and twirled him around, finishing with a bear hug, which forever imprinted on Alfie the correlation between music and adoration.

Finished, he sat back in the chair and closed the lid, his hand resting on top.

"Didn't know you could play," said Mr. Blue. He had sunk into the couch, his torso angled as if he were too tired to sit up.

Alfie shrugged. "I play," he said. "Didn't you see my sax when I got in your car?" The sax was, presumably, hopefully, still in the car.

"Yeah, but. Most kids only play one thing. And badly at that. You're pretty good."

"When can I go home, Mr. Blue?"

The man looked away, then stood, went into the kitchen, retrieved the two bowls and handed one to Alfie, setting off the lamp so it blinked like a lazy strobe.

"Stop asking me or I'll send you back to the basement. Don't be dense."

Alfie took the bowl. Spaghetti and meatballs. He hated spaghetti. He wanted chicken and rice on his own plate and his own fork and his chair and his table and, embarrassingly, he wanted his mother.

Mr. Blue plopped back onto the couch and forked a skein of spaghetti into his gray mouth. "You gonna eat or what?" he asked.

"I'm sorry, I'm not hungry." Alfie placed the bowl on the coffee table and stood by one of the windows. He ran his fingers over the blinds, played with the sash, tested the glass. Single-glazed, old. He could feel, almost hear, the panes shivering against the wind. What would it take to break through?

He walked slowly past the lamp, and its light flared for a second, then dimmed. He turned and walked back with the same result.

"For fuck sake, sit down!" roared Mr. Blue. "What's wrong with you?"

Alfie sat obediently. He now had three pieces of useful information. He just needed to figure out how they fit. Mr. Blue was okay. But that didn't mean Alfie had any intention of staying.

15

"MR. BLUE?" ASKED Alfie.

"You know, you don't have to say my name every time you have a question. There's just the two of us here." Mr. Blue thwacked his empty bowl onto the coffee table and sighed. "What?"

"What are you going to do with me?"

The man lowered his head and stared at his fingers as if counting them. Alfie wasn't sure how old the man was, but he thought a bit older than his father. Mr. Blue wore his iron-hued hair short, an even half inch all around. His skin wasn't so much pale or white as gray, coarse, worn, with deep vertical wrinkles between his brows and framing his thin lips. Despite his age, he had a compact, wiry physique, his movements springy, quick. Alfie did not think he could win a fight with this man. He hoped very much he wouldn't have to.

"Did you know that I used to work with your mother?"

Alfie sat up, alert. How would he know that? Mr. Blue never told him this. "You're a cop?" he asked.

The man shook his head. "No. I was what they call a confidential informant. Do you know what that is?"

Alfie knew what that was, though mostly from television. His mother rarely discussed the particulars of her job. He nodded.

"Your mom, she told me she was a drug ho." Mr. Blue pointed his wolfish chin at Alfie. "Now do you know what *that* is?"

Alfie nodded again, not entirely sure, but guessing from the man's tone, this was a bad thing. An insulting thing. He wondered if a normal boy in his place would feel shame on behalf of his mother. He knew she used to work with drug dealers, but she never talked details, and he never asked because that line of work belonged to his old life, when his father loved him. The day when his father stopped loving him was seared into his guts, into his lungs, so that anything reminding him of the old life also made him queasy, as if he'd drunk too much soda and eaten too much cake.

"You do know what that is?" Mr. Blue let out a mirthless chuckle. "I'd love to hear the dinner talk at your house. Anyway, your mom, the crack ho, figured out I was in trouble. She was right. I was being squeezed like a fucking zit. Everyone wanted a piece of me, cops on one end and the other guys, the not-cops, on the other. If you know what I mean. And that bitch just opened her skanky mouth and lied and lied." He let out a weird sound deep in his throat, a cross between a growl and a moan. "The cops—and by the way, she lied about not being one—told me that if I only introduced her to the right people, I'd be left alone. The guys pressing me from one end would go away, and the cops from the other end would let me go 'cause—and that's how they put it to me—we all wanted the same thing."

Mr. Blue stood and rooted through a corner cabinet, withdrew a fifth of whiskey and flopped back down. He unscrewed the bottle, took a sip.

"Turns out," he continued, "we didn't all want the same thing."

16

Mr. Blue closed his eyes, and Alfie tensed. Could it be that simple? Once the man fell asleep, could Alfie leave? The house was in the woods someplace, but that didn't concern him. One of the things Alfie liked quite a bit about his new life (as in life after Dad) was the Boy Scouts and camping. He'd been cold-weather camping three times, once even sleeping under a lean-to, no tent.

The man shuddered, his eyelids popped up, and those pewter-colored eyes rolled toward Alfie. Two bright spots flushed over his cheekbones, as if he'd just gone running with the wind whipping his face.

"You ever been in love?" Mr. Blue asked.

Alfie shook his head. Love was something that happened between real people, not for him—not the odd boy who needed a spreadsheet just to figure out what to talk about with another person.

"No? How old are you, anyway?"

"I'll be fourteen next month."

"Damn, by fourteen I'd had three or four girlfriends. And they all put out." He squinted at the boy. "You telling me you never got laid either?"

Alfie looked away, his face warming again. It wasn't that his thoughts were sex-free. Some days he thought of nothing else, when walking the halls at school became treacherous—all those denim-encased girl thighs and asses, their long hair grazing their shoulder blades, fanning over their backs.

He wanted out of this man's house. He wanted to go home.

"No?" Mr. Blue squinted at him, appraising. "I'd think girls would be all over you." He burped and massaged his chest. "I did all right though. Then I met Oksana." He shook his head. "She was fucking gorgeous. And crazy. Watch out for crazy girls."

Alfie reflected that he probably wouldn't know the difference between a crazy girl and a non-crazy girl. Was his mother crazy? His father had said she was, called her a crazy cunt. Was Oksana crazy like his mother or a different kind of crazy? Once, when he had a meltdown in fifth grade and his father had to come get him, his father told him he'd end up in a home for crazy people if he couldn't learn to keep a grip on himself.

"We had fun. Me and Oksana. She knew how to live. Good wine, restaurants, the best coke. One time she came knocking on my door at midnight and insisted we go to Atlantic City. And I had to be at work the next day! So what do I do? I said all right, let's go to Atlantic City. We get there and we play poker and she wins, 'cause she always wins, you know? And then we're on the board-walk and it's freezing 'cause it's like February or some such shit and we watch the sun rise. I gotta tell you. I loved that woman."

He glared at Alfie. "That's another thing your bitch of a mother took away from me." He threw the bottle onto the couch and got to his feet, indicating that Alfie should get up. "Come on, that's enough. Go downstairs."

Alfie remained seated. He flicked his eyes at Mr. Blue, then away, lowered his head. He didn't want to go.

Mr. Blue struck Alfie across his left cheek.

Alfie tumbled sideways, then caught himself and sprang up. He didn't want to cry. Wasn't going to cry. Fought to quell his trembling lips.

When the man swung again, Alfie turned and ran down the hallway, paused before the basement stairs, then, as Mr. Blue loped toward him, scurried down and through the door, pressed his back against the dark paneling. The door shut and the lock clicked.

He was alone with the scratchy couch again. He paced the threadbare rug for the next two hours, his limbs shaking for the first half hour, until his mind quieted and his breathing deepened, and when he couldn't walk anymore, he folded into the couch and closed his eyes.

He had made three separate lists in his mind, and he had memorized them. Each list broke down the steps for escape, but each list was incomplete. He needed certain things.

Flipping onto his stomach, he tucked one arm under his cheek and wrapped the other around his waist. Tomorrow he'd try finding what he needed.

For a brief, blinding second, a ferocious rage consumed the boy, and he bit his bottom lip till it bled. For that second he experienced the purest hatred, directed at his mother—who had done something unforgivable to Mr. Blue, who had pushed his father out of their lives; at his father—who was not going to help him, not now, not ever; and at Mr. Blue—because how dare he?

CHAPTER

17

Laney drove home from Noonan's in a haze, missed her exit, had to double back.

Owen Hopper out of prison. Harry dead. Mike scared and running. Owen Hopper knowing her real name.

She'd driven for a half hour before those four persistent thoughts were joined by a fifth. Owen Hopper knew her name, which meant he knew where she lived, and very possibly knew she had a son. And her son went missing after speaking with an older man who might or might not have tried to sell him drugs. Which Owen Hopper always had aplenty. Or at least that's what he went away for.

A lick of fear unlike any she'd ever known grazed her heart, then bit, the pain in her chest briefly violent, breathtaking. By the time she pulled into her driveway, she was near to howling with anxiety.

Mike had given her his passcodes (no questions asked, grabbed her phone and punched in his information). She still needed his laptop to use them, and he told her he'd leave a spare key with the super at his apartment building in Riverdale. They both knew the job would fire him for this if she got careless, and the knowledge vibrated between them, sharp and flinty.

Once home, she dialed Ed Boswell, but his phone went to voice mail. She said, "Ed, it's me. I mean, this is Laney Bird. I was wondering if you found anything else on—" She paused, realizing she'd almost said Hopper's name. But Ed didn't know about Owen Hopper, about the RICO case, or Harry, or Mike. Ed Boswell knew fuck all. "—the older man. The older man by the school who might be dealing. Just, you know. Call me if you find anything."

She searched the house once more, starting with the wreck that was Alfie's room, looking for anything she might have missed. She hoped Alfie had run away. It was a terrible thing to wish, but it was better than the alternatives scrabbling around her head.

After she turned every room upside down and gleaned no new knowledge, Laney buckled to the floor. She lay down, her arms outstretched, her gaze fixed on the cobwebbed ceiling. Was Owen Hopper holding her son? Had Owen Hopper done something unthinkable to her life?

CHAPTER

18

THE FIRST TIME she noticed him, she'd been working as Kendra in Brighton Beach. It was August, and the air hung thick, heavy, the heat so aggressive it seemed to scald her lungs. She hoped to score dope quickly, then wile away the rest of the day indoors. She wore short shorts (the department-issued Glock snug inside an underwear holster), flip-flops, a cream-colored tank with a thorny rose decal over the chest. Her hair was pinned back with rosettes. She envisioned Kendra as a lost girl, a woman in her late twenties who dressed and acted like an adolescent, a girl men (or women) might want to protect or exploit. Either way, it worked. Kendra always made a buy.

That summer and most of the spring prior, Laney and her team had worked a racketeering case, collecting evidence against a tight-knit organization involved in drug trafficking, extortion, illegal gambling, possibly prostitution. Laney's job was to buy as much dope—oxy, coke, Molly, et cetera—as she could from a small selection of dealers working for the organization. No arrests would be made until the team had enough buys to mount a solid case, which meant Laney had the leisure to become a regular without being burned. It also meant she could meet people, earn trust, and hopefully find a weak point. They needed someone who could give them, or at least lead them to, the boss, a Russian-American named Viktor Orlov. Orlov knew how to camouflage. He had no social media presence, and it seemed everyone who worked for him was family. He ran the syndicate low-key, old-school, all communication word of mouth except when it absolutely had to be digital, and then they used coded sentences primarily in English with injected Russian, Ukrainian, Georgian, and, according to a linguist the team contacted, Romany words.

After months of investigation, the team amassed some photographs, some nicknames, enough drug buys to sink three or four of his distant cousins, but Viktor remained elusive.

That day Laney met up with Bunny, a sometime singer and most-time user who had already introduced her to two of Viktor's dealers. Even in the crazy heat, Bunny wore her lemon-yellow wig and denim jacket, towering over Kendra in gold platforms. Together they slogged through soupy streets, past the Russian delis (smells of fried dough, buttery beef, sour pickles), under the elevated train tracks, to a corner on Fifth and Brighton.

Since Viktor's guys didn't text, didn't deliver, and didn't deal from their apartments, Bunny relied on word of mouth and texts from her friends to locate frequently changing drug locations. It was a pain, but Laney saw the wisdom in running a business like that. After all, look how long it was taking her team to collect the evidence. It was a good thing they made regular arrests working other cases. Otherwise none of them would be making overtime, and time is money and overtime is time and a half.

The corner stayed empty, nothing but ice cream wrappers, used condoms, and a dusty pair of purple panties decorating the sidewalk. Laney wiped her forehead with her palm. Maybe she could drag herself the few blocks to the beach and fall into the cool ocean. For just an hour. Or at least get her legs wet. She glanced behind her, making sure Harry was still ghosting, and sure enough he was, steadfast in the unmarked Impala at the other end of the block. Could she convince him to play hooky?

A loud crash and Laney turned, attention fully engaged. A man had burst through a door, smashing it against the wall so hard it ricocheted back against a second man, who hurriedly lifted his arm to keep the metal from banging his face.

She cataloged them as if she were recording descriptions on arrest papers—the first a white male, late thirties or early forties, six foot four, blondish crew cut, gray eyes, white button-down shirt with long sleeves, gray slacks, black leather shoes (expensive), a briefcase (and who carried briefcases anyway?); the second also a white male, late teens, five foot eight, frizzy brown hair, hipster 'stache, black tank top, black-and-white Adidas shorts, Adidas slides.

The first man crossed the street and hurried away, and Laney watched him, thinking. Midday, midweek, on Brighton Street in a heat wave, this man stood out. He should have been in an air-conditioned office somewhere else, yet there he was, his jaw clenched so tight she could see the muscles jumping even as he rounded the opposite corner.

The second man she recognized from pictures at the precinct— an apprentice at the syndicate and Viktor's third cousin. What had just happened between them?

"*Dobrydjen*," said Bunny, who, having lived in Brighton her whole life, had picked up an impressive collection of Russian greetings, curses, and endearments.

The boy squinted at Bunny, his mouth curling down, nostrils flaring. Working this case for months had taught Laney that these Russians would strip you naked at gunpoint and sell your clothes back to you at a thousand percent markup, but as far as they were concerned, men were men, women were women, and anything on the fringes was dirt.

"Marat, right?" Laney said, stepping up to him, lips stretched in a wide smile. She had no idea if his real name was Marat, but it was a decent guess in this neighborhood. He went by Malyish within the gang, but her showing him she knew this would have exposed her as much as her showing him the slim radio taped under her tank top. When she had worked in the Bronx, she'd used Ray or Steve. Everyone knows a Ray or a Steve. Down here, everyone knew a Marat.

He studied her face, her tan legs, smiled back.

"No," he said, "you looking for Marat?"

"Yes." She touched his arm playfully. Contact is personal. It's a shortcut to friendliness. People have a hard time denying you once you've been friendly with each other.

After this, it took only ten minutes to negotiate four dime bags of dope and voilà! A day's work in the bag (ahem), another notch added to the case, and Malyish one sale closer to a lovely stretch at Rikers.

CHAPTER

19

LANEY WAVED GOOD-BYE to Bunny, bringing the radio taped under her tank strap closer to her mouth. "Meet you at First by the boardwalk," she said. It wasn't like she could simply waltz across the street to where Harry sat parked in the shade and get in. That was how undercovers got burned.

She'd done that once, her first week working in the Bronx, and the next time she came strolling onto the set, a junkie named Lala had marched up and down the block screaming cop, cop, bitch is a cop, don't sell to white bitch, she's a cop. And that was the end for Kendra on Lexington and 125th Street.

The heat slowed her but didn't stop her arriving at the rendez-vous point before Harry. She leaned against a tree for the meager shade it provided. It wasn't like him to leave her waiting. Or to stop ghosting. She frowned and punched in a text. She raised her head and listened but heard no sirens. So he hadn't gotten side-tracked by an emergency job.

It was too hot to walk back to the precinct, so she texted him again and headed for the boardwalk. The heat and brightness felt fitting there, the wooden slats rough beneath her thin flip-flops, the beach exuding briny ocean, sunblock, fried food.

She smiled. There were worse places to work. When her phone vibrated, she assumed it was Harry and was ready with a mock reprimand, barely stopping herself even as her brain registered that the call was coming from Theo.

"Laney," he said, his voice tense, shaded with everything from mild panic to fury to a whiff (yes, definitely a whiff) of resentment. "Alfie's had a panic attack at camp."

She took a breath to answer, but he cut her off. "He lost it in the pool. During pool time."

Laney pressed the phone so firmly against her ear that it was heat on top of heat, the electromagnetic waves pulsing through her head. She said—and no, she did not raise her voice—"I told them not to force pool time on him. I told them."

"Laney!" And yes, he did raise his voice. "They're kicking him out of camp! That prick in charge told me he almost called the cops on Alfie. He said Alfie was so out of control, he scratched another kid who tried to help him."

"What?" And now her voice was up too, sharp. "Let them! Let that fucker call the cops! We told them not to make Alfie go in; we told them! I'll be home as soon as I can."

"Oh? And when will that be, Laney? Huh? Is that the beach in the background? Are you on the beach? You're still in drag, aren't you? So what, you need to get back, change, sign out, and then it's rush hour. You won't be home for at least four hours, so don't give me that shit."

"Theo."

"No! I'm dealing with it. I'm going to get him, and—" He stopped, and she closed her eyes, held her breath. And what? And what? "Laney, he was wailing when they called me. He was hysterical. I couldn't get him to stop crying on the phone." His voice was quiet now, defeated.

"Baby, I'm coming home. I'll be home as soon as I can. Okay? Okay? We'll have pizza tonight, okay? And we'll take him out for ice cream?"

In the silence, she heard him breathe, heard his keys clink, his car door close, the engine come to life. "School doesn't start for another three weeks," Theo said.

And what he wasn't saying sat there, pulsing in the air between Long Island and Brooklyn. No camp now and no school meant no painting.

"I'll see if I can take some days off," Laney said.

"Yeah." Theo ended the call, and she squinted into the shimmering brightness above the water.

She'd have to take the days. It was all there was to it. August would be difficult, what with her being low on seniority and all the older cops hoarding summer vacation days since January. She'd have to barter with someone. If she had to, she'd go sick. Her phone vibrated again and this time it was Harry, asking where she'd gone off to.

As she left the beach and walked toward Harry's car, a tall man with a crew cut and white button-down shirt, now without his briefcase, passed her and paused, his eyes narrowing with recognition.

Who knows, if she had gotten into the unmarked Impala right then, subsequent events might have turned down a different path and maybe more people would be alive four years later. But her phone rang again, and she answered, ignoring Harry's car and marching down the block, her words unheard by either of the men watching her and her stiff, furious stride communicating something different to each.

CHAPTER

20

THE CAMP DIRECTOR had called her, castigating her for Alfie's behavior as if she were herself a delinquent, and it was his call that both ratcheted her frustration level and simultaneously kept the watchful man in the button-down shirt from pegging her as a cop.

By the time she finally slid into Harry's car and slammed the door behind her, the man had moved on, having his own business to conduct, and therefore didn't see her getting into the Impala.

With sickening clarity, Laney entertained a quick fantasy of teleporting to the camp director's office and punching his lights out. Not that she was a violent person, but man was she steamed.

She plucked the rosettes out of her hair and tousled the strands into their usual disorder, then fiddled with the vents to send the air conditioning at her face.

"You all right?" Harry asked.

"Yes," she said. Harry was a great partner, but her private life was private. Besides, she never knew how to explain Alfie. "I'm going to bang the rest of the day," she said, not meeting his eyes. If their sergeant had a problem with letting her leave early, she'd make up a doctor appointment. Fake the flu.

They stopped at a light, and Harry glanced at her. "Don't worry about signing out," he said. "Just go, and I'll sign you out at six." Which meant she wouldn't have to make it official. Could pretend to be on the street, gathering evidence. She nodded a quick, sharp nod, not trusting her voice.

He smiled and winked. "Hey, you must be hungry." He reached behind the seats and brought out a brown paper bag, stained at the bottom with greasy circles. "Meat piroshki," he said, then fished out a cruller-sized lump of fried dough wrapped in wax paper and handed it to her. "And cherry cheese for me."

She held the warm pastry in her hands, realizing she was starved, absolutely famished, not having eaten since cereal at six AM and it already late afternoon.

"Thanks," she said. She bit into the soft, buttery dough and wiped at the drippings as they dribbled down her chin. She felt stronger already, capable of handling the difficult evening ahead.

"Good job before," he said, through a mouthful of pastry.

She shook her head. "I'm not getting anywhere close to Orlov. I've been thinking I'll start asking Bunny about him," she said.

Harry drove ahead without comment.

"What?" she asked. "You don't think I should?"

He made a turn onto a one-lane street and stopped behind an idling furniture truck. "I think that's a good idea."

They watched two men unload a white leather couch and disappear into a building.

"What did you think of the guy with the briefcase?" Harry asked mildly. "He almost smashed Malyish's face." He tapped the steering wheel. "He was pissed at someone, for sure."

He put away his mostly uneaten lunch and wiped his hands. Fidgeted as the two men came out of the building, into the truck, and maneuvered a recliner out of its depths. The twitchiness was unusual for him, and she was about to ask if the greasy pastry was already on the way out when he said, "Might be worth following him."

She bit off another chunk of the meat pie. "Okay," she said around the melting dough. "I'll walk around aimlessly until I automagically bump into white John Doe again."

Harry shrugged. "Get your friend Bunny to point you in the right direction."

The delivery truck finally moved on, and Harry stepped on the gas.

"I think if I ask her about both John Doe and Viktor Orlov, my cover is blown." She frowned at him. "Don't you think?"

"Look, we been trying to pin this Viktor guy for how long now? Five months? Six? Nobody's talking because they're all related to him one way or another. I figure we need to diversify. See if Bunny gives you anything on John Doe. Something tells me he's not family. Doesn't have the look, you know? If she doesn't, we bring her in for all those drug buys. Also, since she hooked you up with the sellers, we can probably try to pin sales on her."

Laney busied her hands with the radio taped to her bra strap. True, Bunny broke the law regularly and with adamant indifference. True, Bunny was not her friend. Not even Kendra's friend. Dammit, though.

"John Doe could be Orlov's family too, you know," Laney said.

"I doubt it," Harry said. "Anyway, we won't know until we know, right?"

Right. But fuck if she'd let Bunny go to prison for sales.

21

Sylvan's high school occupied an old mansion on an estate willed to the town back in the thirties. The building, a Georgian sprawl of brick and window with five dormant chimneys rising from the slate roof, had been a country home for a wealthy New York family, the countless bedrooms converted into classrooms. The landscaping still featured limestone statuary, benches, urns, and flowering trees.

This February morning, two days after Alfie's disappearance, the trees stood bare and forlorn, their branches shivering with ice drops, and the statues wore snow bonnets. Students ran past the stone benches and into the warmth of the building as soon as the buses disgorged them onto the cobbled pathways.

Laney perched on one of those benches, heedless of the wet gusts and the frozen slush around her bare ankles. She'd spent the night on the couch, too tired to make it to bed, falling in and out of dread-filled sleep, her mind churning through every event that brought her to her empty house and the empty room where her child should have been. She wore last night's clothes and had forgotten her warm, furry boots—purchased with Alfie in tow at the mall; everything brought him to mind, her entire life was steeped with him—had instead walked to the school in the low-heeled pumps she'd worn to Noonan's, only noticing this when she was already encamped on the bench and her feet numb. She didn't care.

She wasn't sure what she sought (or whom she stalked), but she suspected she'd know when she saw it. Or him. From her vantage point, directly across the main entrance, she scrutinized every student who rushed inside. One of them knew Alfie. One of them had been the last to see him before he disappeared. One of them knew and wasn't talking.

Taken to its logical conclusion, this meant Alfie was involved in something that couldn't be discussed. At least not by a student to a parent. Certainly not by a student to the police.

She ran her fingers through her hair, dislodging icicles that had formed at her nape and crown. The last bus pulled away from the curb and drove around the circular driveway, heading back to the garage. The driver, Vincent, also a retired cop, waved, and she waved back. He'd always been kind to her, willing to pick up her shifts when she had to take unexpected days. She wished, with a desperation born of sleep deprivation and fear, that she was the one driving bus number 182 around that circular driveway. She wished she was warm, her furry boots hugging her feet, her son in a classroom and their little home waiting for them, vindaloo in the Crock-Pot, Netflix queued for their next movie. Her descent into this fantasy was akin to dreaming. For a moment she experienced an absolute calm so complete that when she drifted back to her cold reality, she felt strengthened, clearheaded.

She reached for her phone and checked her messages. Only one, from Mike. *I'm sorry.*

She then checked her Notes app, making sure the codes he'd given her hadn't evaporated in the night, hadn't been part of another fantasy. There'd been a paranoid, shaken look in his eyes that infected her, ratcheting up her already inflamed imagination. Mike had done some digging into Owen Hopper's life since he'd been released and found that the man they sent to prison four years ago no longer had anything to lose. And even less to live for.

She breathed in sharply and looked upward at the heavy sky. A large, dark bird (crow? hawk? buzzard? she couldn't tell) spiraled above the tree line. Whatever might be said of how Hopper's case turned out, he wasn't innocent. He'd been guilty. He'd done plenty to deserve, if not what he got, then surely a portion. Lie down with dogs, as her father used to say. But dammit. Dammit, dammit.

Laney tucked her phone into her pocket and was about to walk home when a side door opened and a boy in a fur ear-flapped hat and olive parka edged out, paused, approached her. Even with the hat down to his eyebrows, she recognized him. It was the boy from the other morning. The one who'd exchanged a baggie of something for cash in the hallway. Jordan Rogers. JP Spankthe-monkey. Her son's friend.

He stood over her, looking down, his face wan and drawn, freckly, a lick of red hair curving out from under that gray fake fur.

"Mrs. Bird?" he asked. He sounded raspy, his voice not yet a man's but not a child's either.

She met his eyes and kept quiet. Always better to wait it out, let the other person—be it suspect, victim, dealer, or lawyer—do the talking.

The boy sat next to her and looked away. The effort of speaking—or maybe the cold—had reddened his cheeks.

"I think I know where Alfie is," he said.

She leaned toward him, her hand almost gripping his, then dropping to her lap. "Where is he?"

"There's this man. I don't know his real name. He told us to call him Mr. Blue."

"Where is he?" Laney repeated, louder.

"I don't want my parents to know," the boy whispered, his face almost completely red now.

She never wanted to shake another person more than she wanted to shake this kid.

"Is Alfie in danger?" she asked, surprised by how level and sane she sounded.

The boy glanced at her, shook his head. He was nearly crying. "I don't know," he said. "Mr. Blue always gave us things, but he didn't, you know . . . He didn't want— He didn't ask us to—" Jordan twisted his fingers together, untwisted. "I saw Alfie get into Mr. Blue's car on Tuesday. It was raining, so I figured he was just getting a ride home." He squeezed his eyes shut as if trying to excise the memory. "Please don't tell my mom."

Laney gritted her teeth in frustration. "Do you have an address for Mr. Blue?"

The boy nodded. "Number forty-two in the Mountain View apartments."

She jumped and ran, wavering between dashing home, grabbing her gun, and getting into her car or running directly to the police station.

In the end, somehow, sanity prevailed, and she called Ed Boswell, yelling out Mr. Blue's address as she sprinted home.

22

MOUNTAIN VIEW WAS a rambling housing development overlooking the Hudson River. It had been started in the eighties and half completed before the money stopped, the resulting clutch of buildings clinging to the hills while the woods encroached on empty lots. At one point, an enterprising band of renters had hacked trails through the new forest, but now even those were overgrown and treacherous.

Laney had careened into the townhouse driveway within ten minutes of leaving her house, two patrol cars sirening in immediately behind. They were in a cul-de-sac, the townhouses flanking number forty-two vacant. She banged on the door as Ed walked up the front steps behind her. Beyond the door, all was silence.

"Who told you about this place?" Ed asked. A second policeman, younger, was now standing at the foot of the stairs, staring at her with curiosity.

Even in her frantic state, something cautioned her against revealing Jordan's role just yet. He'd explicitly asked her to protect him, and a (surely misguided) parental impulse made her cagey. She did not yet know how anything or anyone connected. Getting him in trouble with his parents or even the police was one thing, and she cared diddly squat about that, but placing him in Mr. Blue's line of vengeance? That needed thought. And more facts.

"A boy," she said. "A kid said he knew Alfie and that they used to come here with an older man. A Mr. Blue. He said he saw Alfie get into this man's car on Tuesday afternoon."

Ed waited a beat. Then, "Who's the kid, Laney?"

She glanced at the young cop, back at Ed. "I need to tell you later. I'll explain."

He frowned but didn't press, because now something else caught their attention. In the initial rush of finding the unit and knocking, or maybe due to a particularly muscular gust of wind, they hadn't registered the odor clinging to the air around them. She'd encountered this smell only a few times in her career, and it was never a good experience. She didn't need to ask Ed if he made the same connection because his whole posture changed, his shoulders hunched, and his eyes darted along the perimeter of the house.

As if by silent agreement, they descended the steps and began circling the building, Ed's flashlight out and directed at every window.

Number forty-two was half of the townhouse, one bedroom in back, a living room and eat-in kitchen in front, the windows haphazardly covered with blankets and sheets. The second, mirror half was tenantless—nothing on the windows and thick dust on the floors. Each half had its own garage, down a steep incline at the side in what would normally be a basement.

And it was as they strode down that incline that the stench intensified, and Ed was already pulling his phone out of his pocket even as his flashlight pointed at the narrow garage door windows. Laney had to stand on her toes to see, and what she saw made her chest so tight that dark spots floated before her eyes and she had to grip the rough wood of the door to keep from stumbling.

Inside was no car, no furniture, no suitcases or shelving or paint cans or any other detritus to be expected in a normal, lived-in garage. No, in this space, illuminated only by the dull winter sun and Ed's flashlight, was a bulging shape, covered by a blue tarp. The shape had leaked. The shape had shoes—leather oxfords, one pointing toward the door, one heels-up.

Ed, on his phone, said, "Hey, this is Detective Boswell. Good, yeah. I need a warrant. Now."

He gripped Laney's shoulder and turned her so their eyes met.

"You all right?" he asked.

She nodded, though she had to clench her teeth to keep them from chattering. She'd seen dead bodies before, enough to understand that the amount of leakage happening in that garage meant the body had been there a long time. Certainly longer than two days. But the enormity of realizing her boy had been here, had been coming here, repeatedly, while that . . . while a corpse decomposed beneath him ravaged her, floored her. She didn't trust herself to speak.

"You know that's not Alfie, yes? It's not him."

She nodded again.

"I'm going to get the manager and the keys. By the time I come back, we'll have the warrant. Stay with Officer Ryan."

While Boswell was gone, one more police car arrived, followed by an ambulance and the medical examiner's team in a white van.

When the detective returned at last with the manager and keys, Laney had to step back. She hadn't realized she was pressed against the garage door, as if trying to get through by osmosis.

The manager searched through several sets of keys before finding the one to number forty-two, and they stood in silence, flurries dampening their clothes and hair as he struggled with the lock.

The smell, already strong, enveloped them the second the door slid upward—rot, decomposition, meatiness, human waste. The policemen had their guns drawn, Laney's hand jerking to her hip as well, even though her gun was locked in her gun safe at home.

"Step back," Ed said, but she was as if bewitched, her feet carrying her forward into the fetid darkness.

The young policeman grabbed her arm and pulled, and she looked up at him with wide, bewildered eyes.

"Ma'am, you need to stay back." He held her firmly, shielding her view of the gaping doorway with his bulky body.

"What the heck?" said the manager, craning his neck to look around them.

"Were you familiar with Mr. Blue?" the young cop asked the manager.

"Who's Mr. Blue?" he answered.

They all peered into the garage, Ed's guarded steps echoing inside. Two men in the medical examiner's white jumpsuits walked in, carrying their equipment.

"What is the name of the person who rented this apartment?" asked the young cop.

The manager chewed his lip. "Not Mr. Blue." He drew out his phone and poked at it. "Owen Hopper," he said. "Looks like he moved in about three months ago."

He squinted at the cop, then asked, meekly, "What's going on?"

Just then Boswell, looking haggard and grim, stepped over the threshold and into the colorless daylight.

"Looks to be a male. Maybe five foot nine. Hard to tell by now, but that would be my guess."

He nodded to the young cop to release Laney. Boswell stared at her dirt-and-slush-encrusted shoes, placed his hand on her shoulder.

"We'll find him," he said, and she knew of course that he meant Alfie.

She cleared her throat, pressed her fist against her pursed mouth, waited for her heartbeat to slow.

Then she said, "I know this person."

All three men turned toward her with varying degrees of wariness and curiosity.

"The body?" asked Boswell, sharp.

Laney shook her head. "I mean I know Hopper. He was a CI." She glanced at the manager. "Confidential informant. I worked him on an organized crime case in Brooklyn."

The wind carried the sound of sirens nearing—a strangely ragged effect as the gusts buffeted the wails. To Laney it seemed the sounds were surging out of her past. She couldn't remember ever hearing sirens in Sylvan before today.

"Laney," said Ed, "I'd like for you to go to the station. Can you do that? I think there's a lot you haven't told us."

When she made no move toward her car, he exchanged glances with the young cop. "Officer Ryan can drive you if you'd like," he said.

"What? No, no, I don't need anybody to drive me." She shifted her feet. "May I go inside?"

She would have been surprised if he'd said yes. The garage was now a crime scene, as was the rest of the house, and she had no protective clothing, no training in forensics. Plus, as she had to keep reminding herself, she was a civilian. Furthermore, a civilian connected to the crime scene.

Ed shook his head. "You know that's not possible right now," he said.

She couldn't move, couldn't walk away from that dark opening, the gruesome odor beckoning her. She placed her hand on Ed's forearm, Kendra's personality surging forth, taking over. Make a personal connection. Make it hard for the other person to say no. "Will you take pictures of the body and show me? And of the upstairs? Anything will do." It was an unorthodox request, but not, strictly speaking, an unreasonable one.

Ed stared at her raw-skinned hand on his sleeve, then looked at her. The bags under his eyes seemed bluer, as if he'd been punched days ago and had barely healed. He pressed his lips together, then stepped carefully back inside. She listened for his footsteps, the soft rustle of his jacket against his gun and radio, then the creak of the inside door and his ascension to the rest of the house.

From where she stood, she could see the remains clearly, the medics taking meticulous pictures, measuring. The body lay prone on the cement, a chunk of its skull crushed inward. From the level of skeletonization, she thought it had ceased being someone at least two months ago, probably much longer. She hadn't known she wanted the body to be someone else's until she realized it wasn't Hopper and an utterly unexpected relief flooded through her. Hopper had been seen alive two days ago and therefore could not be the liquefied mass of bone and blackened skin stinking up the garage.

If Alfie had gone with Hopper, as Jordan said, and this body had been Hopper's, with Alfie still missing, the last connection she had to her son would be gone. At least this way, Hopper alive, she could assume Alfie was with him. Further than this, she refused to think.

Her phone pinged with a set of photographs from Ed.

She didn't think anything he chose to show her would be worse than knowing her son willingly associated with a (probable) murderer and (convicted) drug dealer, but her stomach shriveled with despair anyway. Even in the poorest neighborhoods, she'd rarely seen rooms this squalid and desolate. Floors scuffed and filthy under layers of tracked-in, crusty mud, burn marks on the half-collapsed couch, beer cans, empty bottles, candy wrappers, crumpled chips packets, rolling papers, a lighter trapped inside a milk crate, and, unexpectedly, a turntable on top of the milk crate all painted an unsettling picture. Had Alfie and Jordan really been here? Spent time here? With this man? With a corpse's stench permeating the house?

"You didn't know your son was coming here?" asked the young policeman.

She glared at him. "How old are you?" she asked.

He stiffened. "Twenty-three."

"Okay, well, if and when you procreate and produce a teenager, you can ask me that question again."

His features hardened, and he narrowed his eyes. She didn't care. What did it matter what he, what anybody, thought of her mothering skills?

Four more pictures pinged into her phone, her gut shrinking further at the sight of the scrunched blankets in a corner (no bed, no lamp, not even an errant shoe). The closet gaped where Ed had opened it, nothing but hangers and a pile of clothes underneath.

A photo showed garments spread on the grimy floor—two long-sleeved shirts, a sweatshirt, a pair of jeans, one sock, three pairs of boxer shorts.

Any of this Alfie's? Ed texted.

No, she replied.

Other than the corpse, the townhouse was empty, and this offered faint relief. Hopper was not one to play games. If he'd wanted—she shrank from the words stabbing her mind—if he'd wanted Alfie destroyed, he would have done it. Would have made it obvious, a hit.

She felt hungry for the first time that day. She had detective work to do. *I need to go home,* she texted. There was a Notes app full of passwords and codes on her phone, and here she was wasting time.

Boswell stepped out the front door, said. "All right. Go home. Get some coffee. Officer Ryan will make sure you make it there okay. I'll be over as soon as I'm done here. We need to talk."

She was already pulling into her driveway before she realized the patrol car had tailed her the entire way, then parked behind her and blocked her in. So be it. Based on previous experience, she had anywhere from three to eight hours before Boswell would be freed from the crime scene.

She slipped out of her ruined pumps, her feet blue-cold, and ran the shower. A long day awaited. She needed to stay healthy, she needed to be warm, she needed her strength. The hot shower restored some alertness, enough so she wondered if she'd been on the cusp of hypothermia—what with her light jacket and ice in her hair. After, in Alfie's room, she pilfered his dresser for thermal underwear, wool socks, and a black cable-knit wool sweater that had been Theo's, then shrank and got passed down to Alfie, and now fitted her perfectly. Over all this, she wrapped Alfie's bathrobe, then put the coffee on.

Her patrolling life was not so far back that she could leave a rookie cop sitting thirsty and hungry in her driveway, so she brought him a thermos of coffee and a bologna sandwich in a brown paper bag.

"You're welcome to wait inside," she said.

"Oh, I'm good," he said with a smile. If his orders were to watch her and the house, then that's what he'd do, and good for him. She respected a good work ethic.

"Any news on who the body is?" she asked as she passed the food to him through the window. She'd added two chocolate chip cookies to the bag out of habit. She always gave Alfie a treat with his lunch.

"Nothing definite." Ryan grinned and wrapped his hands around the thermos. "Thank you, ma'am. This is very generous."

She patted him on the shoulder. "Well, can you let me know as soon as you can?" He wouldn't, of course. Not until Boswell interviewed her again. But there was comfort in pretense.

"You got it." He started his lunch with the cookie.

CHAPTER

23

As Officer Ryan ate the last of the sandwich and retrieved his phone, Laney texted Holly.

Where r u? she typed.

Shoprite, Holly typed back. *R u ok?*

I need a favor, Laney answered.

As long as I'm home by 3:30 for the school bus, Holly typed.

Twenty minutes later Laney, in furry boots and parka, slipped out her back door and wound her way through the three back-yards separating her house from Holly's. She'd left the lights and the television on. If Officer Ryan or Ed Boswell decided to pay her a visit within the next three to four hours, they'd be disappointed, but she'd take her chances.

Holly handed her a foil-wrapped gourmet chocolate as soon as she pulled out of her driveway. "There are few woes in the world chocolate can't soothe," her friend said, "or at least give you the strength to deal with." She drove away from their street, Officer Ryan, and shortly, Sylvan.

"Laney?"

"Yeah?"

"Now can you tell me why there's a cop watching your house?"

Laney turned up the heat and curled into herself, drew her knees against her chest. "Jordan Rogers told me he saw Alfie get into a man's car."

"What?" Holly snuck a glance at Laney, then turned back to the road. The Tappan Zee Bridge unspooled under them, swaying against the cold gusts.

"I know the man."

"What?" Louder this time.

"I got his address from Jordan, called Ed, and we went there." The edges of the Hudson River had iced over, and the water flowed black and slick between the shores. How scared would Holly be if she knew the truth? "The apartment was empty."

In the ensuing silence Holly leaned forward, her body tensing, her eyebrows knitting. She shot another look at Laney. "So why is there a cop watching your house?"

"The apartment was empty, but there was a dead body in the garage."

"Jesus!" Holly would have stomped on the brakes and pulled over if that had been an option, Laney was sure of it, but they were in the middle of the Thruway and going near seventy. "What the hell is going on? And you tell me the whole thing. I'm getting tired of peeling you like an onion."

Laney placed the chocolate on the dashboard and wrapped her arms around her knees. "You wouldn't happen to have a cigarette, would you?" she asked. Nobody smoked anymore, Laney included, but damn if she couldn't use some nicotine right now.

Holly glared at her, then switched lanes at the GPS's prompt.

"You're right," Laney said. She hadn't spoken of Owen Hopper, of that time, in so long she didn't know where to start. The beginning wouldn't work, since the beginning would lead her to the middle, and she couldn't talk about that. And she definitely couldn't talk about how it had all ended.

"Before I left the force, I worked an organized crime case. This man, Owen Hopper, was arrested." The only one out of the whole gang the city tried and sent away. "He served three years and was released a couple months ago." No one waiting for him and nothing left to lose. "And then he moved up to Sylvan."

Holly turned onto Riverdale's exit. "What are you saying, Laney? That he moved to Sylvan because . . . what? Because of you? He was following you?"

Laney nodded. Another reason to love Holly. She made everything easy. Even difficult disclosures. "I think so, yes," she said. "I think he's been talking to Alfie the whole time, and this week he took him away." She wished her voice hadn't broken on the last word, but it did. She cleared her throat. "He chatted up my son and stole him. But not before killing someone with a blunt object to the back of the skull and leaving that someone to rot in his garage." She put her feet down and rolled her shoulders. She couldn't afford fear; she couldn't afford to be small or weak.

They drove in concentrated silence as Holly looked for parking. After a minute she said, "Oh, honey."

"So. This apartment we're going to, it belongs to an ex-colleague of mine. He gave me access codes for restricted databases, but I can only use them from his laptop and through the VPN the job set up for him."

"Gibberish, gibberish, gibberish job. What are you looking for?"

Laney shrugged. "I'll know it when I see it." They climbed out and faced each other across the car. "Nobody goes through the modern world without leaving a trace. With the right tools, I'd say many, many traces. I'm going to see what I can find on this man."

"Honey?"

"Yeah?"

"You're still avoiding my question. Why did we just escape from a policeman guarding your house?"

"I can't get into the databases from my computer."

"Laney?"

"Yeah?"

"Still not answering the question."

"Are you sure you're not the detective?"

"I'm certainly detecting a lot of bull right now."

They crossed the street and walked up the paved front path to the building's brick facade. In the foyer, Laney searched for the super's buzzer, pressed it. "Look, I told Ed Boswell I knew Hopper. As far as Ed is concerned, I'm now involved in my own child's disappearance. I know the probable kidnapper. Or maybe he thinks Alfie went with him freely, but I'm responsible somehow. Either way, he needs to question me, and he's making sure I stay put." She leaned against the shellacked wall, crossed her arms. "But, as you've pointed out before, Ed is a nice guy and he knows me. He doesn't want to stress me by bringing me into the station for questioning." If it had been her case, she would have been gentle with the parent as well. Even Harry, shit-colored glasses firmly in place, always started with the presumption that parents did not kidnap, maim, torture, or dismember their own children.

Holly dug in her handbag and reapplied lipstick, her mouth a skeptic crease.

After the super peered at Laney's driver's license, gave her Mike Stegner's key, and disappeared back into the dank depths of his apartment, Laney met Holly's stare. "Yes?"

"I'm still detecting plenty of bull," Holly said.

Laney put her arms around her friend and squeezed. "It's all I've got," she whispered into Holly's lavender jacket.

Once in the apartment, Laney started the coffeemaker and rummaged for milk and sugar. She figured Mike wouldn't mind. More than that, he owed her. She'd kept her mouth shut for years, even under pressure.

They settled in his living room, a warm mug before each, his laptop on and connected. Holly blew the steam away, watched as Laney signed in, and said, "You know, you're right about Ed. He knows what he's doing." She sipped her sweet, milky coffee. "You shouldn't keep this to yourself."

But Laney could never tell Ed she was hunting for Owen Hopper on her own. Because if she told him, he'd ask questions, and those were questions she swore she'd never answer. Not with the truth, anyway.

For the next two hours, Laney rooted through Accurint, CLEAR, FINDER—databases she'd used countless times on the job. She scrolled through Owen Hopper's residency records first. He'd moved around frequently in his twenties, had addresses all over the tristate area. In 2001 he settled in Brooklyn with an Oksana Hopper, which was where he lived until Harry arrested him. Laney noted everyone who lived in every residence listed, starting with when Owen moved in and extending for a year after. Being a good detective meant paying attention to details, but first the details needed gathering.

A third coffee saw her through researching all the car registrations under Hopper's name, and then registrations of everyone who had come into contact with him.

She paused, her fingers hovering over the keys. There was one thing she didn't need to see, had been ignoring her heart's clamoring to see because she already knew the basics. The details were not important. Except that they were. Her hands, steady until now, shook as she brought up the case of Otto Hopper, Owen's son. After a moment, she closed the file, stood, and went into the bathroom, where she splashed cold water on her eyes, blew her nose, smoothed her hair, and did her best to put the boy's ravaged face out of mind.

She came back to the living room subdued but determined to finish her research. By two o'clock, she had a spreadsheet hundreds of rows long—a decent start. She was about to search through FINDER again, to check if Hopper had been misbehaving in other municipalities, when the laptop froze and a message popped up from IT.

Hello Mike, the message read, *what are you doing back? Didn't you put your papers in already?*

Laney's heart thumped hard against her ribs, and she slammed the lid down without thinking. Crap!

Holly, who'd been reading on her phone, jumped at the noise. "What just happened?" she asked.

Laney licked her suddenly very dry lips. She had to deal with this. She opened the lid, and thank God Mike was as paranoid as she'd hoped. He had placed a strip of masking tape over the laptop's camera.

The IT message window continued its vigil over her spreadsheet. She began logging out and closing everything. *Hey, Dinh,* she typed, looking at the signature in the message. *Yeah, on my way out today bro. Had to do some last-minute checks for—*What the hell was Mike's new boss's name? She tried desperately to remember. Failed. *—the boss.*

Oh yeah, got ya. Well, hey, good luck!

Thanks bro, she typed, and logged off.

If that didn't raise eyebrows over at headquarters, she didn't know what would. *Bro?* What the hell had come over her?

She disconnected from all the databases and VPN before emailing the spreadsheet to herself, then checked her phone to make sure it had come through okay.

"Let's go," she said, and shoved her arms into her parka.

Holly gave her a curious look but followed her out without saying a word.

It was close to two thirty PM by the time they got back on the highway.

"So let me ask you something," Holly said. "Did I just help you do something illegal?"

Laney reached for the chocolate still sitting on the dash, unwrapped it, and broke it in two. She handed half to Holly. "Not really," she said.

Holly took a delicate bite while Laney popped the entire chunk into her mouth.

"So how well did you know this Hopper fella?"

Too well? Not well enough? How well can you know someone when you're playacting? She'd always been Kendra with him, her entire self hidden away. How much of himself had he hidden?

"He was just someone I worked as an undercover. A confidential informant. He gave us his boss."

"Oh? But he went to prison anyway?"

Yeah. That's what he objected to also.

"It's not like TV," Laney said. "Just because someone works for the cops doesn't mean they get away with their crimes. Hopper got a lighter sentence." Was supposed to get a lighter sentence. He'd known he was playing a dangerous game. He was lucky all he got was a prison term. He could have had his arms and legs sawed off and his torso thrown into the dumpster. She'd seen that happen her third year on the job, and it took years before that blue-bruised carcass stopped haunting her dreams. It had looked like a gruesomely painted mannequin, except for the slick, white bone stubs and the swollen eyes.

Her phone buzzed in her pocket. She looked at the incoming call and crammed the phone back.

Holly glanced at Laney, and her lips thinned. "Who's that?" she asked.

Laney sighed. "Boswell."

CHAPTER

24

LANEY ASKED HOLLY to let her out on the next street over from theirs and walked to her house in the gathering gloom. Ryan clocked her as she neared the driveway and immediately texted, then climbed out of the patrol car. His shoulders squared, one hand a fist by his thigh and the other loosely hovering over his belt, he looked annoyed and ready to act. She could imagine the reaming he'd gotten when Boswell showed up to find the house empty and her footprints leading down the hill.

"Is Ed on his way?" Laney asked.

"Detective Boswell would like you to come to the station."

She'd expected that too, and she opened her car door without protest. She now had fifteen minutes to decide how much she'd share. In theory, the more Ed knew, the more he'd be able to help. She wasn't an idiot, and Alfie mattered more than anything, more than her own safety. If a disclosure from her meant he'd find Hopper and by extension Alfie, she'd implicate herself without a second thought. The only question was whether she could find Hopper and Alfie faster on her own. Putting herself in the cross hairs of Internal Affairs would help no one.

Ryan led her to an interview room and left, closing the door firmly behind him. She wasn't locked in, was free to go, she knew that. But the dingy walls, the stale, airless smell of it, had their effect, and she had to fight against the nervous anxiety cramping her stomach, cooling her fingers and feet. She would try to intuit how much Boswell already knew. The story had been in the news.

The simplest of searches would have brought up Hopper's trial details, her team's reports, the court records. And never mind the notoriety the case generated all over again only six months earlier with Harry's trial. On the surface this was a straightforward situation of an ex-con seeking revenge. It didn't happen often, but it did happen. There'd been a cop down in Florida whose house was set afire by a felon he'd arrested two decades earlier. Being a cop wasn't for wusses, they all knew that.

But still.

Ed walked in thirty minutes later, placed a thick folder between them, and sat down. The day had treated him badly—his hair mussed, an oily sheen to his forehead, a weary slump to his shoulders. He twined his fingers, tilted forward on his elbows. She could tell he wanted to play it aloof and wary but was too tired to carry it off. A twinge of sympathy eased her tension.

"Tell me about Owen Hopper," he said.

"Have you interviewed Jordan Rogers?" Laney countered.

"Yes."

"Do you know where Hopper might be?" she asked.

"No."

They stared at each other.

"What did Jordan say?"

"He said you spoke to him this morning. In defiance of a direct request from both me and his parents that you stay away from him."

"He came to me. I didn't seek him out."

Ed looked at his hands, sighed, and leaned back against his chair.

"Laney." He paused, studying her. "Let's start over. Tell me why Owen Hopper treated your son to drugs, alcohol, and porn for two months. I'm assuming you didn't know about this. Right? I have to assume that, or we're about to start having a very different sort of conversation."

She detected a judgmental current—he would have known if it had been his son, was appalled at her blindness.

"Of course I didn't know!" Her throat hurt, as if she'd been punched. "Ed, of course I didn't know." She covered her face with her hands, took a deep breath, tried to work through that knot in her larynx.

"Then tell me everything you do know," Ed said, and his voice was gentler, softer now.

She lowered her hands, her fingers bending and knotting against her thighs. "I knew nothing until Alfie didn't come home on Tuesday. Everything was fine until then."

He cocked his head. "What about the last time he disappeared? Do you think that was related to Hopper?"

Well, yes, it was so obvious now. Of course he had been high. Her intuition was rarely wrong. But why had he denied it like that? He'd never lied to her before. Except that's precisely what he'd been doing for months. Lying and lying and lying.

She nodded. "Possibly. I had a feeling something wasn't right, but he wouldn't tell me anything. I tried, Ed." She looked away. "We had a fight about it."

He tapped a pen against the folder. "What do you think Hopper wants with him?"

That lump in her throat again, sharp and cruel. What indeed?

Ed opened the folder and leafed through printouts, spreadsheets, reports. "He has no record of pedophilia," he said, his voice even but his eyes averted. They both knew this meant nothing. It simply meant he'd never been caught. "If he wanted revenge against you, he would have attacked you, right? Why befriend your son?"

He closed the folder and looked at her. "Let's back up. How does he know who you are? Or where you live?" He patted the manila folder again. "It says here you worked with him for months as an undercover. He was a useful CI. What happened? Did some-one blow your cover?"

Her stomach tightened again. She didn't want to examine how Hopper knew her real identity. Even now, a year after Harry's indictment, she found it hard to think badly of him and nearly impossible to imagine him willingly exposing her. She decided to sidestep that question and answer the rest.

"Prescription drug fraud. He worked at a dirty pharmacy run by a Russian mobster. He filled any scrip they sent him and filed enough reports with the state drug program so the pharmacy looked legit. Prescription drugs at the counter, street narcotics at the back door. The regulars called that pharmacy *konfetka*, candy." She shrugged. "We were building a case. Then my team raided the pharmacy and arrested Hopper." (Waited until she'd taken a few days' vacation and gone in, tore apart the pharmacy, his apart-ment. She wouldn't have been able to take part anyway, but that's not why they waited.) She clenched her jaw against the memory.

Ed nodded. He would have found out as much from the news reports. He chewed his lower lip as if thinking something over. He said, "I got in touch with Internal Affairs, Laney. They told me some interesting things."

"Um," she said.

Ed held her gaze, and she had to stare him down, had to breathe through it, fight the warmth crawling up her cheeks.

"Well." He stood up, gathered the folder. "If you have any more insights, you know how to reach me."

She stood as well.

"By the way, what kind of relationship did you have with Owen?"

Her heart thumped hard, once, and she froze, felt (heard) her teeth grind against each other.

"Tell me about Harry Burroughs."

She didn't move, didn't blink.

He watched her, waited, then nodded slightly. "When you're ready, give me a call," he said, and left the room.

CHAPTER

25

THE DAY HAD grown gloomier, the pewter sky glowing an odd green. There would be another storm tonight. Where would Alfie be when the storm came? Indoors? In a car? What did Hopper want with him? Her mind circled back to that question over and over as she left the station and started her car. She let it run, cranking the heat as high as it would go. Would Alfie be warm tonight?

Hopper was going through them one at a time, ticking their lives off a list. But he'd not touched her. No, he had, as Ed so pointedly said, befriended her son instead.

Back at her house, Laney tossed a frozen pizza into the oven, brewed a cup of chamomile, and settled at the kitchen table with her laptop. Her phone buzzed, but it was only Holly, asking if there was any news.

No news, Laney texted. Then, *Thank you for driving today.*

Oh please. If you can't break the law for a friend, what's the point of breaking the law?

You didn't break any laws, Holly!

A girl can fantasize.

Laney smiled at her phone and sipped the tea. *Love you*, she texted.

You better, Holly replied. A few minutes later she texted again. *We all just prayed for you and Alfie.* Holly believed in the power of prayer and induced her husband, three children, and any extended family in the vicinity to join her whenever something needed an extra cosmic push.

It can't hurt, Laney texted back.

She then opened Snapchat and looked for JP Spankthemonkey. Because prayer was one thing, and detective work another, and every passing day without her son was a knife in her guts.

26

S HE FOUND JORDAN Rogers's handle on Snapchat and sent an introductory chat. She did this as herself, not Kendra. And no, she didn't care about Ed Boswell's warnings, or anything Jordan's parents might have to say about her reaching out to their son. Their thirteen-year-old had spent two months hanging out in a grown man's apartment getting stoned and drunk. She'd seen him do a hand-to-hand in the school's hallway. And now her own thirteen-year-old was God knew where. Jordan's parents could stuff it.

While waiting for Jordan to notice the chat invitation and hopefully respond, Laney scraped the warmed pizza onto a plate and tore off a chunk. She opened her laptop, then the spreadsheet she'd sent herself from Mike's apartment, and began highlighting rows. Harry had taught her this method: look for connections, the same last names, the same first names, check birth dates, color code everything that looks part of a pattern.

Fifteen minutes ticked by, twenty. She'd forgotten how much she loved this aspect of being a detective. Hell, she loved every aspect of it. She loved the field work best, but this cerebral hunting, this tracking of the spoor a person leaves behind simply by living, stoked the analytical side of her, gave her a sense of power even her gun couldn't provide.

The first time she rode in a patrol car she was twenty-one, fresh out of the academy, and so thrilled that she had to fight to keep from grinning. It had been the culmination of years' long dreaming. While a senior in high school, she'd applied to John Jay College of Criminal Justice. She loved everything about what she studied—whether it was criminal law or forensic psychology. She put in her application for the NYPD in her last year of school and entered the police academy four months after graduation.

Somewhere in the mix she'd met Theo—tall, lanky, blond, blue-eyed Theo with paint-splattered pants and sneakers, torn T-shirts, and beautiful hands that smelled of linseed oil. He painted larger-than-life portraits—eight-foot-high expanses of mottled skin and cracked lips—work she found alienating and off-putting, but grand anyway. He could create something she couldn't, and he did it well, and was beginning to attract notice, a few galleries placing him in group shows to test out the waters.

They were an unlikely couple, introduced accidentally by a mutual acquaintance. Her love for him seemed more than imme-diate, as if he had already been part of her life, her dreams, and meeting him was simply the next step in the relationship. She loved the dip in his bottom lip, his skin (fine-grained, golden), his voice (his voice made her wet the first time she heard it), the way he spoke about politics, history, literature. She related to none of it, but that didn't matter. She adored listening to him.

Her friends rolled their eyes behind his back and laughed, and one by one she stopped seeing them. He was all she needed. He and her work. Her world was perfect.

Those first years glowed in her memory with a grotesque intensity. She'd experienced everything new, good or bad, as a revelation, the world opening its secret layers for her as if lifting away veils. The crazy, over-the-top romance with Theo colored everything else to the point that no human misery could touch her. Abandoned children, abused spouses, murdered siblings,

Mafia killings, car crashes, teen prostitutes, elderly men dead and bloated and half eaten by their dogs—all of it fascinated her equally. She'd come home and sit on Theo's painting stool telling him story after story as he dabbed at a canvas, brush between his teeth and a sodden gray rag in his hand.

Every day she'd rise from their bed perennially yearning for him even as he spilled out of her, shower, put on her uniform, and go to work. The rotating shifts never bothered her the way they did the other rookies—she felt she could go without sleep for days if necessary.

Nothing could touch her, nothing could ruin the hard, glossy, luscious shell her obsession had built around her. And then something did, something penetrated the shell, made its home inside. She fell pregnant a year after graduating the academy. The decision to marry and move in together was barely a decision—they just did it, waking up on a Monday, filling out the marriage license forms, and getting married on a Wednesday. After all, she had a steady job, health insurance, and Theo had neither, and he loved babies, couldn't wait for theirs.

Laney had a hard time believing that had been her life. How was it possible she had ever been that naïve? That in love? She wasn't even sure it was love anyway, but a kind of madness. She used to think that nothing could hurt more than finding out the love had been one-sided. Even as recently as four days ago, she thought that. Nothing could hurt more than Theo telling her he didn't love her, had never loved her, had grown to hate and resent her, even down to the force with which she placed her coffee cup on the counter or the way she laughed (horsey, he'd said, and nasal).

And then her son vanished.

She peered at the Hopper spreadsheet, trying to decide if a Donna Orlov (resident at the same building where Hopper had lived for six months in 1999) was a person of interest or a coincidence.

Her phone lit and she grabbed it, pressed the home button. A notification from Snapchat.

Jordan? she typed.

Mrs. Bird? he answered.

They found a body in Mr. Blue's apartment, she typed. Jordan could use a dose of fear in his life. What was he thinking, going to a grown man's house day after day?

She couldn't quite get her mind around the question of what Alfie had been thinking.

Alfie? he typed, and her stomach flipped at this combination of sentences. She waited. Let him feel scared. Let him feel guilty.

Then, after a sip of tea, *No. It's not Alfie. Now tell me everything.*

The app glowed at her while he typed. Finally, *I can't.*

Why?

Another pause. *You have to promise you won't tell my mom.*

Laney pursed her lips. She'd promise anybody anything to get the information she needed. But for all she knew, this kid was in danger too.

Look, she typed, *that man—the Mr. Blue guy—he's a killer. He killed one person already in that space you say he used to bring you to. Now the best way to avoid being body number two is tell me everything you know.* Strictly speaking, she didn't know for sure if Mr. Blue and Owen Hopper were one and the same and she didn't know if either one of them had killed the JD in the garage. But the chances of there being some random killer/child perverter on the loose living with Owen Hopper and taking down Hopper's enemies were slim to none.

We all knew he was dealing.

How long? she asked. *How long has he been dealing around here?*

Maybe two months? Before Christmas. He saw us at Nuncio's during winter break and offered us a ride home.

Alfie was with you?

Yes.

When would this have been? Had Alfie acted differently during winter break? God, he had a friend and she hadn't known about it. How would she know about him visiting unsavory ex-cons? Except she should have known.

Then where did you go?

His place. He asked if we wanted to go. It wasn't like he kidnapped us. Pause. *Sorry. I mean we agreed to go.*

What did you do there?

He gave us beer and we smoked a joint.

Alfie smoked too? Well, of course he did. Why would he go and keep going if he wasn't interested in the offerings?

Yes.

And then? What did Mr. Blue talk about?

I don't know. Mostly he just asked us about our lives. Pause. *He kind of just listened.*

That's it? How often did you go back?

I don't know. Like maybe ten times?

Like maybe ten or definitely ten?

I don't know. I really don't. We went like once a week. Sometimes twice.

Once a week! Sometimes twice! Where had she been? In her memory Alfie was always home, quiet with homework in his room or helping her with dinner.

And that's all it was? Beer, joints, and oversharing?

Yeah, he said.

She gritted her teeth. *Look, Jordan, do you have any idea why Mr. Blue took Alfie?*

Long pause. He started typing, then changed his mind.

She typed, *Do you think Alfie went with him on purpose?* It was a question that needed asking, but asking it made the pizza turn sour in her stomach. She got up and filled her cup with water from the tap, drank it in huge, thirsty gulps.

I don't know, Jordan typed. *Maybe. They talked a lot.*

What? Alfie talked a lot? With Owen fucking Hopper? Alfie could barely string a sentence together under the best of circumstances, the stutter twisting his face with frustration.

Her fingers hovered with uncertainty over her phone. She had to ask.

Was that all they did? Talk?

Silence on the other end.

Jordan? How about you? Did Mr. Blue ever touch you?

More silence.

Were you dealing for him?

He left the conversation.

She sat down and put her head in her hands. Dammit, dammit, dammit. An extreme weariness dragged at her and she slumped to the table, her forehead against the yellow-checked tablecloth.

Hopper must have been staking her out for weeks before making his move. Watching her, watching her son. Had he stood outside her house and looked through the windows? Had he followed her on her bus route? She thought of all the times she had followed him during that blue-white September three years ago, bulky in her disguises. Had he done the same? He could have been the man waiting for a ride in the supermarket parking lot, the heavyset guy filling a car at a pump next to hers, the dude in the parka handing out flyers on Main Street or the one walking the poodle around the bend from her front porch. He could have been anyone. And then, when did he change his mind? When did he notice Alfie and decide to focus on him?

"Oh, Alfie," she murmured into the tablecloth. "What did you do?"

After some time, her heart rate slowed, the blood receded from her cheeks. She sat up and texted Ed Boswell. *Ask Jordan Rogers about the drugs he's been selling for Hopper.*

Exposing Jordan's secret wouldn't help her cause, but that boy was almost as lost as her own. Perhaps a brush with the law at this young age would conclude his budding criminal career.

27

WHEN ALFIE WAS nine, his father took him to an arts festival in Williamsburg, Brooklyn. Or rather he took him along, since he was trying to secure a meeting with a gallery owner and Alfie's babysitter was out of town.

The arts festival occupied a square mile of old warehouses and factory buildings long since converted to studios and office spaces. Jugglers, acrobats, and musicians claimed corners and performed to the cheers of children and adults, food carts steamed, and the sparkling spring sunlight made the world bright and sharp.

Alfie followed his dad into a building, stumbled, and almost fell because he couldn't keep his eyes from the roiling action on the street. In the gallery, while Theo waited for the owner to finish showing other artists' works to a client, Alfie ran to the window and stuck his head out (no screens or guards on these windows, another wonder). From the sixth floor, the crowd below seemed even more vibrant, and his eyes didn't know where to land, what to watch, all of it exciting.

He stretched his body further into the air, and then someone grabbed him by his belt, was pulling him inside. Alfie looked up at the gray-haired man who held him. It was the gallery owner, the one his father had been waiting to see.

"Mr. Bird," the man said to Theo. "I think it's best if you come back another time. We should talk when it's quieter. Alone." He smiled when he said this, and his voice was gentle, but he held Alfie in place with a stern, firm hand.

Theo glared at Alfie, gripped his shoulder, and said to the other man, "Five minutes."

He led Alfie to the elevator, said nothing while they waited, then more nothing while they descended.

"Dad," Alfie sputtered. He wanted to ask what was wrong, but he couldn't get beyond that one word, his mouth twisting, his palms sweating. Something was wrong, though; his father wouldn't look at him, and his hand remained leaden and rough on his shoulder. Out on the street, Theo planted Alfie onto a curb next to a pretzel cart.

"Wait here," Theo said, meeting Alfie's eyes at last. Alfie knew by the wrinkle between his father's brows that he was unhappy. There was a coolness to his tone Alfie didn't like, and he had to hold back tears, which he could never do. His eyesight blurred, and his nose grew snuffly.

"Stop that," Theo snapped, pointing an index finger at Alfie's eyeball. Alfie fought with himself, swallowed, hard, and managed to prevent a full-on bawl. Theo watched him carefully for a minute to make sure Alfie wouldn't move, then said, "Stay here. I'll be back soon." And with that he disappeared into the building, leaving Alfie perched on the curb's edge.

From that angle he mostly saw people's pants, which were of all different colors and patterns. Eventually, he rose to his feet and walked two blocks to where a juggler was balancing on a unicycle, throwing multicolored pins, balls, and fruit into the air. Alfie edged his way through a crowd and sat on the ground next to a group of little kids, their parents a wall behind them.

The miraculous thing happened as the light waned and the juggler stepped down, picked up three torches, lit them, climbed back onto his cycle, and began to throw them into the air. In the blue twilight, the torches danced and flared, black smoke fluttering around their bright centers like inky gauze. And then the juggler opened his mouth and placed the flaming tip of a torch inside. Alfie gasped, pressed his hands against his chest, as if in an attempt to stop the fire from descending into his own lungs. He watched, mesmerized, as the evening came and the juggler put all three torches one by one between his lips, then breathed streams of yellow fire into the darkening air.

His father found him before the act ended and shook him, grabbed his wrist, dragged him toward their car, which was parked fifteen long blocks away from the festival.

"I told you to wait," Theo said through his teeth, his face so rigid Alfie forgot his disappointment in missing the rest of the fire eater's performance. His father was angry with him. His father was often angry with him, and no matter how hard Alfie tried to be good, he kept failing.

"I'm sorry," Alfie said. He had to run to keep up with Theo's long stride, and he was getting a stitch in his side but was afraid to complain.

They drove home in silence, except for when Alfie remembered to ask his father how the conversation with the gallery owner went. Theo shrugged, his brows knitting and his mouth turning down. "I can't very well get a deal with a gallery if I only have time to paint one painting every six months," he said.

"Can I help you paint?" Alfie asked.

At this, something in Theo's face softened, crumpled, and for a terrible second Alfie thought his father would start crying as well. Just when Alfie felt a sympathetic lump form in his throat, Theo reached out and ruffled his son's hair.

Some pressure lifted then, leaving Alfie tired and hungry but no longer close to tears. He spent the rest of the evening reliving the juggler's amazing feats, and when Theo had cooked Alfie's turkey burger (on a potato bun, with ketchup, one pickle slice, one tomato slice, the only way he could eat it; any other way felt impossible), he took his bath, put on his pajamas, and asked for the iPad.

Starting that evening, Alfie added the study of fire to his already beloved study of music.

CHAPTER

28

A FEW WEEKS BEFORE Theo left, Alfie, who was ten and a half
by then, was performing research in the backyard.

Theo was painting, locked in the bedroom he'd turned into a
studio, and had been for hours. Alfie knew better than to knock
or call or disturb his father in any manner whatsoever.

His mother had gone to work yesterday and still hadn't come
home, though she'd called a few times to wish Alfie good-night
and ask him if things were okay. As always, he told her everything was fine. He couldn't remember the last time she'd spent the
weekend with them, but he didn't mind. It gave him more time to
experiment and nobody to question or stop him.

Only the squirrels and the neighborhood cat paused to observe
as he held a lighter to a spray of Aqua Net and measured how
far the bright flame whooshed. He did the same with a can of
WD-40. Then with black spray paint, aiming at the hedges, the
sharp-leaved holly, the stone pathway laid through the grass. The
WD-40 sprayed furthest and hottest, and he wrote this down in
his notebook.

He didn't notice the smoke spiraling out of the studio window
until he'd stuffed the Aqua Net, WD-40, and spray paint into a
plastic bag along with his notepad. Only then did he realize the

burning smell was not coming from the singed shrubbery or the lawn but from his house.

He dropped the bag and ran inside, skidding along the wooden floor toward the locked studio door. He knocked, then kicked at the door, but heard nothing. Grayish tendrils furled out from under the paint-spattered wood, and Alfie panicked, his mouth so rigid he couldn't have screamed his father's name even if the entire house was engulfed.

He stepped back, then ran full speed at the studio door. The wood cracked but bounced him away. He did this two more times, then a third, then again. The burning smell had turned into something oilier, more acrid by the time the frame splintered and he shoved his way in.

His father slept, sprawled in the leather armchair that had been Alfie's uncle's, an empty bottle of wine at his feet, oblivious to the odoriferous smoke obscuring the corner where he kept his rags. His latest painting, inches away from the rags, was also beginning to smolder. The cloths, soaked with linseed oil and thrown to the floor carelessly, had begun to oxidize (Alfie learned later during another bout of research). With no air circulation inside the pile, heat had built up for days before finally combusting.

The floorboards were already charred. Alfie gaped at the heap for a second, then ran to the bathroom, grabbed the bucket from under the sink, filled it with water, ran back to the studio, and dumped the entire bucket onto the rags. Then, for good measure, he seized the wool Mexican blanket that had always hung on the studio wall, threw that onto the steaming rags, and stomped on it. His father had owned the blanket since his own childhood (he said). Alfie's studies taught him that wool was one of the most flame-resistant natural materials and was good for smothering flames; he had developed a habit of keeping a water-logged wool sweater with him when experimenting in his room.

Theo woke with a jerk and turned an outraged, bleary eye at Alfie.

"What the hell?" Theo rose from his chair, staring in horror at the black, oily mess on his floor, then at the broken lock. "What the hell are you doing?" he screamed, and grabbed Alfie by the arm, wrenching him off-balance so that Alfie tripped over his own feet and would have fallen if his father hadn't lifted him.

He tried saying something, tried to explain, but nothing came out of his mouth except saliva.

The bottom of the new painting was ruined, blackened with smoke and smeared with soot. The painting itself was of a monstrous mouth, open, red on the outside and brownish black on the inside, and it scared Alfie the way fire never could.

Theo dragged his son out of the studio and into the living room, then smacked him on the side of the head. "I told you to leave me alone!" he screamed. "I just asked for a few hours to myself, and you couldn't give it to me! What's wrong with you? Huh? What's wrong with you? Why are you like this?" And all the while he shook Alfie so that his teeth clacked and his upper arms bruised.

Alfie was beyond speaking, beyond trying to save himself. All he saw was hatred in his father's eyes, and it was the coldest, hardest thing he'd ever seen. He didn't even realize he'd started to cry until Theo yelled at him to stop.

"Just grow up!" Theo screamed. "Why can't you grow up! Stop bawling, for fuck sake, just stop it!"

Theo let go of him and slumped to the couch, his head in his hands. When Alfie tried to touch his shoulder, his body was so stiff, so rejecting, that Alfie sank to the floor and put his own head in his hands in despair.

By the time his mother came home, so tired she slurred her words when she told him she loved him and hugged him, Theo had thrown out the rags, washed the floor, and replaced the studio lock. Neither one of them mentioned what happened.

Not in so many words, anyway. But when Theo made his announcement three weeks later, Alfie knew it was because of him. Because he hadn't been able to explain. Because his father hated him.

CHAPTER

29

IN RETROSPECT, ALTHOUGH the spreadsheet Alfie created to narrow down possible friend candidates guided him to Jordan—
skinny, shifty, quick in all the ways Alfie wasn't but also just
enough geeky and philosophical for them to always have something to discuss—it was Alfie's spectacular failure at the fall talent
show and subsequent suspension that drew Jordan to him.

Alfie had practiced repeatedly in the backyard, though to be
honest, he made sure his mom was asleep or running errands when
he did. He followed all the safety instructions listed in the videos
he'd seen on the web. He even texted with an experienced fire
breather, who gave him useful pointers. He never had a problem,
not once. He never burned his fingers or his lips. He made sure
to wipe his mouth and face after every time he swigged the tiny
amount of kerosene needed to aspirate onto the lit torch.

Yes, he knew his mother wouldn't have allowed it, so he didn't
tell her. He figured she'd see him perform at the talent show and
then she'd know how careful he'd been and she'd forgive him.

But of course he didn't count on the show taking place
indoors. It wasn't supposed to. It was supposed to be outside, at
the park bandstand, on a Sunday, with food trucks and a DJ. But
the weather turned nasty, and rather than postponing the event,

the organizers moved it to the auditorium, the food vendors stinking up the hallways as they delivered paper plates heaped with
sausage and peppers, gyros, and empanadas.

He knew he should have withdrawn his name. But he had
practiced for such a long time, and he was good, the flame
whooshing from the torch as if he were a dragon—beautiful
and strong. Onstage, he placed his saxophone case on the floor,
opened it, and withdrew a torch, his little jar of kerosene, his
cloth, his lighter. The principal, who had been standing to the
side of the auditorium, was slow to react, his face first bemused,
then alarmed, then downright panicked when Alfie lit his torch.
He was still running down the aisle as Alfie tipped half a table-
spoon of kerosene into his mouth and blew a fine mist with all his
might, producing a gorgeous, ten-foot-long yellow flare. Which
ignited the curtains.

He was almost arrested. His mother was livid, took away his
phone, iPad, and laptop privileges for two weeks, and he was suspended for three days. But it was worth it.

Because there he was with a real, bona fide friend. Jordan made
it seem easy—this being-friends thing. He talked all the time. He
talked about the Snapchats he'd had that day or the night before,
about the Marvel multiverse and how Loki was a more powerful
god than Thor because Loki was smarter and could shapeshift,
about how the whole Batman versus Superman thing was completely false because why would they ever fight each other, it was
just a made-up war, not really real. He talked about Judy Bennett
in Algebra II and how he saw that she had a red welt on her thigh
through the rips in her jeans and how he thought it was razor
burn. All Alfie had to do was nod or shake his head and the conversation would continue.

They were together a lot that fall and winter—during lunch,
after school, at the football games, Alfie in his band uniform,
Jordan in his trademark black sweatshirt and jeans, though they
never visited each other's houses. They were together when Mr.
Blue approached them, and Alfie always thought it was Jordan

who drew the man's attention, what with his nonstop mouth and easygoing ways.

He was wrong about that, as he'd been about so many things. Alfie wondered how it was possible to go through life being as wrong about so much as he always seemed to be.

Alfie and Jordan were getting pizzas in the parlor on Main Street (Nuncio's, Jordan's favorite, though Alfie preferred Bella Theresa's on Third), and this guy sitting behind them jumped into their conversation. They tried to ignore him, raised their eyebrows at each other and waited for him to shut up, but he knew the most interesting stories and they couldn't help listening. He told them about Mr. Cooper at the high school who got fired for slamming a freshman boy into a locker early one morning. And about Dawn Pinelli who babysat for the football coach and then got caught on surveillance emptying his medicine cabinet and liquor cabinet and, most fun of all, his gun cabinet. Once the man had their attention, he asked them about themselves, what they liked. He fell into the rhythm of their dialogue effortlessly, theorizing perfectly sound opinions on the best Skrillex versus deadmau5 (Mr. Blue preferred deadmau5, and Alfie totally agreed). When he offered to drive them home—it was December, below freezing, raw and windy, and they were a good forty-minute walk from their respective houses—they said sure, great. And when he said he had to pick something up from his apartment and would they mind, they said no they wouldn't, and once there, he handed them a couple of beers and dropped a needle—literally, the guy had a turntable—on Nosaj Thing, and that was that.

CHAPTER

30

A T THE TIME it seemed the decision to focus on Hopper and bring him in as a CI was one the entire team undertook. But really, when she tried to remember, it was always Harry who'd pushed for it.

"Put the word out," Harry had said. "Ask the regulars if they know who he is. I'm telling you, he's going to be the one. He'll give us the rest of them. My gut tells me so." Harry's gut had solved hundreds of cases in his career and he was fond of it, not shy about giving it credit.

Laney, no less desperate for a proper break in the case, saw the sense in what he said and asked Bunny and a few others to keep an eye out for the tall, older guy with the blond crew cut. Besides, she had no further leads. She'd be making dime-bag buys for a year before they had anything near felony counts on any one of the Orlov dealers, and they still would not have Orlov.

"Him?" Bunny asked, perfect eyebrows rising. "The really old dude?"

"Well, he can't be more than midforties. Why, do you know him?" Laney asked.

"No!" She *tsk*ed. "What do you want with him?"

Laney rolled her eyes, then asked if Bunny had any dope on her (she knew she didn't, could see from the sheen on Bunny's forehead and the slight trembling in her hands that she was jonesing, needing a fix, and soon). This led to another buy from Malyish, followed by a well-deserved hour in a fiercely air-conditioned bar with Harry and Mike.

"I saw our white John Doe today." Harry sipped his Scotch. "Over by Baikal. He must live in the area."

"But what makes you think he's part of Viktor's group, though? Maybe he's just another dope fiend," Laney said.

Harry shrugged. "I got a feeling. He doesn't have the dope fiend look." He patted Laney on the back. "How's Alfie doing?"

She gulped down half her lager. "You know. Good." She nodded. Her son had been quiet since the swimming pool incident at camp back in August and the subsequent expulsion. Subdued, wouldn't talk about it, but clung to her when she was home, sometimes even sitting on her lap when they ate dinner. Theo'd say, you're too old for that, sit in your own chair, but Alfie would remain glued to her thighs and she allowed it, and in the end Theo would frown and pour another glass of wine.

At last, three weeks after she'd first seen their John Doe, Bunny sauntered over and asked Laney for a cigarette. Laney always made sure to have a fresh pack, just for sharing.

"So, that guy you've been ogling?" Bunny lit the cigarette and inhaled deeply.

"Yeah?" Laney tried to sound bored. With Bunny, a jaded vibe worked best.

"Turns out he works in a pharmacy."

"Ooooh, that explains the nice clothes."

Bunny snorted. "What nice clothes? That JCPenney bullshit he's got going on? Really?"

Laney shrugged.

Bunny looked at her and shook her head. "He's in with Viktor Orlov."

Laney bit the inside of her cheek, feigned a confused frown. As far as Bunny was concerned, Laney knew nothing about Orlov.

Bunny said, "Stay away from him. And"—she paused for extra drama—"he's married. With a kid."

Laney had to look across the street so as not to give away the excitement galloping within her. All these months, and here, potentially, the weak link. A man involved with their target. A man with a family. Family made a person weak.

Harry was right. His gut had killer instincts.

She looked back at Bunny and winked. "I like 'em better married."

Bunny laughed, then grew somber. She stomped out her cigarette and placed both hands around Laney's biceps, bending down so their eyes were level. "I'm serious, baby. Stay away from him. Those Russians are no joke." She straightened and flipped her long hair off her shoulder. "Just saying. Woman to woman. You don't want to get mixed up in that shit."

"I know." Laney frowned. "But you know how it is. I like him."

"Baby, you don't know him! You just saw him the once! What's the matter with you?"

Laney thought that standing on a corner waiting to get done by a drug dealer might begin to answer that question. She said, "You wouldn't happen to have his name, would you?"

Bunny sighed, then stuck a Post-it note on Laney's chest before walking away, her hips swinging lusciously atop long, glossy legs. Owen Hopper's name and phone were on that yellow Post-it.

After that, all they needed was a half hour's worth of checks and they knew where he lived, where he worked, his wife's name, his son's, his car, his license plate number, his moving violations, his wife's parking tickets. As they suspected and hoped, he was no relation to Viktor Orlov. His wife was Russian, but she arrived in the U.S. back in the midnineties, her entire family remaining overseas. If cornered, his only familial obligations were to himself, his wife, and his son. He was perfect.

All they needed next was to pin something on him. It had to be big enough to potentially send him away for a year but not so big that being a CI couldn't save him. A small sentence could be negotiated away with a trophy as substantial as Orlov in return.

They decided to begin with surveillance.

CHAPTER

31

SEPTEMBER UNFURLED ITS mild breezes, chased away the oppressive heat. For six days she played the role of a homeless woman, padding her body with pillows under shapeless clothes she'd rubbed with dirt. It was a peaceful week, sitting on a park bench in the sun, facing his building. When he went to work, she followed, pushing her shopping cart full of trash. A few times she followed his wife and son.

The son was a couple of years older than Alfie, and she found herself studying him, sometimes following him when she was meant to trail the father. The boy had both a sweetness and an intensity to him that reminded her of Alfie, and Hopper was endlessly caring toward him, spending hours in conversation with him, shooting hoops, playing chess in the park after work.

The boy took after his dad in looks and tastes—a blond, gray-eyed, gangly teen in skinny jeans and expensive sneakers. Despite his father's love and attention, or maybe because of it, Laney had a feeling she wasn't going to be the last cop showing an interest in him. Once school began, he cut classes to ride the subways, jumping on top of cars only to flatten himself just before they screeched into a tunnel. The second time she followed him, her maternal instinct overwhelmed her and she took pictures, printed them, and left them in the Hopper mailbox. As far as she could tell, that was the last of both school cutting and train jumping.

Most mornings she lingered on a stoop next to the pharmacy where he worked.

"Goddammit," she told Harry midweek back at the precinct, "your gut should have its own pension."

"Oh yeah?" He grinned, leaned back in his chair, popped a pretzel into his mouth. "Bingo on our guy Hopper?"

"Every morning, carloads of people are unloaded at the pharmacy. Eighteen yesterday, twenty today. They go in all together, like a tourist group, and come out all together a half hour later. *Then* the dopeheads start arriving, like clockwork. The really shabby ones who are about to shit themselves go into the alley behind the pharmacy."

Harry extended the bag of pretzels, and she grabbed a handful, then continued. "So I go to the alley and shuffle over to one of them—you know him, Guppie—the one with all the pockmarks?"

Harry smiled and nodded.

"I say, you holding? And he says, nah, I'm waiting. And I say, for what, and he says, just wait. And what do you know? Guess who opens the back door and comes out for a cigarette break, except he's got everything you want—he's got oxy, dope, coke, whatever." She crunched on a pretzel. "I think we can bring him in just based on what I witnessed today, but we'll need a few buys to seal the deal."

Next week, wired up with the ghost kit, she listened in as one of their newer undercovers, Kyle Thompson, went into the pharmacy where Owen Hopper worked. She strolled past the alley, made sure she'd have a clear, unobstructed view, crossed the street, leaned against the brick wall of a storefront accountant office, and shook out a cigarette.

The pharmacy was owned by an octogenarian immigrant from the Soviet Union, a man who'd served ten years in the gulags for political reasons and been a refusenik in the seventies until he finally managed to escape the motherland and land in Brooklyn.

Now he suffered from diabetes, heart disease, rheumatoid arthritis, varicose veins, asthma, and depression and rarely inspected his place of business, leaving the running of it to Hopper.

They had timed Kyle Thompson's visit a few minutes before the truckload of patients arrived. Kyle milled between the aisles, his blurred outline winking in and out of view, bought a bottle of vitamins and left, walked to the end of the block, then turned back. When the first junkie sidled into the alley behind the store, he followed. Kyle was too much of a novice (his hair too short, his physique too well fed and healthy) for him to play anything but what he was, a suburban working-class guy, and the act worked; his buys were usually quick and efficient.

He joined the junkie already waiting and squatted against the wall. Laney couldn't see their faces clearly, but her view was good enough for her not to worry. Through her headset, she heard Kyle's soft breathing and his "Hey, man" to the junkie.

When the back door opened and Hopper stepped out, the dopehead, dispensing with niceties, creaked to his feet and said, "Two perc tens."

Hopper ignored him and faced Kyle, his posture stiff, shoulders squared.

The junkie shifted his feet and stared at Kyle too.

"Hey," Kyle said.

Hopper nodded.

"I saw your post on Craigslist," Kyle said. Hopper listed his inventory online but in posts so cryptic that they had to show them to one of their other CIs for translation. He changed it every day or so, another curious detail setting him apart from Viktor's associates. He'd made himself traceable. At the time she thought this meant he wasn't so smart, would be an easy win. Later, of course, she understood Hopper was simply following orders, never questioning their origin or purpose.

Hopper said nothing.

"I'm Kev," Kyle said, which was his entirely unimaginative undercover name. "Craigslist? I asked if you had thirty mgs and you said sure." His posture was relaxed, easy. He was just a contractor taking a half hour out of fixing someone's kitchen to get done. "You said thirty bucks each, right?"

Hopper nodded.

Kyle fished three hundreds from his jacket pocket and held them up. The junkie stared at the cash, and even from across the street Lanie suspected he was drooling, though she couldn't be sure due to his general decrepitude.

Hopper went inside, then a few minutes later came out with a small paper bag, handed it to Kyle, took the cash, and turned to the junkie, who, still staring wide-eyed at the undercover, had to be prodded to produce his paltry scrap of bills.

"Positive buy," Laney said into her set.

"Great job!" Harry said once they were back in the office. "Criminal sale of a controlled substance in the third degree." He handed her a bag filled with *chebureki*, still hot from the fryer, then bit into one himself.

"Lamb?" Laney sniffed the pastries, and Harry nodded, wiping the juice from his mouth. She fished out a turnover and nibbled the flaky corner. "I guess we have him," she said.

Harry and Mike brought Hopper in the next day, waiting for him to leave work before approaching and asking him to come with. He refused at first. They were in plain clothes, the unmarked Impala parked at a meter a few cars down, and they told him they'd have no trouble calling a patrol car and having him arrested right then, in front of everyone. So do it, he said, and stomped away. But they wouldn't leave him, matching his stride, and as they all walked, Harry and Mike pointed out two of Viktor Orlov's cousins staring out a deli window. What do you suppose they'll think, Harry said, if they see you carted away in a police car? What do you think they'll do? Hopper shrugged, said I don't fucking care, and Harry smiled his thin smile, only his lips stretching, and said I believe you care.

Hopper slowed, stopped, squinted at the two detectives, and said, "Fine, but I'm not getting into that junker that's screaming it's a cop car. I'll walk."

Laney watched Harry and Mike question Hopper on camera in the small interview room at the back of the precinct. He could never know she was a cop. As far as Hopper was concerned, Laney would also be a confidential informant, another person caught up in the drug world and stuck between prison and an offer of clemency.

"We have enough evidence to put you away for a while," Harry said. "Could be nine years. That's a long time in your kid's life."

Hopper sat in his uncomfortable chair calmly, his arms crossed. "So why am I not arrested yet?" he asked.

Mike said, "You want something, maybe? A coffee? Tea? I think we have soup in the kitchen today."

"I'm fine," Hopper said.

Harry sipped a soda. "Look," he said, "it's clear you're smart. You have a nice family. We'll take you, but we don't really want you." He put the soda down and leaned forward. "You know who we want."

Hopper looked down, his first indication of unease. "I have no idea who you want," he said.

"No?" Harry cocked his head. "We want Viktor Orlov."

Hopper tensed, his shoulders squaring, his hands twisting into fists, evident even in the gray surveillance footage. He said nothing, wouldn't look up.

"Owen," Harry said, "you sold felony-weight controlled substances to an undercover. Other undercovers can testify to you possessing and selling multiple weights on multiple days. Depending on the DA's mood, that's anything from one to nine years. Add one to nine years for each occurrence. We can arrest you today and you will never see your son graduate from school. I doubt he'll go to college or anything. Hard when your dad's in prison. Not providing."

He sat back and picked up his soda, sipped again. Said amiably, "Or who knows, maybe that crazy-hot wife of yours will get remarried and the new guy will pay for college. It happens."

Hopper raised his head, but there was a steadiness to him. He was listening, hard.

"Putting you away will give us nothing. Orlov will have another guy in that store tomorrow. If we close down that store, he'll go somewhere else. We need to get him."

Hopper looked up at the camera, and Laney shrank back. He seemed to be staring directly at her. After a moment, he placed his elbows on the metal table and faced Harry. He said, "Viktor is a smart guy. He keeps himself to himself. I don't know if I can help you. Even if I wanted to. Which at the moment I don't know if I do, since you haven't told me what I'll get."

Mike said, "If you give us enough information to put away Viktor Orlov, we may be able to persuade the DA to put you on probation, seeing as it's your first offense."

"Probation will not help much if I'm dead. Which is what I will be if I give you what you want." The tendons were jumping in his jaw. "Just arrest me now. They'll take care of my family."

Harry held up his hands, palms out. "Hold on, hold on there. You seem almost eager for prison." He smirked. "Family life getting to you? Need a break?"

"Fuck off," said Hopper. "I can't help you. Just do what you need to do and fuck off."

Mike said, "I think you misunderstand us. We don't expect you to testify or anything. Nobody will know it was you. Just keep doing what you're doing. We'll send another confidential informant to work with you. Get them acquainted with Orlov's men. If you can, introduce this person to Orlov and the CI will make all the buys. When it's time to testify, you're out of it."

"Are you serious? Nobody will know?"

"Not unless you blab," Harry said. "You don't strike me as someone who blabs. Do you blab?"

Owen looked at Harry, then Mike, then Harry, then the camera.

Something cold coiled and turned inside Laney's gut. Excitement (because the hunt was about to start), apprehension (because the hunt was about to start), and maybe a touch of pity (because didn't she know him by now?).

"It's just a recording," Harry said, never taking his eyes from Hopper.

"Okay," Hopper said. "I've got everything to gain and nothing to lose, right? Isn't that your point?"

Mike clapped him on the shoulder. "Exactly our point, my man. You sit tight. I'll be back with some forms and we'll get started."

For the first couple of weeks after this, Hopper gave them dreck. The names and numbers he wrote down led to dead ends, abandoned apartments, absent dealers, empty storehouses.

"Douchebag's fucking with us," Mike said.

"Wants to play that game, we'll raid the pharmacy and arrest him today," Harry said.

"Wait until Saturday," Laney said. She knew from her surveillance that Hopper's son, Otto, played varsity basketball on Fridays and Owen always went, escorting his flashy wife to the bleachers, buying them all hot dogs and pretzels. It was a completely stupid, unreasonable, unprofessional reason to hold off an arrest, but something in her wanted to see them all three together, happy like that. If he was going away for years, he might as well get one last, beautiful night with his family.

As it turned out, Owen did not get to see his son play basketball that night, but he did get an extra two months with his wife and son due to Viktor Orlov's calculating nature.

That Friday afternoon, two men in black tracksuits approached Hopper as he walked home, their bodies tautly muscled, wiry, their feet nimble as they directed him off to the side and then down the steps leading into a building's inner courtyard.

Laney, in her homeless-lady drag for the day, schlepped her shopping cart to the top of the steps and crouched. It never ceased to amaze her how easy it was to be invisible. Make yourself dirty and fat, layer torn, shabby, filthy clothes over your body, rub oil into your hair, and voilà! No one looks at you. Even the criminals look away.

The acrid stench of urine drifted upward from the tunnel leading into the courtyard. She could hear voices but had to strain to decipher the words. They had stopped in the tunnel, the two men flanking Hopper, closing in on him, their bodies coiled, ready to strike.

Hopper, to his credit, did not back down, did not cower. The tendons in his neck bulged as he talked, his face glistening with sweat and worry. Laney held her breath, every cell listening.

They knew about his visit to the station, and he swore up and down, on all the saints and his mother's life, that he'd said nothing, would say nothing, what did they take him for, he would gladly serve time rather than betray them. In the end, despite the fact that one of the men had shoved him, sending him pinwheeling awkwardly into a filthy puddle, they left him alone.

They bounced out of the tunnel, sleek and quick, heedless of Laney's bulky form against the wall. Hopper emerged a few minutes later, his slacks stained, his white linen shirt torn at the sleeve. One look at his eyes and Laney knew he was ready for her. He had the face of a person watching his house burn. In one unlucky month, he'd lost Orlov's trust and was looking at years in prison.

With her by his side, all he had to do was continue standing his ground with Orlov, protest his loyalty, all the while feeding her everything he had. He could put Orlov's entire family away and remain untouched.

Later, after she'd showered and changed into her street clothes, she joined Harry and Mike for a pint at their local.

"He's going to work with us properly now," she said. "He's about to crumple. Between those McThuggers and the two of you squeezing him, he's ready to pop."

"You sure?" asked Harry.

"Like a cannoli."

Mike gestured for a second pint. "Well," he said, "in that case, it sounds like it's time for him to meet Kendra. Officially."

She grinned. Yes, time for Kendra to leave the shadow world and enter the world of the noticed, the observed, the heeded.

They didn't need a scared informant, who might tell them anything, might lead them into a trap, might clam up altogether. And they didn't need a dead one, which was sure to happen if Orlov got the idea Hopper was betraying them. They needed a sneaky one whose best interest coincided with theirs.

32

O N THE DAY Laney was to officially connect with Owen Hopper, she almost didn't. She waited at the precinct for Harry, who was uncharacteristically late, and tried not to check her messages. Alfie had had an episode two days before, something to do with his locker and him not being able to open it in time, and then being marked tardy in math class, and then panicking. The nurse called, the principal called, the guidance counselor. Laney felt an involuntary anxious spasm every time her phone pinged. The way she was feeling that day, she was better off burying the phone in her desk drawer. Theo would have to handle anything that happened, because if she wasn't *on*, wasn't one hundred percent focused, she'd blow her cover. And if she blew it while Hopper was introducing her to Orlov's men, she'd be screwed.

She swiped a bit of gloss on her lips—mauve, because Kendra liked mauve. The sticky, strawberry-scented balm put her in mind of Theo's latest work, and she ran her hands through her hair in irritation, her fingers snagging on the jeweled bobby pins she'd threaded through.

Theo had started a new series of paintings—canvases six, seven, eight feet tall featuring enormous mouths. Pink, coral, red, umber, black, cracked, glossy, toothless and overly toothed, these orifices screamed and moaned at her whenever she entered his studio, and for the first time his work unnerved her. If she were to be honest, which she wouldn't be, not even with herself, they revolted her.

The days of perching on his painting stool, yakking away about her adventures while he painted, were long gone. She didn't even know when that had stopped, but he'd gotten into the habit of locking the studio door when working. She knew he needed his painting time, so she left it alone. Consequently, she hadn't been able to discuss her case and her doubts about it with anyone. Kendra's personality was usually uncomplicated for Laney, but something about Owen Hopper, or the seriousness of the next phase, the high stakes, rattled her.

She needed another, deeper angle. She couldn't just be chaotic, dope-sick Kendra; it wouldn't fly with the Russians. She'd kept her thoughts to herself for obvious reasons. Nobody wanted a waffling undercover on a case this big. She couldn't, wouldn't botch it up.

When Harry arrived, forty-five minutes late and out of breath, Laney leaned back in her chair and crossed her legs. Said, "What, no Danish? Not even a *churro con chocolate*?" She squinted, took in his flushed cheeks, dilated pupils, flaring nostrils. "Harry, are you exercising? Are you exercising *and* on a diet?" She almost laughed, the relief of finally starting the day rushing through her, a bright and fresh feeling, her qualms at rest for now.

"You're funny," Harry said, shrugging off his jacket, the top of his gun visible over his belt. "Damn BQE. Two trucks broke down, one after the damn other. A fucking parking lot for three miles." He'd already signed in, had the case folder in his hands, riffled through it, then dropped it on his desk.

"Whenever you're ready," Laney said. And here it was, the excitement, the thrill, coiling within her, warming. Of course she wouldn't fail. Kendra always made a buy. And if this time the buy was pounds instead of ounces, tens of thousands instead of tenners and twenties, she could do that too.

Harry looked at his feet, glanced around. They were alone in their corner, heaps of empty space surrounding them. He sat facing her.

"How are you feeling?" he asked.

"Like the fucking queen who's going to take Orlov down," she said.

He didn't smile in answer; his eyes somber, his face, though glistening (from what? his run? had he really run to the office?), seemed haggard, the eye sockets sunken, a raw-looking welt on his neck slithering into his shirt collar.

She sat forward. "What?"

"Laney, there's something I need to tell you."

Heart thumping, hard, her hands and feet ice-cold. "What?"

"I know you've been on this case from the beginning."

She frowned.

"But Orlov's guys are vicious. Hopper isn't one of them, and we know that. I'm not talking about him." As if she'd objected when she hadn't. She held her breath. "I'm talking about the others. They're violent as shit, and you can't fight them." He raised his hand, again as if she'd objected. "It's simple biology. Every one of them can fuck you up, and no amount of karate or Krav Maga is going to save you."

"What are you saying, Harry? You don't want me to go ahead?"

He stared at her, stubborn. "I'm saying that maybe we get Thompson to go instead. You've got a kid to think about."

Kyle? Kyle was too new. He didn't have the imagination or the experience to roll with it if something came up.

"Are you serious?" she asked. Neither one of them moved. Why was Harry saying this? Had he sensed her doubts? "Kyle will fuck this case up the ass and back. He has no idea how to talk to anyone. He screams cop."

"He's not so bad. He's been doing it for six months. And he has a hundred pounds and eight inches on you."

"No offense, Harry, but take those eight inches and shove them up your crack." She jumped to her feet and jerked her handbag over her shoulder. "I'm the only person for this case, and I don't have the slightest idea why you're sitting there and not driving me. Maybe you're the one who needs to sit this one out? Should I ask Mike to ghost me instead? Or Kyle?" For some reason she made air quotes around Kyle's name, and that didn't even make any sense, but that's how she got when she was mad.

Harry held her eyes for a few more beats, then looked away, rose to his feet, patted his pockets, grabbed his jacket and headed out. She followed.

Later, in the car, as they neared Hopper's pharmacy, Harry grinned. "I had you there, didn't I?"

She turned to face him, bemused.

He patted her knee. "Nothing like being told you're not good enough for something to make you want to fight for it," he said.

Realization (and relief, and gratitude, and annoyance) hit her all at once, and she had to look out the window so he wouldn't see all that in her face. Yes, Harry was a good detective. And he was an even better partner. Later, after she'd started making the bigger buys and the captain praised her in person, she found out she hadn't been the first choice to work with Hopper after all. Harry had fought for her, had to convince the bosses she was the only person for the job.

And even later still, she realized his reasons for fighting for her had nothing to do with her abilities and everything to do with his perception of her loyalties. Which perception was, as always with him, utterly accurate.

33

AFTER HIS ONE visit to the station, Hopper refused to come back. I'll tell you everything, he said, but you gotta come to me. I'm dead otherwise. And since nobody wanted a dead CI, especially not one it had taken nearly half a year to find, everything he gave them had to come through Laney from now on. They told him there'd be another CI coming but didn't specify who. Keep doing what you're doing, Harry told him, be yourself, and we'll take care of the rest.

That first day, she bought three hundred dollars' worth of oxy and Ritalin from him. The second day, twice that. The third day, she asked if she could talk to him in the back room.

"I have a business proposition," she said.

"I'm good," he said. "I don't need any more business."

"Maybe then I have a proposition for your supplier."

At this, he stopped what he was doing and looked at her, taking in her smooth hair (she'd changed the style, brushing it down over her forehead for a sleeker, more professional look), her fitted blouse, her slacks. She could almost hear the gears churning in his head—was she the CI sent by the cops? Or was she just another small-time dealer wanting in on an operation?

"Come back tomorrow at one," he said.

He always closed the pharmacy from one to two, and that's when she showed up the next day, carrying a slice of pizza and a can of orange soda in a grease-spotted brown paper bag.

They met in the back office, his pastrami and Swiss on rye spread out on the scarred oak desk and her pizza cooling on her lap. The office, for decades the domain of the octogenarian Russian immigrant, was decorated with an American flag, a black-and-white photograph of the octogenarian as a young man, and a color one of him in front of the Statue of Liberty.

Hopper bit at his sandwich, chewed quickly.

"What are you looking for?" he asked.

Laney sat up straighter, moved her pizza to the cluttered desk. Some grease dripped onto a receipts pile and she let it. A little of Kendra's chaos was good; it suggested a believable irreverence. She had discussed her persona and angle with Harry and team for days before settling on a plausible story. Harry was adamant that she couldn't play the buyer herself; the Russians would never trust a woman. Or maybe they would, he'd said, but not quickly.

When he first suggested this, Laney bristled. Would she always have to prove herself, work harder, be tougher, and still have to endure colleagues and perps alike judging her based on her reproductive organs? She was small in stature, yes, but so was her father, who had weighed in at 145 pounds at his heaviest and barely broke the five-foot-six mark, neither of which stopped him from amassing over three thousand arrests in his career. Prior to becoming an undercover (when the arrests she facilitated had to be attributed to detectives working with her or else blow her cover), she'd had the third-most collars in her command.

"He's right," Kyle the newbie chimed in. "You're too pretty. They won't believe you."

As Laney was about to shoot something back about Kyle's own dubious believability, Harry interrupted. "You have to work with them, Laney. Give them what they expect to see."

Her pulse slowed, and she broke eye contact with Kyle and looked through the grimy precinct window—women in form-fitting skirts and heels, men in shirt sleeves. Even the children and the elderly dressed along strict gender lines. She glared at Harry. She could pretend he was being a dick, but he was only being honest. She'd have to figure out how to work within this culture. She'd learn how to be the right person for this assignment. The only person.

"I'll tell Hopper I'm buying for my man," she said. Besides, it wasn't her job to educate anyone in the finer points of gender equality. Her job was to buy drugs.

Harry nodded. "Good. Who's your man?"

"Runs a discount store in Buffalo. Supplies all the college students with oxy, dope, blow, Molly, Vicodin, Ritalin, Adderall, Fentanyl, et cetera, et cetera. Our old connection fucked off somewhere and we need a new one."

The guys agreed. "That would work," said Mike. "You could even use that as an excuse if you're in a hairy situation. You can say you need to talk it out with your old man."

Harry smiled. "I like it. Why Buffalo?"

She shrugged. "College town. Kids do drugs. Also, it's near Niagara Falls. Have you ever been there?" She'd always wanted to go, but when she wasn't working, Theo wanted time to paint. Then there was Alfie, who would eat only the three foods he allowed himself, prepared just the right way. Somehow they just never went.

Harry shook his head.

"Me neither," she said. "So a person can dream, right?" That was the thing about fake identities. She could be anybody, from anywhere.

Harry sat back, his shoulders relaxing. "Okay, so your guy is a mover and shaker in Buffalo, and you make buys for him. Sounds convoluted, but that's good. Mundane stories are the easiest to double-check."

She said, "I'll make sure he'll be able to verify what I tell him anyway." Easy enough to get fake business cards for the discount store, a burner phone with that number. Let Kyle the believability expert answer it if anyone ever calls.

Now, sitting across from Owen Hopper, Laney felt Kendra taking over, loosening her limbs, her lips quirking in a flirty smile. Kendra, unlike Laney, knew her appeal and didn't mind using it. Not at all.

"Oxy to start. Adderall, Ritalin. I'll need dope, coke. Molly if you have it." She popped the tab on her soda and sipped.

"Is that it?" he asked, but with a smile, amused.

"College kids," she said, smiled back. "Mommies and daddies are bleeding cash into their kids' pockets and the kiddies are breaking down our door at all hours."

He balled up the paper bag from his sandwich. "Our door?" he asked.

"Yeah, me and my husband. Up in Buffalo. It's pretty there, you know? But yeah, we're looking to do more business. Or rather, business is booming and our supplier can't keep up. So I'm, you know, looking around."

He glanced at his phone. "I got to get back soon," he said.

She sat forward. "How are you getting around iStop for the scrips? We looked into that, but the state counts every fucking pill."

Hopper chewed the inside of his cheek. Laney wondered what he was thinking. If he suspected she was the CI, he'd answer her questions, since that was the agreement he made at the precinct. If he decided to believe her story, he might give her the brush-off.

She said, "Hey, we've got cash. We'll buy from your supplier, or from you, no problem. I'm just curious."

"Yeah," he said. "Whatever." He cocked his head at her. "So what do they have on you? You got caught selling? Buying? Someone OD'd?"

It was okay if he knew she was the one feeding his information to the police, as long as he didn't realize she was police herself. She was Kendra with him. And Kendra was never honest.

"Honey," she said, "I just asked a question. If you don't want to answer, no big deal, but I got ten K that needs spending, so you tell me what you have for me."

He looked away, his face tired all of a sudden. He said, "We have a doctor. Name is Bruce Shulman. He's a GP, married to Orlov's niece. It's a very simple gig—anybody around here on Medicaid who needs extra cash goes to Orlov and he sends them to the GP. He prescribes them painkillers, whether they need them or not, and he enters the information into iStop. Each patient gets thirty bucks for the trouble of going to the doctor and getting the scrip. I put the scrips into the system and log everything into the New York database. Insurance, mostly Medicaid, pays for the pills. If the person is an addict and they have the money but their insurance won't cover the meds, they come to me. It's theoretically legal, or at least we make it look legal."

"That's brilliant," she said. "If I didn't know about the other stuff going through this place, I'd say you're practically squeaky clean."

The corner of his mouth twitched. "Yeah. You can't prove the patients don't need the pain meds. Then I fill the scrips, the patients fuck off to wherever they spend their days with their thirty bucks, and I sell the pills. Thirty apiece, and twenty-five of it goes to Orlov."

"And Shulman? What's his cut?"

Hopper grinned. "Orlov takes good care of his family. Nice cars, nice clothes, jewelry, vacations."

"All right, sounds good. Maybe I'll make an appointment with Dr. Shulman." She picked a gob of cheese off her cold pizza and rolled it between her fingers. "All those kiddies coming to me for the oxy and the Vicodin eventually come to me for dope. So that's on my grocery list as well."

He glanced at his phone again. "There's a load coming in from the West Coast on Wednesday. I will put you in touch with a guy named Oskar Koshka." He stood up. It was near two PM.

She gathered her uneaten lunch and dumped it into the trash can. Together they made their way back to the front, and he opened the door, letting in the smells of dust and gasoline, ocean and incense.

A skinny girl with too much makeup over greasy skin and overbleached hair edged into the alley behind the shop, glancing at Owen, her eyes sharply hungry.

Laney watched her merge with the shadows, wondered how old she was. Sixteen? Seventeen?

"Do you feel superior to her?" Owen asked, and the question was so unexpected that Laney responded with an incredulous little laugh.

But then she peered at the darkened, stinking alley. Would Kendra feel superior to that girl? The answer came easy. "Yes," she said. "Of course. She let something own her."

Hopper walked back into the coolness of the pharmacy, the door swinging shut. She followed him as he shouldered open the back door, handed the junkie girl her fix, pocketed her cash.

"See now, I don't think of it that way," he said. "Not everyone is that in charge of themselves. Some of them are so young. They think they're invincible, that they'll never be like that. They'll never sell their bodies." He went behind the counter and retrieved an empty pill bottle, began filling it. "But they do."

"Everyone has a choice, Owen," Laney said. "I have a choice. My choice is to give them what they want. If it wrecks them, that's on them. I make my decisions and they make theirs."

He peeled a label off a sheet and stuck it onto the bottle. "All of our decisions come down to survival," he said. "Really, in the end. For all of us. The dopeheads come to me because if they don't get their fix, they'll die. Or feel like it anyway. You come to me because if you don't give the cops what they want, they'll take something away from you. Something you need to survive."

She picked up a candy bar and placed two dollars on the counter between them. "And you? How did you end up in all this?"

He pushed the dollars back to her. "Just trying to survive, Kendra. Just trying to survive."

Five days later, following his introduction, she bought the biggest batch of heroin she'd ever seen. The transaction took place above a law office, and the seller, Oskar Koshka, along with his two bodyguards, was not only happy to take her cash but treated her with a flirtatious deference that made the whole experience feel like an odd date.

"Adding the husband was a brilliant touch," Harry told her after he'd vouchered the dope. He'd volunteered to do the vouchering for her, since she was still finishing her buy report, her expense report, and they all wanted to go home.

Months later, when questioned about the discrepancies between her reports and the vouchered drugs, she said she'd been tired, preoccupied with domestic drama, couldn't remember the details.

But that day the adrenaline from the buy pumped through her. It had gone so easy, she didn't know why they all worried. At this rate, they'd get every one of Orlov's guys in weeks, a couple months at most. They had evidence to put away five of them already—Malyish, Koshka and the two bodyguards, and Bruce Shulman, who had written enough bad scrips for Kyle Thompson (and for once, Kyle's wholesome suburban looks paid off) to earn himself at least five years and a hefty fine.

"Reeling in that big fish!" said Harry, and clapped her on the shoulder.

"I'm not counting fish sticks until they're chopped, breaded, and fried, but I can sure smell the batter," she said, already stepping into the elevator to begin the commute home. Her own family waited—her strange, imperfect, and utterly beloved family. When she was in this kind of mood, on the heels of a success, she told herself she did this job to protect her loved ones, to provide for them, to cocoon them within the strength of her love.

Harry, who knew her better than anyone, called out to her as the elevator doors closed, "Keeping the world safe."

CHAPTER

34

AND YET, THE case stalled after that auspicious beginning.
Meetings fell through, sellers grew cagey and walked away.
She wondered if her cover had blown and she not known it, if
Hopper had ratted her out and then strung her along.

Despite all the time and money spent, they had no hard
evidence against Orlov, nobody who'd risk their lives speaking
against him.

"One more week," Harry told her as they hunkered in a Chi-
nese restaurant, a bowl of dumplings over ramen noodles before
him, pepper beef for Mike, a plate of fried wontons for her. "If we
can't get something on him in that time, we're off the case, all of
us. They're interviewing some cops who can speak Russian." He
shrugged. "Probably not such a bad idea."

She stabbed her chopstick into a wonton, then again, without
eating. "I can do this, Harry." Though she didn't know how. Should
she be tougher? Or more feminine? Should she flirt? Or threaten? Be
professional and aloof? Where was she stumbling? She didn't know
how she could have read the signals for last week's buys so wrong.

The next meeting, tomorrow night, had to be it. Hopper had
set it up, introduced her to one of Orlov's cousins, was going to
have Oskar Koshka vouch for her legitimacy. It was supposed to

be the final one—the real deal, Orlov in the room, half a kilo of coke, and bam, case closed.

Harry put down his fork and looked at her, hard. "I don't think you should go," he said. He wasn't kidding either; she could see it in the grim set of his jaw, his stiff shoulders. He'd been short with her, with everyone, all day.

Heat flared in her face, and she had to bite her words. She didn't want an argument now.

Mike said, "Harry, it's all set. We'll have a team surrounding the place."

Without looking at Mike, Harry said, "It will take us more than ten minutes to get to you in that apartment if something goes wrong. At least let Thompson go with you."

She shook her head. "Where's all this coming from, Harry? Relax! We're almost there. This one is it. Besides, they know me. They expect me."

Something passed over Harry's eyes—disappointment? regret? fear? She couldn't read him. This wasn't like the ribbing a few weeks ago. He meant it. Maybe he had a right to doubt her ability after the way things had been going, but fuck it. She simply couldn't let him cockblock her chances. Not now.

"She's right," Mike said. "It would be suspicious if we added Kyle to the mix this late."

Neither Harry nor Laney acknowledged Mike's words. Laney said, "What's the matter, Harry? Did Cynthia start doing your horoscope chart again?"

He pursed his lips.

"Or mine? Did she do my chart?" But he didn't smile back, remained cold and severe, and a stinging irritation made her short. "Chill, Harry. I know what I'm doing."

She threw a twenty on the table and stormed out of the restaurant, desperate to have the last word lest he try to pull rank or, worse, get Mike to do it for him.

The buy was to be in an apartment on Tenth Street, sixth floor. Laney had prepared with more care than usual, her excitement a warmth in her middle. She'd noticed the Russians favored black leather, with sporty twists for the men and pop-star enhancements for the women.

She chose a tight, waist-length, black leather jacket, red top and skirt, and black booties. Even as the weather turned nasty and a cold, lashing rain detonated the night in a rumble of thunder and lightning, her mood remained determined.

But when she got to the apartment, the vibe was all wrong. She felt it as soon as one of the four guards locked the door behind her and leaned against it.

Unsurprisingly, everyone in the room looked exactly as expected—black leather coats over shoulder holsters over black tracksuits over black sneakers, crew cuts, and flattened noses. Alarmingly, Orlov wasn't there. Instead, a man she'd dealt with before, one of Oskar Koshka's nephews (and Orlov's second cousin) loomed before her in the empty apartment.

That was another thing—she'd expected someone's home, but this was obviously a vacant rental, commandeered for the night. She didn't like this at all. In a home you could deflect uncomfortable conversations any number of ways, furniture could be useful; in an outdoors buy spot, you could run. In an empty apartment with a locked door and an armed droog plastered against it, you had to be alert. Make that fucking alert.

The man, Marat Djugashvili, examined her, eyes scraping over her short hair, her jacket, her leggings and boots, then up again. He smiled. Rather, his lips thinned and his teeth gleamed (an American smile; the dude at least spent enough time in the U.S. for that), his eyes remaining cool.

She unzipped the duffel and exposed the top layer of cash. Ten thousand dollars this time, enough for half a kilo of coke, maybe a third if he was in a haggling mood. Either way, the sale would cost him and his guys twenty years.

Zipping the bag closed, she shifted her weight, letting it rest on her hip. Ten thousand dollars was heavy.

"That is small bag," the man said.

She grinned. He was making it easy. Getting him to voice the details of the sale out loud was half the battle.

"Half a kilo," she said, "for ten K, as agreed."

He shrugged, spread his hands. "There is snag."

Her stomach churned, and for a second she thought the light in the room dimmed.

"Oh yeah?" If she appeared unconcerned, it would come off fake, raise eyebrows. It was too early to play at being pissed. She settled on cool and dissatisfied. "What kind of snag?"

The man beamed, and this time the smile reached his eyes, which were a pale, tigerish brown.

Her skin was alert now, her ears, every part of her energized and waiting, and the pull to leave, to rush the guards at the door, shoot her way out, fought with the desire to see this through, to win. At that moment the thought of buys and sales was buried under a nearly animalistic need to triumph over this man.

Her hand traveled to her hip, where her gun waited, small, smooth, loaded inside its hidden (but already snapped open) holster.

Harry would be hearing all this. He was certainly on his way toward her, with backup. Ten minutes. That's it. She had ten minutes to figure this out.

The man reached inside his jacket pocket, and she widened her stance, planted herself firmly into the floor, a solid triangle. She tested ninety-eight out of a hundred on her last qualification at the shooting range. She'd kill this perp in an instant if he pulled a weapon.

Instead, he retrieved a box and extended it to her.

She didn't move, the adrenaline rush so intense she felt the letdown like a wallop. One of his guys took the box, walked the five paces to where she stood, and placed it in her hands.

It was a box of chocolates. Perugina Bacis. As it happened, her mother's favorites.

"What the fuck is this?" she asked, her voice betraying her.

"Like I said," the man said, "change of plans. We just received a shipment of these."

"What?" She felt sluggish, stupid. Where was Harry? Was he hearing this?

The second guard handed Djugashvili another box out of his own jacket. Djugashvili opened it, removed a bonbon, unwrapped it, popped it in his mouth, and chewed with visible delight.

"Ten tons of this shit," he said around the goo in his teeth. "Company hire stupid driver. Who leaves truck idling while he goes for piss? We drive away truck. Now we look for buyer. You want buy? I give good price."

Laney stared at the blue-and-gray box in her hands. What was she going to do with ten tons of chocolate?

"We agreed on cocaine, Mr. Djugashvili, not candy." She let the box fall to the floor.

The man frowned. "Is good chocolate," he said. "Make good money. You buy for fifty percent off retail, sell at profit. Easy money."

When she said nothing, he said, "Fine, sixty percent off retail. That's eighty thousand for the ten tons. Really good fucking deal."

Desperately, she attempted to regroup, fast. She had only the ten thousand on her, which meant that if this guy agreed to sell her a part of his load, she'd still end up with two hundred fifty pounds of chocolate. Grand larceny whether she bought everything or just the portion she could afford, but in the smaller amount, only third degree. Since Djugashvili had no priors, there was a chance he might not see any jail time at all. If she managed to buy the whole lot, it would bump the case to second degree and jail time.

But . . . crap!

"Ten thousand now and the rest next week. I'll buy the ten tons."

Djugashvili opened another chocolate and bit off the hazelnut nipple. "No. Everything or nothing. Now."

"Ten thousand now, the rest in two days."

He smoothed the translucent wrapping under the foil and held it to his eyes. "You know, they have these things on each piece." He squinted, then guffawed. " 'A mom's hug lasts long after she lets go.' " The rest of the chocolate went into his mouth. "My mother was whore. She still giving hugs in Tbilisi. You know Tbilisi?"

She shook her head.

"No? Why would you, right? So!" he clapped his hands. "We have deal?"

"Ten thousand now. The rest in two days," she repeated.

He waved his hands. "Fine, fine. Deal."

Three of his men disappeared into a back room and began bringing out boxes while one of them lifted the duffel bag, slung it over his shoulder, and left the apartment. She wondered if Harry was outside already, in the hallway, on the stairs. They would not arrest any of them yet, since the plan had always been to get Orlov, then rope in the others with all the evidence they'd collected. Arresting anybody too soon might spook the boss. But standing in this empty room with a goon behind her and four in front gave her a headache. She wanted them gone so Harry and team could sweep in and take the goods.

Nobody was moving.

"Well, see ya in two days," she said. "Same time, same place?"

None of them said a thing, but stared at her, their bodies rigid with tension.

"Unless you guys want to bring this to my place for me, it's best you get going. We're done here," she said.

More silence. She felt the breath of the guy behind her on her neck and, despite all intent to keep her cool, lashed out, her elbow jabbing backward, her body compressing, ready for battle.

Then the lights went out.

She pulled her gun at the same time as something hard hit her head and she stumbled to her knees, a riot of leather arms swinging around her face, a fist connecting with her cheek, though she managed to turn just enough to make it a glancing blow. More furious than scared now that the worst was happening, she jumped to her feet and lunged at the nearest dark form, shoved her gun into a chest, but before she could pull the trigger another blow struck her temple and she crumpled to the floor, seeing and hearing nothing, a blackness gulping her into nothingness.

35

SHE WOKE IN the ambulance, the EMT calm and soothing by her side as the blaring, rain-dazzled streets rushed past the windows.

"How're you feeling, Officer?" He checked something on a monitor, smiled at her with encouragement.

"Like an elephant sat on my head," she said.

"Ha-ha, yeah." He peered at her eyes, at the side of her face. "We're just going to check and make sure there's no concussion, but you look good."

She swallowed, just now becoming aware of the soreness all around her eyebrow, her jaw. "I doubt it," she said.

Later, after the scans showed she'd sustained nothing worse than bruising and a black eye, she called Theo. "I ran into some trouble," she said, her mouth stiff from the battering. "I'll be home in a few hours."

The ER doctor said they'd keep her overnight, but she wanted to be home. She needed Theo's turpentine-stained hands around her, his comfort, his love, and to hell with this case for a while. She couldn't bear to think of the beating she got. She hadn't been able to defend herself. Some cop she was.

Theo's silence seemed accusatory. "What happened?" he asked after a moment.

She didn't know. She had a vague memory of Harry bending over her, but he hadn't come to the hospital, and neither had Mike. She only knew she'd been knocked unconscious. If Harry had been in the hospital with her, she would have bucked up, made light of the situation. But alone, with only Theo listening, the enormity of her failure tormented her, and she blurted, "I was jumped, Theo. They robbed me."

This time the silence seemed shocked. "Where was your backup?" he asked.

Yet another thing she didn't know. "They got me out," she said. "I think Harry and Mike got to me before . . . It could have been worse."

"You think? Laney, what happened tonight?"

But she was so tired all of a sudden, barely able to string thoughts together, slurring her words. "I'll tell you when I'm home," she said.

"Laney."

"Yes?" God, she craved him next to her.

"Laney, you can't do this anymore."

She held the phone away from her ear. The phone felt hot, unpleasant. "Please, Theo, please let's wait until I'm home."

"There's other ways of being a detective," he said. "You don't have to be an undercover."

She grunted. "Later, Theo. Don't harp on me now." As she said this, Harry walked through the door, heard her, paused uncertainly at the entrance. She hung up without saying good-bye and gestured for him to come closer. Speaking with Theo made her tired and distressed, another disappointment to an already disastrous night. With a depth of feeling that surprised her, she wished for her mother's quiet, comforting presence and felt even more wretched at its permanent absence. When she spoke to Harry, her voice rose unpleasantly.

"What the hell happened, Harry? Why weren't you there?"

"The radio stopped working," he said.

The implication sent a lance of pain up her jaw. "Did you get any of the conversation?"

"About half. Once we realized you weren't transmitting, we moved in, but we had to break the door down." When she turned away from him, he said, "We had to arrest them. We had no choice at that point."

She slapped the mattress in frustration. "My cover's blown, Harry. That's it. I'm burned on this case." She didn't think she could feel any worse, but there it was, the helpless anger mixing with the pain and the fatigue, a hot, sharp slurry in her chest.

"We arrested you too," he said.

"You what?"

"We made them think we responded to a shots-fired call and we arrested everyone in the room, including unconscious you."

"Shots were fired?"

He nodded, narrowing one concerned eye at her. "Your gun, Lane. You fired. You put a nice hole into the wall."

"I did?"

He sighed and sat on a chair next to her. "Lane, your cover is most likely solid. But you're done with this case. You can't go back in. You're going to go on medical leave for a few days at least. Okay?"

She peered at him in confusion. His words made sense, but his tone was all off, and she was too exhausted, too enervated to understand the disconnect.

"Do you think Hopper set me up? You think he was in on it?" Strange how much she wanted the answer to be in the negative.

Harry moved his shoulders, something between a noncommittal shrug and a loosening maneuver. "Don't know, Laney. We've brought him in. If he was, we'll get it out of him."

Shifting sands. That's what this felt like, without end. She needed at least one clear, solid thing in her life. "I'm not going to talk about this now," she said. "I want to go home."

But even that wasn't easy. She'd fired her weapon, albeit accidentally, and that precipitated a slew of paperwork and an interview. Internal Affairs took her gun for testing, and she had to wait for them to return it, and for everyone on the team to be questioned. Their stories were checked and cross-referenced, their radios examined, reports filed.

By the time it was all done, the sky was morning-bright and she was nearly hallucinating.

Harry had stayed with her throughout, and when she finally changed into her street clothes and staggered outside, he drove her home.

CHAPTER

36

THE FIVE DAYS of medical leave passed as if in a fever. It had been so long since she'd spent so many consecutive days with Theo and Alfie that she felt a stranger, a visitor to their daily lives. When Alfie first saw her bruised face, he rushed to her and pressed his slight body against her, burying his forehead into her shoulder. Later, as they sat on the couch watching one of his favorite shows, he placed a small, cool hand on her swollen cheek, a surprisingly soothing gesture.

Each day she woke early and made him breakfast, an indulgence of waffles and eggs, French toast, and hash browns he'd associated only with Fridays and Saturdays—her usual days off. Her first day home, Theo stayed by her side. They went for a long walk, chatted, cooked dinner together. They avoided the subject of her undercover career and she was grateful. Once they were sure their son was asleep, they had sex—a coupling first tender and cautious, then quick and heady, and finally violent in a way that left her panting, sore, and uneasy.

On her second day, Theo was polite but taciturn, and she told him to go paint, he didn't need to babysit her, she was fine, just needed rest. But she couldn't rest, had lost the knack for it over the years of working long hours. By her third day she called Harry.

"What's the news?" she asked.

"Don't worry about anything, Lane, just get better. We'll talk when you come back."

"Jesus! Tell me, Harry. What's happening with the case?"

She heard movement, as if he were walking somewhere, then a door closing. "They had to let Djugashvili go," he said. "We have the chocolate as evidence, 'cause it was obviously stolen and we know who it was stolen from, but we have nothing connecting him to the actual theft. He claims he had no idea where the goods came from and he was only trying to unload it. That brings it down to possession of stolen property. He made bail."

"You're kidding." She had gone outside, wanting the cold on her face after the stuffiness of the house. "What about the assault? And what about him telling me that he, or I don't know, his guys, stole the truck."

"Technical malfunction, Lane. I told you. None of that got recorded. We have your word against his. That will have to do once it goes to trial, but for now he made bail. Even with the assault charge."

"And the money?"

"Gone. We weren't able to find the fifth guy or the cash."

"Fuck, Harry."

And it was all her fault. She'd allowed them to rob her, overcome her. The case was falling apart, stalled, going nowhere. All those years trying to prove that she could be as tough as any of the guys, that she could take on the effin' mob. She closed her eyes. All she proved was that everyone who ever doubted her was right.

"Look, try not to think about it, okay? Spend some time with your family."

She ended the call and walked back to her silent house. But she wasn't used to being home, couldn't think what to do with herself. Grabbing a bottle of wine from the rack, she knocked on Theo's door, then turned the knob. When he didn't respond, she knocked again.

He jerked the door open halfway and stared at her from a gaunt, pale face, his thick hair messy and paint streaked. Over the years, his pretty-boy beauty had crystallized into a sculpted, linear handsomeness, the planes of his face long and sharp, austere. His lips were a dark, burgundy extravagance within all that pallidness, as if painted, wine stained.

She held up the bottle. "Take a break?" she asked.

He stepped back so she could come in, and there were those mouth paintings, moaning and screaming and gaping at her. She walked quickly toward the window, perched on the sill, waited for him to open the bottle, pour a few inches into a cloudy glass, and hand it to her.

"What happened there?" She nodded toward a blackened patch of floor. Dirt? Soot? Had there been a fire? Alfie hadn't said anything to her.

He walked out, returned a few seconds later with another glass, filled it halfway, put the bottle down. "I spilled some lamp black," he said. "I tried to clean it up, but it left a mark."

She peered at the dark smudge, about ten inches in diameter. When this room was her brother's, it'd been carpeted cobalt blue, a color both electrically bright and cold. She'd been glad to see it go when Theo redid the floors. This was his room now, and if he was okay with paint on the hardwood he'd so carefully restored, then who was she to complain?

"I think I'm off the case," she said.

He sat down on his painting stool and swirled his wine. "And you don't want to be?" he asked, a clipped reproach in his tone.

"It's my case, Theo. I worked it and worked it. I know everyone in it."

"You were beaten and robbed, Laney." He looked down, then at his latest painting. She could almost feel his need to pick up a brush and fix some error. He leaned toward the canvas, his eyes squinting. Soon he'd need glasses. He said, "You have a child, you know." He pressed his thumb against an inch of paint and smeared it downward. "What should I tell Alfie about your black eye? Or the next black eye? Or when they shoot you to death?"

She gulped the wine, barely noticing the rich bouquet, the velvety roll of it on her tongue. "You'd both be very well provided for if they shoot me to death." They told Alfie she'd been careless, had fallen and hurt her head and now needed a few days to feel better. "Theo, I want to get those guys. Don't you see? They're bad." Although those were her genuine thoughts, voicing them to her husband made her feel simplistic, and she elaborated, "They create addicts out of people. Out of children!"

"Nobody is created." He glanced at her, then back at his painting. Raised a brush and touched another inch of canvas. "Everyone creates themselves."

When she left the studio, he said, "Close the door," and continued painting, a dab of vermilion on his cheek from where the thumb he'd used to blend the paint had brushed against his skin.

37

ALFIE'D NOT BEEN allowed out of the basement for two days. The only way he guessed at the passage of time was the content of his meals—Wheaties in the morning, canned soup for lunch, canned pasta for dinner, as predictable as a bus schedule. Mr. Blue had given him a freshly emptied bucket along with a roll of toilet paper, then shut the door in his face when he tried to object (beg, he was ready to beg, but didn't get a chance).

He felt filthy and thirsty, though not hungry. His anger was a hard, hot tumor in his stomach and food wouldn't sit right, giving him cramps or making the return journey as soon as he managed to swallow some. Not that the food was anything great anyway: tomato soup, gelid in a pool of water meant to dilute it, microwaved SpaghettiOs, Cup O'Noodles.

He wished he knew what the plan was. Not knowing what was in store tortured him more than not being able to wash or the enforced idleness, more than the loneliness, more than the lack of light and air. He thought he could handle anything as long as he knew what was coming down the bend.

So when the door opened this time, he rushed it, shoving his body into the opening. "Please let me come up," he said. "Please."

"Get back!" yelled Mr. Blue, and pushed him so hard he fell on his ass, gracelessly, painfully.

"Please," Alfie said again. "Please." Maybe it was the way his voice broke, or the tears he fought to contain, or the way his whole body trembled, but Mr. Blue relented, his face darkening with emotion. His captor turned around, lurched upstairs without looking back and without locking the door.

Alfie bounded after him, taking great, hungry gulps of fresh(er) air even as his soul seethed with resentment. He'd never begged anybody for anything his whole life. Not even the kids on the school bus when they shoved him around all through middle school. Not even his father when he packed his three suitcases.

"May I use the bathroom?" Alfie asked. "May I wash?"

Mr. Blue regarded him with defeated, hurt eyes, bottom lip jutting, then nodded. "Fuck it. Go. You're too big for that window anyway." His breath carried a familiar pungency, and it wasn't until Alfie had stripped and climbed into the shower that he connected the odor to alcohol via half-buried memories of his father's afternoon meanderings through their house. Mr. Blue was smashed.

The hot water smelled nice—steam and a chlorine tang reminding him of swimming pools. He scrubbed his hair and skin, then stood under the shower head with his face upturned and eyes closed.

When Mr. Blue banged the door open, Alfie jumped and clambered out of the bath, his skin immediately goose-pimpled. He clamped his teeth lest they begin chattering. Vicious drafts wafted through the tiny window, around the vanity, and from under the tub, blowing freezing air upward over his legs. The man peered at him, knit eyebrows at odds with his otherwise blurred, almost tearful expression, then turned away. Alfie barely had time to grab what he needed from the cabinet under the sink and fold it into his clothes before Mr. Blue looked at him again.

"Enough of that," he said. "Hot water isn't cheap."

Alfie dressed quickly, managing to hide the item inside his pant leg, pulling his sock over it.

"I'm s . . . sorry about the hot water," Alfie said.

In the hallway, Alfie contemplated the front door again, but the heavy bolt lock was still drawn and latched. He'd have to break through with an ax or find a key. Nothing had changed with the windows either—each of them nailed shut with plywood. The only reason he knew it was daytime was because the miserly bathroom window had allowed an anemic light through its frosted glass.

Mr. Blue had rekindled a fire in the wood-burning stove, and the living room had a thin, grayish haze of smoke. Alfie bent toward the stove.

"I think you used green wood," he said.

The man scoffed, then waved Alfie's words away and sagged onto the couch, sipped from a can of beer. Clicked a lemon-yellow lighter and lit a joint. "What do you know from green wood. Huh?"

"Well." Alfie reached to the firewood strewn on the floor and lifted a heavy branch. The man flew at him so fast, Alfie barely had time to drop it, shut his eyes (involuntarily, embarrassingly) and raised both hands.

"I just wanted to show you something," he said quickly, but Mr. Blue had him pinned against the wall anyway, directing boozy fumes and skunky breath into his face.

"You want to go back downstairs?" the man roared.

Alfie shook his head. "No, sir."

Mr. Blue let go of him and took another sip of his beer from a can he'd miraculously held on to even while manhandling Alfie. The boy crouched and, without lifting the log, peeled back a bit of bark. "Look." He pointed to the tender wood underneath. "See how it's so smooth and kind of moist? Firewood needs to be seasoned for a while before you can burn it indoors."

Mr. Blue kicked the log out of his hands. "The fuck you know about firewood?"

"I learned it in Boy Scouts."

The man sat back down. "Boy Scouts?" He eyed Alfie up and down as if trying to see evidence of Boy Scout material. Then he grabbed an unopened can, popped the tab, and extended it to Alfie. "Have a drink, Boy Scout."

Alfie took the beer and perched on the edge of the armchair. The stove was still smoking and the heat it generated was weak, unhealthy. Even this close to the fire, Alfie's breath puffed out of his mouth like translucent gauze. The thing inside his sock hadn't fallen out, was pressing against his calf, and his heartbeat slowed.

The man cocked his head at Alfie. "You know," he said, thick voiced. "I had a son. Once."

Alfie waited. He never knew the right thing to say under normal circumstances, and his circumstances lately had been anything but. Did Mr. Blue just tell him his son had died? Should he offer condolences? Maybe the son wasn't dead. Maybe the son ran away, just like his mother probably thought he had. And anyway, he didn't know this other boy, this son. How could he have a proper emotional response toward a person he didn't know?

The man said, "His name was Otto. He was about your age when your cunt of a mother fucked my life up good and proper."

The mention of his mother unsettled him, a collision of worlds that didn't make sense, and he now knew even less how to respond. He sipped the beer. It was warm and rancid tasting, but he swallowed anyway.

"Otto was a great kid. Never cried if he got hurt. Stoic, you know? A real little man." Mr. Blue made a weird sound—like a choke and throat clearing all at once.

"Mr. Blue?" asked Alfie. Somehow he'd sipped his way through a quarter of the can, and it seemed easier to talk now. "What is your name? I mean, it's not really Mr. Blue, is it?"

The man sucked his teeth, then shrugged. "Fuck it. It's Owen. Call me Owen. Owen, Oksana, and Otto. The Triple-O family. That was us."

Alfie drank more. He was thirsty, and the beer was refreshing on his throat, though every time he stopped drinking, his thirst came back stronger. "Triple-O," he said. What kind of thing is that to name your family? Although, for all he knew, everyone did this. Did his mother have a name for them? The Looney Birds?

"The plan was, I'd move us. Somewhere out of the city, you know? Far away. Oregon maybe. Emigrate to Canada, I don't know. Somewhere. And your mother was all for it. She said, you gotta get your kid away from here. Like she was all caring and shit about my kid." He shook his head. "She said that. And you know what happened next? No? She didn't tell you?" He threw his empty to the floor and picked a fresh can from the side table. Popped the tab. Sipped. Burped. "They arrested me. Waited until no one was home, went in, planted shit all over. Made it look like I was some kind of big-time crime boss. I swore up and down the stuff wasn't mine, but who's going to listen? Hell, I put my entire life on the line for those cop pigs."

Alfie choked down the warm dregs of his beer. He didn't want to drink more, but he was still very, very thirsty. "Owen?"

"What?"

"What happened to Otto?"

Owen stood on unsteady legs and tottered to the wood stove, opened the latch, releasing more smoke, and threw two logs inside. He did this without gloves, and Alfie saw ugly red blisters form on his palms. The man either didn't feel the pain or wanted to feel the pain.

"My boy." Owen's voice was small, phlegmy. "He died. That's what happened. He died because I went to jail. I went to jail because of your mother."

He turned toward Alfie, burning branch like a torch in his blistered hand. "And here you are. Why should your mother still have a son when she took mine away?"

He advanced, and Alfie stepped back. Strangely, for the first time since he met this man, he understood him. Grief and loss he got. Alfie tried to remember what people told him when his father left. But he didn't think "it's his loss" or "he'll be back" would be appreciated (or accurate).

Instead, he said, "It will be okay."

Owen swung the burning branch, the fire sputtering and thick, gray smoke coiling from the tip. "What? What are you talking about?" He coughed. "I have nothing to live for anymore!"

Alfie considered using the thing in his sock right then, but he hesitated, and the moment passed. The angles were all wrong. It couldn't work.

And so Alfie did the one thing (he thought) helped his mother when she became upset. The one thing he'd done every night that entire first year after Theo left, his mother sobbing, sometimes in her bedroom, sometimes while cooking their dinner or sitting in the backyard. He stepped up to Owen and wrapped his arms around the man's middle, then placed his head on his shoulder.

Owen froze, arm lifted in midair, the fire on the log's tip faltering, fading, turning black, then releasing more gray smoke. His chest rose and fell in ragged breaths.

Alfie pressed the man's body closer, buried his face in his neck. He knew no words of sympathy, no comforting platitudes. But he recognized pain and he offered solace through acceptance, because even though Owen had kidnapped him and locked him away and was obviously unhinged, his sorrow was a clean, clear thing, an understandable thing, and Alfie would never withhold comfort from someone who needed it.

They stood like that for a long time, swaying gently to relieve their weight from one foot to the other. The branch stopped smoking. The fire in the stove's belly died, leaving gray wood and lumpy ash behind. Owen dropped his arms and let them hang on either side of Alfie's, then lowered his head so his chin rested on the boy's crown.

"My son needed a father," Owen said. "Every boy needs a father to keep him in line. To set an example. Otto needed that more than most."

Alfie released his hold and extricated himself, then slumped to the floor. He sat cross-legged, his head in his hands. Fatigue dragged him downward, every limb as heavy as if double, triple the gravity pulled at him.

"My father left," Alfie said. He never talked about Theo, not even to his mom. Especially not to her. "I don't know where he is. He doesn't even call me on my birthday."

Owen continued to stand over the boy, as if movement was unthinkable, unbearable. "Maybe he's dead," he said. "Or maybe he's in prison. It's what your mother deserves. To have no one."

Alfie raised his head and met Owen's eyes.

"Will you kill me?" he asked. There was a time, once, about a year after his father left, when he wanted to die. He had gotten in trouble in school—a moment of anguish over some failure that marked him as disruptive, sent him to the principal. His mother came to get him, and although she didn't reprimand him, the defeat in her eyes cut him deeply, and he'd cried with self-loathing and desolation, unable to see any brightness in his future. He whispered his death wish into her ear that night, his chest tight and his heart sore. He knew he said something untenable when she grabbed his shoulders and shook him and told him he should kill her first in that case, because how could he expect her to go on living. His mother's misery sobered him, and he calmed. She needed him. Therefore, he couldn't kill himself. Therefore, he'd just have to keep going.

But now he realized he wanted to live for purely self-centered reasons. He wanted to keep breathing. He wanted to play music. He wanted to go to a concert, at least once in his life. He wanted to grow and then grow old. Very old.

Owen stared at him as if thinking this over. Nodded.

"How?" Alfie asked.

The man looked away, then walked to the TV cabinet and opened the glass door. He withdrew a leather pouch roughly the size of his hand, untied the string that held it closed, and removed the contents. A syringe. A plastic baggie filled with a light-brown substance. A small, metal measuring cup. A green rubber ribbon. He opened the baggie and tipped the contents into the cup, then added a few drops of water from a plastic tumbler that'd been standing on the cabinet. He patted his pockets for something and, not finding it, disappeared into the kitchen, then emerged with a long-reach Butane lighter, held it under the metal cup, and waited. Alfie watched, mesmerized, as the man let the lighter drop, stirred the cup's contents gently, dipped the syringe in and pulled an amber liquid inside.

"Like my Otto," Owen said.

Alfie had seen Jordan try this a few weeks ago, but he'd abstained, always saying, "No, thank you," unwilling to ever again feel out of control. Had Owen been trying to kill him even then?

"I don't want to die," he said.

"I don't expect you do, no. But it has to be done. Your mother needs to feel this. What I've felt. Fuck. Still feel. It's unavoidable."

But yet Owen held the lethal syringe without making a move toward the boy. He could have overpowered him easily. Alfie had some wiriness to him, but not the kind of strength to fight an adult man eighty pounds heavier.

Alfie said, "I'm scared." Because he was. Because a part of him didn't think Owen would really kill him. Because a part of him couldn't believe he would die like this, now, and the discrepancy between his childlike belief in his invincibility and the grown man proclaiming otherwise made him ill.

Owen nodded again. "It's to be expected. Why don't you lie down on the couch? You'll be more comfortable." He tangled the green ribbon between his fingers, one-handed, knotting and rearranging it, shaking it loose, tangling again.

Alfie placed his hand on the thing he'd taken from the bathroom cabinet. The door was still bolted and padlocked. The windows were still nailed blind. The only other door led to the basement, and Alfie would never go down there again.

And he was still unsure. Owen could have killed him many times. Could have forced an overdose on him when Jordan conked himself out, could have run him down in the street instead of kidnapping him. Alfie looked away lest the man guess his thoughts. He never quite knew if others saw through him, could read his plans from his expressions. He often believed his mother knew what he was thinking, and before that believed the same of his father. So why not all adults?

The fact that other people had no clue of what happened in his mind had been a difficult one for him to learn, and he still wasn't totally convinced this was the truth. But if Owen wanted him dead and hadn't taken the opportunity to kill him yet, then maybe he was hesitating. And being hesitant was another thing Alfie knew plenty about.

"I missed my father at first," Alfie said, and got to his feet. "Then I figured he was off to live a new life."

He placed his hand in his pocket.

"I didn't mind him leaving after a while. I didn't mind." He was always a terrible liar, and the flatness in his voice undermined his words. It was clear from his tone, from the warmth in his face, that he had minded a lot. Still minded a lot.

Inside his pocket, he wrapped his fingers around the lemon-yellow lighter.

But Owen didn't seem to notice. Not the lie, not the movement. His eyes had a swollen, red look to them, and his mouth was slack, open slightly. When he spoke next, he was gentle, almost kind in his tone. "Lie down, Alfie. Let's get you comfortable. I'll even tell you a story if you want." He smiled. "Otto loved when I told him stories. Oksana was terrible at it. She was not a reader. She had no patience to sit and tell stories while the little guy tried falling asleep." He shook his head, as if a particularly memorable night came to mind. "He always asked me for more. More, more, more, Daddy."

Owen patted the back of the couch. "Come on. Lie down. You're a good boy. I can tell you're a good boy. You don't deserve to die, but neither did my Otto. He was a good boy too. The best. Why should she have you when I don't have him? It's not right."

He smiled and patted the couch again. "Come on. I know you believe in what's fair, Boy Scout. I know you understand why this is right. It's the equalization method. Each side of the equation must be made equal."

Alfie said, "I'm cold. It's cold in here. Can I have a blanket?" And this was true. His words puffed white as he said them. The room was freezing, easily below fifty degrees now.

Owen frowned. "Okay," he said. "I'll get you a blanket. Lie down."

And Alfie did. He placed his head on a stinking, flattened throw pillow and curved his knees up to his chest. His right hand on the lighter, his left hand over the can in his sock. He had time to rehearse the maneuver in his head three times before Owen came back with a stiffened crocheted blanket gritty with dirt and dust.

38

E D BOSWELL CALLED Laney late in the day, startling her from an ethics dilemma. She didn't think Theo deserved to know about Alfie's disappearance, but the moral (pain-in-the-ass) part of her had been nagging that she should at least try contacting him. She'd been staring at the same web page for an hour, Theo's name listed in a tasteful, elegant font next to his horrible orifice paintings. It was his gallery's site, and she only needed to dial their number and pass on the message. They'd take it from there. She need not speak with him if she didn't want to; he could get his information from the police. And yet she hadn't moved, her phone dormant by her hand until Ed rang.

The house had grown dark and cold, and she wondered if a power line had gone down, knocking out the heat. She'd need to go to the basement and check the boiler. With numb hands, she answered the phone, her voice scratchy and weird sounding.

"Hi, Laney," Ed said. "Are you okay?"

She stared at the phone. Was she okay? Really? She cleared her throat. "Yes, Ed," she said.

"Good. I was wondering if you had a minute. I'd like to stop by."

"Yes," she said. Then, "Did you find something?"

"Erm. Nothing about Alfie, no. I'll be there in a few minutes."

She flipped the light switches—dead. She'd need to call the power company and report the outage. After digging through the closet, she lit some candles and torches. The stove started with a match, and she had time to put the kettle on for coffee and set two cups on the kitchen table before he pulled into her driveway. A polite man, he wiped his feet on the welcome mat and asked if she'd like him to take off his shoes, something he hadn't done the first time he came by. She wondered if this meant she was no longer a suspect.

He kept his coat on, unbuttoning it so it flared awkwardly over the kitchen chair when he sat. His suit was rumpled and too small, obviously bought when he was younger and thinner.

"Thank you," he said, stirring sugar into his instant coffee. He put down the spoon, his face guarded and watchful. "Do you have someplace to stay tonight? They might not fix the power until tomorrow."

"I'll be fine," she said.

"You can stay with us. Allison will be happy to have you."

She wondered if he made the offer knowing she'd never accept. "Thank you, Ed. That's kind. No, I'll be fine. There's plenty of blankets."

"Okay then." He tapped a finger on the table. "We have an ID on the body at Hopper's apartment."

Well? What was he waiting for? "Okay," she said.

"We've identified the body as Victor Orlov. That was your racketeering case, right?"

She nodded, her teeth grinding with distress. He knew perfectly well it was her damned racketeering case. She was sure it was all in that thick binder he'd had with him the last time he questioned her at the precinct about her connection to Hopper.

"Laney?"

"Yes," she said. "Orlov was my case."

"Right. May I ask how well you knew him? Did you ever meet Orlov in person?"

She coughed, her throat so dry it took two tries and a gulp of piping-hot coffee to get the next words out. "I did, once, yes."

"I see. And this was during the case you worked with Owen Hopper?"

She nodded.

"I'm here confidentially, Laney. The Orlov murder case is still open, with Owen Hopper as our primary—and, frankly, only—suspect." He sat back, as if debating what to say next. "There's something else. He didn't die in Hopper's garage. He was killed elsewhere and then dumped in the garage." He shrugged. "I don't know why Hopper kept the body. Seems creepy. But we're estimating he died sometime at the beginning of December. The NYPD had a missing-person report on him as of November twenty-eighth, but it was nothing but dead ends until now." He smiled briefly. "So to speak. Laney, it's not just Hopper who knows your real identity. Your name and address were in Orlov's phone. His wife gave us the passcode. We're assuming his entire crime family knows who you are." He looked away for a second, picked up his spoon, tapped it on the edge of his mug. Placed it on the table again. "I'd like you to come and stay with us. Please. It's not a good idea for you to be alone. Especially now."

She rose from her chair and placed a hand on the wall to steady herself. Cold. She was cold, her fingers numb.

"Why, Ed? So I can drag your family into this as well?"

In the dark, with only the candles lighting his tired face, he was a solid bulk, warm and serious. "My family is used to it," he said.

"If Orlov knew my name and where I lived all along and wanted me dead, I guess I'd be dead already." She met his eyes. "But I'm not."

"Laney?"

"What?" Hopper had moved to Sylvan just after killing Orlov. She imagined him driving around with a murdered Russian mobster in his trunk, renting an apartment, moving in, transferring the rotting body to the garage. She suspected Orlov was the one who gave her up to Hopper just before Hopper killed him. And the only way Orlov would have known her real name was through the NYPD, and it sure wasn't her who told him.

"Laney, a lot of people seemed to know who you were. Can you tell me anything about that?"

She laughed, surprising herself, a dry, cackly guffaw. "I can't tell you how he knew my real name." She could though, because the answer was obvious, and not just to her, but to anyone who had looked through both Owen's and Harry's case files. Ed was looking at her with concern and that insufferable pity he seemed to reserve just for her. Yes, she could tell him it was Harry Burroughs who sold her out, or maybe even Mike Stegner. She could admit to being a gullible and idiotic detective on top of being a failure as wife and mother. But she didn't want to. She didn't want to show her soft underbelly to anyone ever again.

Ever.

"I'm sorry, but I must ask again. How is your son connected to Hopper and Victor Orlov?"

Laney realized she was outside. She had no memory of walking down her hallway and out the door, but there she was, on her iced-over porch steps in Alfie's sweats and wool socks, her body so cold she was shaking. Boswell stood behind her, propping the door open with his foot, his hand on her arm, steadying her.

"I don't know," she said. "I wish I knew, but I don't."

He was saying something, tugging her back into the house, but her mind had muted him, instead going over the details of Alfie's last month.

"Jordan," she said, interrupting him.

Boswell had managed to maneuver her indoors and closed the door. Gently, he led her to the couch and sat her down, then crouched in front of her.

"Are you saying little Jordan Rogers is connected to Victor Orlov?"

Sluggish. Her mind trawled from thought to thought—Owen Hopper and his voluptuous, painted wife, his wolfish son. Harry and his shiny new Mustang. Harry, dead of an overdose from the drug he hated most in the entire world. Mike, gone. Orlov, murdered. And her son, her Alfie, who knew where.

"Laney." Boswell was lifting her hand, wrapping her fingers around the coffee cup, leading it to her lips. After a few gulps she forced her mind to settle, to focus on the man in front of her. He was important. He was supposed to help. She had to hope he could help.

"Hopper gave them drugs." *Gave it to them.* Of course he gave it to them. It was never about selling the drugs or hooking them or their friends. It was always about her. He had known who she was all along. Because Orlov told him.

She gripped his sleeve, wringing the loose fabric in her hand. "He's not after Alfie. I mean, he's after Alfie, obviously, but his target is me. He wants to hurt me, and he's doing it by going after my son." She let go of him, her hands tugging her hair. She had to focus.

"Why?" Boswell asked. "Why through your son? What does that mean? Why not attack you?"

She stopped, the realization hitting her like a cold wave. "He wants me to feel what he felt."

"When? What he felt when, Laney?"

She slapped her hand against her mouth. It was one thing to think this but another altogether to put it out into the universe. To name it. He gripped her wrist and pushed it down, away from her face.

"What he felt when?"

"When his son died," she said.

CHAPTER

39

SHE'D MET VIKTOR Orlov only once, a dinner date arranged by Hopper two weeks after the chocolate heist fiasco. Hopper called her a dozen times after she got jumped, never leaving messages. During those weeks, Harry and Mike visited him at home, a move so threatening he didn't sleep for seventy-two hours afterward. Or so he said when she finally picked up her undercover phone after coming back to the precinct.

"Kendra, I swear, one more visit like that and I'm dead."

She had gone outside so he wouldn't hear the precinct's ambient noise.

"Fuck," he whispered. She could hear him shutting a door. "Listen, I didn't know Orlov was going to mess with you like that."

"I know," she said, because that's what Kendra would have said.

"Are you okay?"

"Nothing broken," she said. "I tried to pop one of them but missed. Too bad."

"Yeah," he said. "Too bad. Look, I need to speak with you."

She almost groaned with frustration. She was off the case, officially. Desk duty until everyone figured out where to put her. "No, Owen. I'm not . . . I can't talk to you anymore. They won't let me."

"Do you still work with them?" She understood he meant if Kendra still worked for Harry and Mike. She paused, as she wasn't sure anymore. She certainly was no longer privy to their cases, mostly spending her time doing checks for the various detectives at the precinct. They treated her fine, smiled and asked how she was doing, but gone were the lunches and the conversations, and she wasn't sure if it was them all being busy or if something else kept them from her.

"No," she said. "I don't. I'm leaving for Buffalo in a few days. I can't stay here anymore."

"Shit! I need to talk to them, but I can't be seen with them again. Can you imagine how that looked, when the cops showed at my door? I had to force my wife and kid out of the apartment for two days after they left, just in case. I need to get a message to them, and I can't do it over the phone. I won't even tell you over the phone."

"What is it?" she asked anyway.

"Can you meet me?"

40

S HE MET HIM at a bench on the boardwalk, the November
day cold and gray, the wind wet, but not so strong that they
couldn't eat their sandwiches.

He grimaced when he saw the fading bruises along her temple
and cheek.

"Fuck, Kendra," he said. "I swear I didn't know that was going
to happen. You know I had nothing to do with this, right? They
told me they'd sell you the coke." He shook his head. "Fuckers. I
can't believe they did that to you." Emphasis on the *you*.

He looked shaken, thinner, older, his corned beef on pumper-
nickel untouched on his lap. The tattoo winding above his wedding band rippled as he tapped his fingers. It was the names of his
wife and son in an elegant spiral. For a confused moment Laney
felt envious of his wife. Theo would never have gotten her name
tattooed anywhere on his person, least of all his hands.

She glared at him. "Why are you surprised? That they did
this to a woman?" She snorted. "They're criminals, Owen. As are
you. As am I. What kind of code of honor do you expect? Exactly?
Hmmm?" She regretted her words immediately. She was stronger
than that, she was her father's daughter, not a princess, not a delicate flower. Why take it out on Hopper? She believed him (mostly)

when he said he had no clue she'd been jumped. Things happen. You can't control every situation, no matter how hard you prepare.

She picked at her meatball hero. Perhaps she snapped at him because she didn't feel like herself. Her whole body still hurt, her face ached, and life had grown increasingly weird at home—Theo quiet and remote, Alfie clingier than ever. Also, that burn spot in the studio bugged her. She didn't buy Theo's bullshit about spilled paint and she couldn't get a proper answer from Alfie. Their evasive silence worried her. Without acknowledging she'd been wrestling with a decision, her mind had announced its verdict that morning. She'd quit her undercover gig and transition to straightforward detective work. Maybe go to a squad. She had options. Yes, she loved her job, but Theo was right. She couldn't keep placing herself in danger. She had to put her family first.

"I might be a criminal," Hopper said, "but that doesn't mean I'm not a gentleman."

"Okay, so you always hold the door for a lady and you always pick up the check." She tore a piece of bread off her hero, kneaded it into a tiny ball. "Could be that's your problem."

He frowned. Wrapped his uneaten lunch and shoved it back into its bag.

She said, "You know. We've talked about this stuff. You dress your family nice. You feed them nice. You take them nice places. Nicer than you can afford on your salary." She should stop talking, but something had gotten a grip on her. "Maybe if you weren't such a gentleman, you wouldn't have to be a criminal."

The line between his brows deepened, and he held her stare. "Why did you become a criminal, Kendra?" Cool voice, not angry, but sharp, irritated. "I mean, if we're playing the how-we-got-to-this-moment-in-time game. What's your story? Why are you hundreds of miles from your husband, buying for him, nearly getting yourself killed? Hmm? What's he holding over you?" He squinted at her. "No, he's not holding anything, is he? You just love him. And you'd do anything for him." He turned away, shrugged. "I don't know why you think you're so different from me."

Her face warmed at this, and she bit into her sandwich to hide her emotion because she'd allowed the conversation to get personal. His words were truer than he could possibly guess. No, she was definitely not herself today.

When she didn't answer, he said, "One good thing came of that mess. That's what I needed to talk to you about. Listen, Viktor trusts you now. He knows you were arrested along with Djugashvili." He glanced again at her fading bruises, then slid his eyes to his lap with a wince, as if trying to erase what he saw.

For the next few minutes they sat in silence, her cheeks slowly cooling to their usual paleness, his knee jiggling up and down.

Then he said, "Orlov agreed to see you. He has a kilo of coke he needs to unload fast. He'll meet with you tomorrow. You have to get that message to the cops. Today."

And despite her soreness of body and mind, her frustration, at his words her heart thumped harder. She was off the case, and she'd need permission to go ahead. She might not be allowed. But as she busied herself with disposing the rest of her lunch, she entertained a moment of hope.

Let it happen, she said to herself. Let it come through, let me succeed. This last time, let me win, let me get the bad guy and I'll quit. I'll sit at a desk for the rest of my career.

As for the disquiet squeezing her chest, wasn't it simply indigestion, bad food swallowed quickly?

41

THE MEETING WITH Orlov took place in a restaurant called Baikal, amid the clatter of serving dishes, Eurodance thumping out of speakers, and extravagantly dressed diners shouting over the din.

She wasn't supposed to be there. Had been explicitly told to leave it alone, no one trusted Hopper's information anymore. The captain said no, the sergeant said no, Harry said no, and Kyle the newbie said, "How about I go?"

And then, just before she left for the day, Harry brought her a bag of shashliks wrapped in pita and took her aside. Wire up tomorrow, he said, keeping his voice low, his face neutral. It's our last chance. I'll be just outside, we can't let this one go. Mike is behind us on this if anybody asks. Let's get Orlov. I know you can.

She could have kissed him, she was so relieved. She'd get her one last chance to make this right.

Orlov sat with his back against the leather of a padded booth, which itself was at the far end of the restaurant, giving him an almost 180 view of the establishment. He wore a white shirt, no tie, top four buttons undone and exposing a whorl of tattoo on his chest, a gray suit, and Adidas Sambas. Laney noted the Rolex and the thin gold chain around his throat. A graying crew cut and sea-glass-blue eyes completed the Russian mobster look. She'd have known him for what he was even without the photographs hanging up at the station.

If she succeeded, Viktor Orlov was looking at ten to life, and the rest of his family would fall into her waiting lap like ripe plums.

She'd never worked a buy this big before; the stakes had never been this high. The thrill had kept her sleepless, and she'd risen that morning jumpy, glowing, laughing at something Alfie said without remembering it the next moment, giving Theo a deep, hungry kiss before throwing her Kendra clothes into a duffel and driving off to work.

A leather gym bag stuffed with twenty thousand dollars rested on a chair next to her. She hadn't asked Harry what lie he'd concocted to get her here. And she sure as hell was not going to question him why he needed the secrecy. She didn't care how she took Orlov down. She just wanted to be the one to do it.

She needed to negotiate the buy, needed Orlov to sell her a kilo of coke, or as near as he would be willing for the cash. If he asked her to go somewhere else, somewhere private for the transaction, she'd go. If asked to count the money, she'd give him the bag. The conversation would be recorded through the wire she wore under her red vinyl dress, and as soon as Harry felt they had enough evidence, he'd barrel in and make the arrest.

She sipped the sweet, red wine Orlov ordered for her and smiled. A heap of platters hid the round table between them—rosy beet salads, pickles, eggs deviled with caviar, buttered and peppered pelmeni, grilled kabobs tossed with glistening tomato slices, thick slabs of dark and white bread—and neither one of them had touched a crumb. Orlov had emptied half a liter of vodka and showed no sign of it, his posture as pugilistic and tense as when they first sat down.

"Mr. Orlov," she said.

"Viktor, please."

"Viktor." Another smile, a not-especially-discreet glance at her phone. "I need to be somewhere in about a half hour. So maybe we can conclude our business?"

He grinned and drank another mouthful of vodka. He'd been like this all afternoon—taciturn but friendly, avoiding any direct reference to the reason for their meeting. She'd been ready for danger, for a physical assault, subterfuge, trickery, but this sly discretion was driving her batty. Fine, she would walk away. See if he would go after her then. Twenty thousand in cash wasn't big money, but it wasn't nickels and dimes either. It would keep him and his cousins in Adidas footwear for at least a year.

She slid her phone into her purse, stood, and hefted the leather gym bag onto her shoulder.

"Viktor, I believe we have misunderstood each other." She turned to leave. "You know how to get in touch with me if you decide to work with me."

"Kendra," he said, and she stopped. "Please sit down."

She pretended to vacillate, then sat.

"You haven't eaten anything," he said. "This caviar is like the food of the gods. Ambrosia. Have some."

She laughed. "Viktor, I gotta go." Time to switch tactics. She leaned forward, pointed a bejeweled index finger at him. "Shit or get off the pot, as my pop used to say. Do you have coke for me or not? Tell me how much you want for it. I'll give you twenty thou for a kilo." He'd been sliding away from her innuendos for over an hour, and she was growing desperate.

Whether due to her inexperience, bad chemistry, or plain evil luck, Viktor Orlov glinted his blue eyes at her, finished the vodka in his glass, and said, "You mistake me for someone else. I am aware that illegal sales go on in our neighborhood, but I know absolutely nothing about them. I am deeply offended by your assumptions." He rose to his feet, placed his cloth napkin on the table. "I wanted to treat you to true Russian hospitality. I did not expect this ridiculous slander." And with that, he walked away, leaving her at a table laden with uneaten food and a bag glutted with unspent cash.

"Fucking Hopper," she said, stunned, as she climbed into Harry's car. "Did he lie to me? What just happened? Did someone tip Viktor off?"

"Like who?"

She *tsk*ed in irritation and said, "Harry, he knew exactly what was happening. He knew I was recording him, or why the ridiculous speech? Who was he talking to?"

Harry scowled, then nodded. "Someone tipped him off all right. He knew you were bugged."

They drove in silence, stopped at a red light. She said, "You think Hopper is playing games?"

"I wouldn't be surprised," Harry murmured.

She believed the failed buy her fault for a long time. She hadn't put Orlov at ease enough, or she didn't see the lies in Hopper's face. She heard what she wanted and ignored all else. The only thing she managed to get that day was Orlov's straight-faced denials. On tape.

By the time she understood that was the entire reason for the dinner invitation, she had no choice but keep her mouth shut.

CHAPTER

42

IT TOOK LANEY nearly three hours to drive home from Brooklyn to Long Island after that absurd dinner with Orlov. Three accidents, one after another, snarled the BQE, bedeviled the LIE, closed lanes. She crawled forward, a few feet at a time, all the while replaying in her mind the fruitless strategies she'd attempted with the mobster sitting across that loaded-down table.

Everyone fails, and she had failed plenty in the past—that time her cover had blown in the Bronx and she had to move to another command or risk deadly violence. Or the time she had accidentally gotten into a random guy's car after a buy because the car was exactly the color and make of her ghost's. She still cringed (and laughed) at the driver's shocked expression when suddenly presented with a disheveled crackhead in his passenger seat.

But for the most part, she'd been good. Good as a rookie, walking a post in midtown. Good when she joined the Street Narcotics Unit. Ultimately very good as an undercover. The failure with Orlov's case didn't sit well with her. She'd done everything right, more than right. She'd put extra hours, mounds of effort into catching this family, and nothing had come of it.

She inched forward, exhausted in body and mind, longing for her little house and its painterly odors, its quiet. She wanted to share a bottle of wine with Theo, do a puzzle with Alfie. She wanted to stuff all thoughts of Owen Hopper and Orlov and Harry into a trunk, close the lid, shove it under the bed. Or better yet, off a bridge.

By the time she arrived home, dinner time had long since passed, and Alfie, showered and pajamaed, was sprawled on the couch with a graphic novel, Theo sketching in the armchair by the standing lamp.

"Let's go to the beach for the weekend!" she said. The day had been the last of her shifts for the week, and she could probably take an extra personal day. She'd do whatever she had to in order to spend time with her husband and son. Real time, not an hour here, an hour there. And away from the house, so that they could all be together, properly—no chores, no painting.

Theo looked up. God, he was beautiful. The creamy light contoured his cheekbone, flicked over his sculpted chin and nose, played with his tousled hair.

"It's November," he said.

"Indoor water park resort," she said. "There's one just outside Philly. Let's do it."

Alfie put his book down. "Water park?" he asked, tripping slightly on the p but finishing the word.

She smiled, the thought gripping her now. "Yes, come on. I'll see if they have rooms. Okay?"

Alfie clapped his hands. "Yes!"

Theo turned back to his sketch pad. "If that's what you want," he said.

Fate smiled on Laney that night, whether as compensation for the previous weeks or as a last handout of happiness before the shitstorm to come. She booked three nights at CoCo Key Water Resort in Pennsylvania and spent the next couple of hours folding towels, bathing suits, snorkel masks, and beach shoes into duffel bags.

The following days were infused with humid, chlorine-scented languor, evenings at the resort's bar while Alfie slept in their room.

They rested, ate, watched their child play. She wanted to tell Theo about the case, no reason why she shouldn't. But every time she started, he'd look somewhere to the side of her left ear and hold his body stiff, as if waiting for her to stop talking.

And even then she didn't guess. She thought he was mulling over the latest technique he'd been trying out—something with beeswax that made the house smell strange, a combination of varnish and sweet resin. It wasn't working the way he expected and he'd been staying up nights, the only time he had to himself, he said, to get it right. He always longed for his brushes and paints when they went away. She understood that.

Nothing seemed to draw Theo out of his moodiness, and Alfie was Alfie—silent, watchful, even in an inner tube, floating down an indoor river.

Still, the getaway helped. The distance from work gave her much-needed clarity. It wasn't her place to save the world. It wasn't up to her to apprehend every murderer and drug peddler. The job was the job, and life was life. She'd known too many cops who fused the two and lost everything bright in their existence. Cops who could only get through their off-duty hours by drinking themselves numb, who worked thirty, thirty-five years until even the NYPD didn't want them anymore, then died a week after retirement.

She returned from the long weekend restored, having forgiven herself, mostly, for her failure. There'd always be more cases; she'd solve some and blunder others, and she was okay with this. She had to be. Anything else was vanity.

The next day, her son off to school without complaint for a change, her talented husband busy on a new canvas, she left for work with a light heart.

She signed in and headed to the locker room when the captain passed her, stopped, turned, placed his hand on her shoulder.

"Good work, Elaine," he said. "You did good."

She smiled, uncertain, but ready to take the compliment. "Sure," she said.

Mike wasn't at his desk, and neither was Harry.

She powered up the computer she shared with the night-shift detective and turned to the sergeant on duty. "Hey," she said, "what are you still doing here? Pulling a double?"

The sergeant looked like he was easily doing a triple, his eyes reddened and the skin under them bruised.

"Yeah," he said. "What happened to you? You weren't at the raid?"

"What raid?"

He sipped from an enormous mug of coffee with a baby's footprint decal over blue text—*My dad might be a cop, but I walk all over him.*

He said, "That pharmacy you've been working. Your guys raided it. Raided the CI's apartment too." He whistled. "He's going away for a loooong time."

Adrenaline surged through her body before her mind fully processed what she just heard. Why hadn't Harry told her? Even if he was above her in rank and maybe didn't need to, still, they were friends.

"Did they get Orlov?" she asked, too loud.

He blinked, startled. "No," he said. "Just the pharmacist."

Her fingers tripping and missing keys, she logged into the system. No messages from Harry. Nothing on her phone.

What the hell, Harry? she texted, watched as the text was delivered, watched the three dots as Harry began an answer, watched the three dots disappear as he stopped without answering.

Mike Stegner didn't answer her text either.

This didn't make any sense. She pulled up the arrest paperwork and sat back in stunned frustration. Harry had arrested Hopper for prescription drug fraud, illegal possession of controlled substances with intent to sell, the sale of controlled substances, and then got a search warrant and found heaps of contraband at Hopper's apartment—backpacks full of cocaine, over a hundred thousand in cash, suitcases stuffed with firearms.

She knew none of it was Hopper's. He was absolutely manic about keeping his family out of his dealing. Even if he'd lied to her about his level of involvement, he would have never, ever put his wife and son in the kind of danger that comes from storing suitcases full of firearms. She was sure of it. And if it wasn't Hopper's and Harry knew it too (he must have) and arrested him anyway, then why? Whose contraband was it?

The day dragged after this. Neither Harry nor Mike responded to her texts or calls. Further digging revealed that Hopper's wife had disappeared along with the son.

Later, she'd look at that day as the turning point. Before that day, she had been a hardworking detective with a good marriage and a lovely home. She had great rapport with her partners and loved her job.

On that day she found out her partner had executed a plan that made no sense to her, a low-level criminal was suddenly the ringleader, the drug lord was an upstanding citizen, and at home there was Theo and the three suitcases, and a silenced son.

After that, she didn't have it in her to pursue Harry's reasons for pinning the entire case on Owen Hopper. She wasn't even sure if Harry had done the pinning or if someone else had. She couldn't get a minute alone with any of her teammates.

Surely the raid was one big, huge cock-up. Harry would find the evidence to prove all those bags of coke and firearms were planted, most likely by Orlov himself, and refocus his investigation where it belonged. But the case wound its way through the justice system, with Harry testifying to everything he'd seen and found with a confident, steady voice and easy posture.

Surely Theo would call her on her birthday, or at least send a card. And when her birthday came and went without a word from Theo, she thought, okay, he needs space. Fine. Then Christmas neared, and still no call or package. Afraid to believe Theo would not send his only son a Christmas present, she'd bought a card, just in case, wrote as closely as she could in Theo's graceful, angular script, added a gift certificate to GameStop, and mailed it from Manhattan. Alfie took it to his room silently, and she never knew if he'd guessed.

The holidays that year were the worst since her parents died. Thanksgiving at a diner with Alfie, Christmas at the mall. She hoped two hours at a Dave & Buster's plus a movie plus pizza and ice cream would make up for their sheer solitude, but they didn't. Midnight found her in Alfie's room, holding him as he cried and heaved and finally ran to the bathroom and vomited pizza and ice cream into the toilet.

And through all this, she had to work. She had to drive to her precinct, sign into the system, run checks on suspects and crime scenes. She had asked for a transfer to a detective squad in Queens, a closer drive from Long Island, but transfers take time. Meanwhile she was back on buy-and-busts, ghosting. Everything that used to be so exciting, so meaningful (she was making the world safer!) no longer meant anything. Her team's buy rates slipped lower and lower. She found she didn't care.

At the precinct, Harry typed up his reports, went out on cases, avoided her, and all the while she watched him. And the more she watched, the less she cared about what she saw. Because if she allowed herself to care, then what would that say about the only job she'd ever wanted? About Harry, who had been her mentor, her best friend, her partner?

Two months after the raid, Alfie had his meltdown in the mud and Laney resigned.

Three months after that, she was driving a school bus in upstate New York, and her son would not leave her side when she was home.

So be it, she told herself. She'd changed her life. She'd moved on. She rarely discussed her old life, except sometimes with Holly, and only because Holly loved crime dramas. Her friend couldn't believe Laney had lived the life she'd only seen on the TV screen.

It wasn't until a year after the raid that the Internal Affairs Bureau contacted her and asked if she would meet them. The two IAB officers drove to Sylvan and sat in her living room, drank her coffee, and asked her about Harry and Mike and the Orlov case. They asked and asked, and the more they asked, the quieter she got. Their questions turned a spotlight onto her own actions, and now she was obliged to ask herself—did she really not know? Not see?

She answered the only way an ex-cop and a cop's daughter could answer—with selective silence. Harry, she said, had been an exemplary detective. No, she never saw anything untoward. No, she never heard him say anything odd. Of course she never saw him take evidence from a scene. Definitely not plant any evidence either. Why had she quit so soon after the Hopper raid? That's personal, but if you insist, divorce, a bad time. Yes, she'd call if she remembered anything. Yes, she'd keep their cards. No, she had nothing else to add.

CHAPTER

43

FOUR DAYS AFTER her son vanished, and one hour after she found out Orlov had known her identity all along, Laney decided to go visiting.

She changed her clothes—black, loose-fitting slacks, blue shirt buttoned to the throat, a thick, blocky sweater, also black. She combed her hair and parted it to the side. No makeup. No perfume. The mirror reflected a tired woman nearing middle age—colorless skin and lips, red-rimmed eyes.

Good. Not threatening. That's what she needed to be where she headed next.

Her car was warming when Holly tramped along the snow toward her, leaving deep hollows, her tiny besweatered dog shivering in her arms.

"How's it going?" Holly leaned into the driver-side window. She looked done in by the dreary February gloom, broken vessels under her eyes, a deep worry line between her brows, and her thin hand trembled under Buster's belly.

"I need to go somewhere," Laney said, then, "Hey, you all right? What's up?"

But her friend shook her head and grinned briefly, becoming her usual cheerful self again. "Any news?"

"I'd tell you if there was." Laney sighed. Rubbed her eyes. "Obviously." She reached out and petted the little dog under its chin, and it squinted, straining toward her fingers. "How about you?" she asked, because clearly something was up. "How are the kids today?"

"Oh, you know, the usual. Basketball games, birthday parties. It never ends." Holly shifted her eyes sideways in guilty discomfort, then looked back at Laney. "I'd rather go sleuthing with you any day."

Laney snorted in spite of herself.

Holly stepped away, little Buster yelping as if she'd squeezed him too hard. She patted him and he licked her thumb. "Lasagna will be done in an hour. Want to come over?"

"Maybe later." An evening in Holly's warm, child-filled, husband-enhanced house sounded both horrifying and maddeningly appealing. "I'll call you."

She backed out, fishtailing slightly on the ice, and aimed for the road that would take her to Long Island.

The late Harry Burroughs had grown up in Rockville Centre, Long Island—summers at the beach, clubbing long before he reached legal age, construction jobs until he spent one winter too many out of work. Then community college and the police academy. He was Laney's senior by eight years, though it didn't show. He'd remained an exuberant, youthful man well into his thirties and only settled with a girlfriend after his thirty-eighth birthday.

The image of him spiking a vein at the age of forty-four, when he hadn't even as much as smoked a joint his entire life—not even in the clubs, not even at the shore when he was fifteen and beautiful and could have had anything he wanted for free—that image was impossible. Did he die in his living room? In an alley? Was Owen Hopper the last person he saw? What thoughts did dying Harry think?

Under all this festered an ache Laney barely understood. It's acceptable and rational to mourn one's parents, a brother, a failed marriage, even the loss of a beloved career. But Harry was so many conflicting things, she didn't know where he belonged. He'd taught, and helped, and made many a workday glitter with humor.

Yet he betrayed his oath. He betrayed her and put her in mortal danger. She'd loved him and trusted him, and now all she could see was the shit-stain he'd left over every interaction. Of all the things he did wrong, that was the one she had the hardest time accepting—that whenever he guided her, supported her, bought her a round, made her laugh, through all of it he'd been ready to sacrifice her life for a new car.

Laney rang the buzzer of Harry and Cynthia's condo. The forty-mile drive had taken over two hours, the traffic constipated over the bridges and down the LIE.

The lights were on, and she could hear a television's faint murmurs. Even if Cynthia had not been home, Laney would have waited. Through the night, if necessary.

Footsteps, then a swish at the peephole. She felt Cynthia standing at the other side of the door—a cessation of sound.

"Cynthia," Laney said. "I need to talk to you."

The door opened, but Cynthia didn't move aside; stood with her arms crossed over her chest.

"What do you want, Elaine?"

Was this woman still jealous of her? Even now?

"Cynthia." Laney tried to smile, realized it wasn't working, cleared her throat. "Please? Can I come in?"

The woman breathed out sharply and moved aside, gesturing for her to enter. Laney removed her boots in the hallway, taking her time, cataloging everything she saw. Generic photographs of beaches and sunsets on the sage-green walls. Thick, Persian rugs on polished hardwood floors. A kooky juxtaposition of bland Ikea TV stand and what looked like antique bookcases, ornately carved mirrors, a mahogany dining room table, midcentury, well kept.

Other than the TV stand and those dumb photographs, there was nothing of the Harry she'd known in this expensively furnished apartment. But, as she'd been finding out lately, she didn't really know anybody in her life. Was she going to visit Holly's house one day to discover a basement BDSM sex chamber?

She tried that smile again, her face nearly breaking in the process. "Cynthia," she said. "Did they take Harry's laptop?"

Cynthia narrowed her eyes. "Why?"

This was thorny. She'd debated approaches to this conversation during her entire tortured drive. Cynthia loved Harry. Had truly, madly, obsessively loved him. Laney knew all about that kind of love. But how much had Cynthia known about Harry and his secrets? How did she feel about them now that it was too late for excuses and explanations?

"I think I know who . . . did it to him," Laney said. She couldn't say *killed*. The word stuck and wouldn't come.

The other woman pursed her lips, said nothing.

"Do you think you know, too?" Laney asked, her voice softening.

Cynthia turned away abruptly and walked toward the window. It was dark now, the streetlights refracting through the cream curtains. "He lied to me," she said after a while, then nodded, as if giving herself permission to go on. "He said he was at work." Her voice wavered and she tilted her head up, took a deep breath. "So many nights. So many nights he said he was at work. But he wasn't. I checked. I don't know why I didn't confront him. I figured he still came home to me. He told me he loved me. He was generous. He took me to Italy. He bought me flowers every other day, like clockwork." She shrugged. "Yes, they took the laptop, but Harry deleted everything before he gave it up. Not that it helped him."

"Where did he store the stuff he deleted?"

Cynthia shook her head. "It's gone, Elaine. He erased it."

Laney didn't want to push this woman (too much), but she was tired and desperately worried. "We both know he'd never completely erase anything he might need later," she said. "Please. I need to know what he was doing." And with whom, and what he told them, and what they knew, and the degree to which they held Laney responsible.

"It's all in the news," Cynthia said. "Everything you need to know."

Impatience twitching within her, Laney said, "No, nowhere near. I need serious details, Cynthia. Please. Is there another laptop he might have used? A thumb drive?"

Silently, without looking at her, Cynthia disappeared into a bedroom and came out a minute later holding a phone.

"He asked me to hold on to this. I don't know how he found out when they were going to get the warrant, but he knew," she said. "He told me to stay with my parents for a few weeks, and that's when they searched the apartment."

"The detectives didn't ask for it?"

Cynthia rolled her eyes. "He had more than one phone, Elaine. He gave them his regular one."

She placed it on the dining room table and sat down, turned away from Laney, withdrew her own phone, started tapping and swiping.

Laney powered it up and stared at the lock screen.

"Would you be able to guess at Harry's password? Or do you know it?"

Without looking up, Cynthia said, "He wasn't very creative with passwords."

Laney waited. Then, "His birthday? Your birthday?"

"Reverse shield number plus initials."

"Have you looked though it already?"

Cynthia said nothing, but her shoulders tensed and her tapping grew more aggressive.

For some reason the obviousness of the password demoralized Laney even more. The man who helped wreck her career and put her in harm's way time and again hadn't even bothered with a strong password.

Well.

He had two email accounts, one immediately accessible from the home screen, the second one hidden in settings.

The first account opened right away, and now she knew that Harry liked Japanese porn, MMA, and Alex Jones.

But when she switched to the second account, a password screen popped up, and the shield number didn't work this time. She turned to Cynthia again.

The other woman raised her head, her brow wrinkling. "What? Did you find something?"

"Do you know the password to his other mail account?"

Cynthia's eyes were dark and tired and resentful and mean. "What other mail account?"

Laney tapped her fingers. "He had a second account."

"I didn't find it when I looked." Dry, cool tone.

Time for honesty. "Cynthia, please tell me everything. What do you know that didn't come up in the trial? You must know something. You were the closest person to him."

The ensuing silence was charged, Cynthia's body so tightly coiled that Laney was afraid to touch her lest she lash out.

"You need to leave now," Cynthia said, without looking at her.

"What do you know, Cynthia?"

"You must go."

"Are you in danger? Cynthia? Look at me! Tell me, are you in danger?"

The woman darted a pained glance at her. "No more than you."

"My son is gone," Laney said, not as a trump card but because that's why she was there, because that's why she did anything now. "He got my son." She reached and placed her hand on the other woman's shoulder. "You know who I mean, right? You know who has him? Owen Hopper." Not a question. A confirmation.

"What? Alfie? Why would anybody take Alfie?"

Laney waited, her throat working and her face prickling under Cynthia's worried stare.

And then Cynthia's face banged shut, grew paler. "I can't help you," she said.

Laney released the breath she'd been holding. The words, when they came, were barely audible. "It's my son, though. My son. You really won't help?"

Cynthia got to her feet, her body in that fighting stance again.

It seemed to take Laney an hour to walk the twenty feet to the front door, and just before leaving, she said, "You have my number. In case you change your mind." And then, with the door already open and her foot over the threshold, "If you still hate me, I get it. I do. And if you're scared for yourself, I understand. But it's my boy. My baby. It's my baby. If there's anything at all in those emails that can help me find him, I need to know. Don't you see? I know Harry was working with Orlov, but maybe there's something else there. Maybe there's a place they all went to or, I don't know, where they took hostages. I don't know where he took my son, Cynthia! I need to know!"

Cynthia paled, then shook her head. "I don't have the password," she said.

Laney drove home through traffic, construction squeezing the highway down to one lane, through the accidents, her eyes dry, burning. Halfway there, on the Palisades, she nodded off, then snapped awake when her right wheels hit the gravel on the shoulder, and she drove the rest of the way with the windows wide open and the radio set to the hard-rock station at top volume.

Even so, as soon as she coasted into her driveway and turned off the ignition, she placed her arms over the steering wheel, dropped her head onto her arms, and closed her eyes. The sleep overtaking her was dark and absolute, a passing out in its purest form—she'd crossed from consciousness to oblivion, no thoughts, no dreams, no feelings.

'Round eleven, Holly, out yet again with her dog (always an excellent excuse to see who on the street was awake and who wanted a chat), rapped on her window, startling her into a blurred alertness. She stumbled out of her car, stiff and freezing, thirsty, her mouth dry, her stomach hurting.

Wordlessly her friend walked her into her house, guided her to her bedroom—barely used since Alfie disappeared—removed her boots and her jacket and her belt, slid her under the heavy covers, disappeared, then came back with a glass of water. Laney wondered if the power had been restored yet, was about to ask Holly, then immediately forgot, her mind circling back to Cynthia instead.

"Alfie's going to die," Laney croaked. "Nobody will help. Nobody." The words felt like a fire in her throat, enflaming her face, whooshing down into her chest and bowels.

"Shhh." Holly held the tumbler to her lips, and she took a few sips of cold water. Her friend sat on the edge of the bed. "Your son is smarter than you think." She leaned down and kissed Laney on the forehead. "He takes after his mother."

PART THREE

CHAPTER

44

SHE OPENED HER eyes to feeble early-morning light only to wish that black absence absorb her again. But something was different today. She shifted under the bedclothes, felt the clammy wrinkles of her slacks and blouse.

The house was warm. She smelled coffee. She trundled down the stairs and peeked into the kitchen. That answered the question of whether the power lines had been fixed. Holly must have checked the thermostat and preset the coffeemaker before she left last night. It was just after six thirty AM.

Laney looked for her phone, found it in her jacket pocket, typed, *How do you even know how to set that coffeepot? I could never figure it out!*

She poured a cup and sipped, carrying it with her to her room, where she sat on the bed, back against the wall, her hands wrapped around the warmed ceramic. A while later, her phone pinged.

For shame! I bought that for you two years ago! You're telling me you never programmed it?

Laney typed, *Thank you.*

Holly: *Eat some breakfast. I checked and you have bread. Make some toast. Life is better with toast.*

Laney: *Maybe.*

Holly: *I get it. But you can't help anything if you've starved your-self to death, right? I know you have eggs too. Eggs and toast. Now go get a shower.*

Laney grinned at her screen.

Holly: *Every problem has a solution.* Then she added a thinking emoji.

That was Laney's line. She always thought anything could be dealt with. Anything. She had honed this philosophy in a game of what-ifs she and Theo used to play.

He'd initiated the game early in their relationship. What would you do if your house burned down? What if you were traveling in another country and someone planted drugs on you and you got arrested? What if someone hacked your bank account and stole your identity? What if you got a terminal illness? And if the solu-tion was out of your hands, you could always take yourself out of the equation. Suicide was an abstract, the occasional final move.

The grimness of the game was the point, a way to exorcise anxieties. He was unfailingly calm afterward. They never touched on the real problems—what if your career tanks because you're spending all your time taking care of a small, demanding child? What if you don't love your wife anymore? What if you don't love your son anymore? What if you want out of your marriage? Your life?

And now Laney asked herself the question she'd been afraid to face for five days: What if Alfie is dead?

The answer was clear, clean, easy. She had her off-duty revolver, had filled out forms and made sure to qualify every year so she could continue carrying it. She hadn't though—hadn't carried it, not until now. But she knew it was oiled, ready, strapped into its holster inside her gun safe. She imagined coming home after Alfie's funeral (this was important; there couldn't be any doubt of his death) and removing the revolver from the holster. Lying down on her bed.

Incredibly, this macabre fantasy steadied her. She had never considered suicide, not ever, not even when Theo left, not through the trouble afterward. But the idea that she wouldn't have to suffer, wouldn't have to go on eating, walking, talking, working, all the time knowing her son had been killed because of something she'd done or failed to do, soothed her.

After she scrubbed yesterday's sweat and fear from her pores and hair, she dressed in her own clothes, not Alfie's, not Kendra's— jeans and a green turtleneck, a fitted oatmeal cardigan.

Then she went to the kitchen to fry up some eggs and toast.

CHAPTER

45

AFTER SHE ATE and washed her plate, she cleared the kitchen table, opened her laptop, and retrieved the spreadsheet she'd been analyzing the day before.

On a piece of loose leaf, she began jotting notes.

- Owen Hopper was released from Groveland Correctional Facility in upstate New York four months ago.
- According to what Mike told her, by the time he was released, he had the names of the two cops who raided his apartment and their addresses, plus the knowledge that Kendra was an undercover. It wasn't clear if he knew her real name at that point.
- Two months ago, he confronted Viktor Orlov and (probably) murdered him by smashing in his head. She didn't know if Orlov gave her up, but she was certain Hopper knew her real name and address by the time he decided to transplant himself to the Hudson Valley.
- Sometime shortly afterward, Hopper drove to Sylvan with Orlov's body in his car, rented a one-bedroom apartment in Mountain View, and dumped the body in the garage.

- Twelve days ago, Owen Hopper somehow managed to in-
  duce Harry Burroughs to inject himself with a lethal dose
  of heroin. Or, more likely, Hopper did the injection.
- Five days ago, Alfie got into Owen Hopper's car.

She had to stop there. Stand. Pour another cup of coffee. The
eggs and toast briefly threatened a return visit, then subsided. She
sat back down and gripped her pen.

She went through the entire spreadsheet again and red-
highlighted anybody with the last name Hopper. Then pink for
anybody with his wife's maiden name, Gulyansky.

After a half hour she paused, her mouse hovering over a Jane
Hopper. She searched for that name in the sheet, found three separate entries. About ten years ago a Jane Hopper had lived at the
same Brooklyn address as Owen, though in a different apartment.
Four years ago she was no longer listed at that address but rather
in the Bronx. Now Jane Hopper lived upstate in Narrowsburg.
Laney brought up Google Maps. Narrowsburg was about an hour
and a half north of Sylvan. Maybe two hours in bad weather.

She then switched to the sheet listing automobile registrations
and violations, realizing she'd seen this name already. There. Nine
months ago, a traffic violation near Dansville for Jane Hopper.
Another search in Google. Dansville was about ten miles from
Groveland Correctional Facility.

Fifteen minutes later she had strapped her holster around her
waist, the familiar heaviness of the gun pressing into her hip,
crammed her feet into her boots, and lifted her jacket off its hook.

Ten minutes after that she kicked her car tires in frustration.

The temperature had dropped close to zero overnight, and
though it was in the twenties now, her car doors were frozen shut.
Her key wouldn't even turn inside the locks. She ran back into the
house, grabbed a lighter from the junk drawer, and held her key in
the spluttering flame. After this treatment it turned, but the doors
still wouldn't open. Up until this moment a smidge of hope had flut-
tered within her. Or at least a smidge of resolution. She had her first

useful piece of information in days, and she was going to drive to Narrowsburg and pay good old Jane Hopper a visit. An unthreatening, composed visit. That's all. But she couldn't even get that going.

She spun on her heel and marched down the hill to Holly's house, knocked, and only then realized it was Sunday, and therefore Holly's day to be elbow-deep in trays of sausage and peppers for fifty.

When no one answered, she climbed down the steps and wondered if holding the lighter to her car doors would open them, melt them, or explode the car.

"Laney? Are you okay? What happened?"

She turned to see Holly, in black yoga pants and pink sweater, poking her head around her half-open doorway.

"Sorry! I forgot it was Sunday! I was just wondering if you had any deicer for cars."

Holly stepped onto her porch and squinted toward Laney's car. "Doors frozen?"

"Yeah." Laney looked around the empty driveway. "Where is everyone? Are you actually alone?" Holly's house was so rarely empty that Laney wondered if something bad had happened, then experienced a brief pang of guilt for being so inattentive.

"Come inside, won't you? It's freezing."

Laney hesitated, but her car doors were not going to unfreeze on their own. Her friend's house was uncommonly quiet.

Holly hurried to the back and closed a door, her face rosy and furtive, then rooted in a kitchen drawer before retrieving a slim deicing stick.

"Here," she said. "Hopefully it still works." She peered at Laney. "Are you feeling okay?"

"Yeah. Yes. Why are you alone?"

Holly pianoed her fingers over her throat. "Oh, it's Oliver's grandmother's birthday. She's like ninety. Or a hundred. I can't remember. I packed him and the kids off with my peppermint chocolate cake and, erm . . . you know." She giggled. "I said I was sick." Her eyes shifted to the floor.

Laney glanced at that closed door, then stopped herself. She just couldn't. She'd pry the real answer out of Holly some other time. After Alfie came home. In one piece. Alive.

"Okay, well. Thanks for the . . ." She held up the deicer.

"Wait, where are you going?"

Good question. She could lie. Say she needed to run to the grocery store for more coffee. But (and this was yet one more thing she missed about Harry) she really wanted someone to bounce ideas off. "So, you know all that information I downloaded from the computer in Riverdale? I think I may have found a connection to Hopper. Like, I think I found where someone lives who used to live with him and then visited him in jail. And it's not that far from here." She cleared her throat. "Relatively speaking."

"You're kidding." Holly stared at the deicer. "You're not doing this alone, are you? Are you going to tell Ed?"

"Tell him what? It's not a bad hunch, but it could be nothing. And even if this Jane person is a sister or an aunt or even his mother, it doesn't mean that's where he is right now."

Holly followed her outside. She said, "But you're driving up there?"

"Might as well. Sitting here doing nothing is eating my brain away."

Holly touched her forearm. "Give me ten minutes. I could use a field trip."

Laney frowned. "You can't come with me."

"Why?"

"One, you're home, erm . . . relaxing . . . on your own for a change. Two, it's three hours round trip! Maybe for nothing. And three, if it's something, there's a murdering, kidnapping felon on the other end."

Holly grinned. "Well, I've been missing some excitement in my life lately. Thinking about time to spice things up."

A week earlier Laney would have balked at taking a civilian (she simply couldn't stop thinking of herself as something other than that) outlaw hunting, but now she couldn't muster the authority to make anybody do anything they didn't want to. Also, she realized she was happy to have Holly along. Might have walked to her house for this exact purpose.

"Bring a thermos," Laney said. "It's a long drive."

About twenty miles in, the car warm and quiet, Laney's phone chirped. She rooted for it in her pants pocket, drew it out, and handed it to Holly.

"Who's it from?" she asked. She hated looking at phones while driving, had seen too many crashes with drivers' hands wrapped around them as they were hefted into an ambulance.

Holly peered at the screen, smirked, then looked at Laney. "Who's Cunty Burroughs?"

Laney grabbed the phone and glanced at it, handed it back to Holly. "It's Cynthia. Can you read her text to me? Passcode is 587231."

Holly quirked her mouth. "You know you can have the phone read it to you, right? You just have to set it up."

Laney rolled her eyes. "Just read it to me, will you?"

Holly held the phone close to her face and squinted. "She says, 'Harry was a lying bastard. Be careful.' The phone chirped again. "She just sent an attachment. Should I open?"

Laney nodded.

"It's a bunch of messages. A ton of them."

Laney pulled over onto the shoulder, flicked on the hazards, and took her phone back. The reception here was terrible, but with some cursing and maneuvering, she was able to scroll through the emails Cynthia had forwarded.

"Fuck," she whispered, flipping through message after message. She took ten minutes to skim the lot, then put it down. She'd have to read them in detail later.

"Are you going to tell me?" Holly asked. She'd plugged her phone into the car's charger and had spent her time flipping and tapping through her own messages while Laney read hers.

"Fucking Harry," Laney said.

46

S HE DIDN'T KNOW why she was so shocked. No, not shocked. Devastated at how much more twisted the truth was than she suspected.

"One of my ex-partners worked for the mob," Laney said. She might as well tell Holly everything at this point. Her head drooped against the car seat, eyes half-closed. "The Russian mob. I didn't know." Except of course she had. Toward the end. It had been so obvious after that raid. "I didn't know then. He was the one who arrested Hopper."

"Are you serious? That's nuts!" Holly's eyes widened.

"So, about a year ago, he was indicted on all kinds of charges—racketeering, drugs, I don't even know them all." Yes, she did. But the list's scope exhausted her. "He was arrested and then suspended. Six months ago there was a trial."

She rubbed her eyes. Internal Affairs had wanted her to testify, but she told them she knew nothing, saw nothing, couldn't help them, and eventually they decided not to waste time with her. At least in their eyes, she was clean. How she looked to herself was another story.

"He was found guilty. His sentencing hearing was supposed to be sometime in the fall but kept being pushed back."

"Oh my God. You never said anything. I think I remember this case in the news. I never thought that was anything to do with you!"

Laney shrugged. "Yeah, well, not something I like to think about." She looked at Holly. "After he was found guilty, all his cases were suspect. All the evidence he had been responsible for was now tainted. That included the case with Owen Hopper. In fact, it was the Hopper case that got Internal Affairs curious in the first place, and that was the one they investigated. They found Harry had planted all the evidence in Hopper's apartment. They proved it."

"But why? Didn't you say Hopper was just an informant?"

Laney sat up straighter, buckled her seat belt, and switched gears. Time to get driving.

"Looks like the mobster we were going after paid Harry to frame Hopper. For everything. That way the investigation against him would end." She pulled onto the highway, then glanced at Holly. "Hopper is not innocent, but he wasn't guilty of all the things Harry pinned on him. So, because so much of the evidence was now unusable, they let him out."

"Jesus."

"The first thing he did was find the mob boss, because that's who issued the order to frame him. Hopper must have known that all along. By the time he smashed a hammer into the guy's head, he also knew I was one of the people who put him away. He definitely knew who I was, my name, and my address. The second thing he did was move up here and start a relationship with my son. And the third thing he did was somehow corner Harry while he was waiting for his sentencing hearing and kill *him*."

They drove in silence for a few minutes. Then Holly said, "I can't believe this."

It felt cold in the car, an underground kind of cold. Laney's fingers and toes ached. She turned up the heat.

The messages Cynthia sent her went back five years—Harry and Orlov mostly, sent between Harry's Gmail and a VK account, the Russian version of Facebook. Harry had been on his payroll at least that long, tipping him off whenever there was to be a raid or a concentrated series of buy-and-busts. The messages hinted at things that hadn't even come up at trial, things that would have sent Harry to prison for a few lifetimes. Orlov had fed him information about rival gangs and he'd raided them, stole cash, drugs, then sold the drugs to Orlov. He'd tinned Orlov's guys out of arrests, fixed parking tickets, worked a bizarre upside-down security for Orlov's men when they burglarized warehouses and businesses. There were hints at homicides in those messages, at least two. She searched for Hopper's name and found three email exchanges detailing his frame-up. Three emails. Enough to destroy two families and at least one life.

She searched for herself within that mass of messages, found dozens of references, and then had to stop reading. Harry had used her real name from the very beginning. There had never been a time during her months of buying from Orlov's men that they hadn't known who she really was. Apparently, the only people who had been in the dark about her role were Owen Hopper and her.

She shook her head. He hadn't even bothered to disguise his own name properly in his communications. He'd been so sure of everyone else's stupidity. At their blindness.

Well, he'd been right about her stupidity. Her blindness.

Harry. Her friend. What was it? Did he really need the extra money so bad? The job didn't pay great, not as much as the suburban police departments, but Harry had been nearing twenty years as a second-grade detective when he was arrested. With the kind of overtime he did, he was making plenty, three or four times the national average yearly salary. Was it the power? The idea that he could do anything he wanted to anyone he wanted? What else did she not know about people? Her naïveté plagued her. In the end, she was the reason Alfie was who-knows-where in hell-knows-what trouble. All because of her misplaced loyalty, her silence about her suspicions, her inability to think badly of people she loved.

She *had* loved Harry, in her own way. Not like she'd loved Theo, nothing like that. But more than once she had found herself fantasizing that if she'd worked with her dad, he would have been like Harry—smart, larger than life. Safe. Of all things, that's how she'd felt around Harry.

She could never trust her own feelings again.

The sky had darkened as they drove, turned a wolfish color, and now a thick, swirly snow was beating against the windshield. She didn't want to cry, felt that if she did allow herself the weakness, she'd be useless for the rest of the day.

But her nose grew stuffy with moisture anyway; her eyes watered, her throat hurt. She wiped at her face and told herself to buck up because if she could take her son being gone, she could take her ex–best friend being a liar and a criminal. She could take him being dead. She could take knowing she'd been so mistaken about him. She could.

Holly handed her a tissue and she blew her nose, dabbed at her eyes.

"You think guys leak like this when they're upset?" Laney asked, because she wanted to talk about anything other than Harry and his betrayals.

"It's okay to be upset," Holly said. "You can cry. I won't judge."

"No, you won't. But fuck that. Harry fucked his life all on his own. He deserves to be dead."

"But you're not crying 'cause he's dead, are you?" Holly wasn't looking at her, had her body turned away. "You're upset that you didn't read him well enough?"

She glanced at Holly. "You don't have some kind of sex chamber in the basement, do you?"

Holly's eyes rounded. "What?"

Laney shook her head. "Never mind. I'm beginning to think everyone around me has a secret life."

"Well, most people have some kind of secret."

"Well, I'm an open book. Husband left me, my son is an odd-ball, I tell everyone about this shit. What's the point of hiding anything? Why, what are you hiding?"

Holly stared at the windshield, the corner of her mouth twitching. "If I tell you, will you call Ed and share what you've discovered?"

"I'll think about it."

Holly opened her mouth, and Laney raised her hand. "Wait. If you're going to confess to dead bodies in your backyard or crush-ing small animals with your high heels, I don't want to know."

Her friend swatted at her, *tsk*ing. "Oh please. I should be that interesting. No, my biggest secret is"—she cleared her throat, her cheeks reddening as if she were a child—"I write stories."

Laney furrowed her brow. "Yeah?" Why would that be a secret?

"Erotic stories."

"Oh."

"For a romance publisher."

"What, like *Fifty Shades*?"

Holly turned her face toward the window, her fingers tapping at her throat. "Sort of. Yes, kind of like that."

They drove in silence for a few minutes. "And you get paid for that?"

"A little, yes. You know, wine and chocolate money." Holly laughed her tiny laugh, and Laney found herself laughing as well. Perfectly poised Holly, typing away about tumescent body parts. "Expensive wine and chocolate," Holly amended.

"Why the heck would you keep that a secret?"

Flapping her hand at Laney, Holly said, "Can you imagine the small talk at the Girl Scout den meeting? Please." She rolled her eyes.

Laney slapped the steering wheel, and the car swerved on the icy road, fishtailed, righted. "What's wrong with me? I thought Theo loved me and loved his life until the moment he told me he'd rather slit his wrists than spend another day as my husband. Harry was a fucking felon. My son, my only son—and God knows, if there's anybody I should understand, it's him—spends his afternoons with a dealer, doing God knows what, 'cause I sure don't know, and then runs off." She could barely speak, the words wrung out of her in a spray of spit through tense lips. " 'Cause I don't really know if he's been kidnapped, do I? Maybe he did go on his own? Maybe he ran away. Maybe he chose to go with Hopper."

Holly shook her head. "No way. Alfie is like a vampire; he needs his native earth around him when he sleeps. There's no doubt in my mind he would have never left on his own."

Laney cut a glance at her friend. "What do you know from vampires anyways?"

"Oh come on. I write erotic romances, remember? Lots of people like to read about erotic vampires." She shrugged but then grew serious. "Laney, you can't ever fully know another person. Don't beat yourself up for it."

"I just don't know how I can be pretty good at detective work and so unbelievably blind when it comes to people I care about. It's downright uncanny."

"If it makes you feel any better, I don't believe I know my husband's dark secrets." Then, so soft Laney barely heard, "He definitely doesn't know mine."

"Oliver has dark secrets?" Steadfast, gentle Oliver?

Holly snorted in exasperation. "Everyone does!" She turned and pointed at Laney. "Even you do." She held up her palm. "And don't feel you have to tell me about it."

They drove in silence for another ten miles, and then Laney said, "You're right. I do." She touched her friend's knee lightly before putting her hand back on the wheel. "Don't feel you have to tell me yours either."

Holly didn't respond right away. Then, "Just cut yourself some slack, will you?"

The snow was going through a personality crisis as they drove, going wet and soft, turning to gray sluices of rain, then back to flurries. According to the GPS, they were within ten miles of their destination. They exited the highway and were now on a two-lane narrow route climbing up a mountain. An old, overgrown forest rose on both sides of the road—snow-topped pines, bare maples and birches with a thicket of brambles blocking out any light between the trees. The light, already as gray as stone, had darkened further, and Laney flipped the headlights on. The GPS clicked and told them they had lost the signal.

A shiver ran through Holly, and she tugged her scarf closer around her throat. "Who would live up here?" she asked, peering at the empty road, the encroaching woods. "It's so lonely."

"Some people hate being around other humans," Laney said. "If this Jane Hopper grew up in some tight-ass quarters with everyone on top of everyone else, she might want nature and solitude. Think about it, for years all you have is concrete and crowds, the stinking subway, trash everywhere. And then, this." She wouldn't have been able to live anywhere this isolated herself, but she could see the appeal.

"Who do you think she is? Your guy's sister? Mother? Aunt?"

Laney had been contemplating this ever since she noticed the connection between Jane Hopper and Owen Hopper. "Someone close," she said. "Someone who didn't mind the drive to visit him."

The road curved sharply again, the snow growing icy, and Laney slowed. In the past six miles they hadn't seen a single off road, not one driveway or house. And so when the gravel entrance appeared to the right just as they came out of another curve, Laney shot right past it. She screeched to a stop, put the car in reverse, and backed up to the path, which, she saw now, was a driveway, a mailbox crooked and snowed over at the corner.

Her heart quickening, she took her foot off the brake and turned in. The driveway was long, and so overgrown with a canopy of pines that they might as well have gone into a tunnel. One hand on the steering wheel, she unsnapped her holster and made sure her gun was accessible.

As they pulled into a clearing, she slammed the brakes so hard that the car bucked and they both jolted against their seat belts.

"Oh no," said Holly.

"Fuck!" said Laney. It took her painful moments, way too long moments, to unstrap herself with fingers gone numb with fear, and she shoved the door open, stumbling out, her feet skittering on the iced gravel.

The house before her still smoldered. Half of it was gone, blackened skeletal frames pointing to the sky. The other half stood awkward, blind, its glassless windows gaping and dark. Somewhere in the back of her awareness, Laney heard Holly dialing 911, saying something, then cursing.

"There's no signal," Holly said.

Of course there wasn't. The reception even in Sylvan was uncertain. Up here, in these mountains mobbed with trees, they would be lucky if they could get a satellite phone to work.

"I think I'm getting something." Holly crunched over gravel, her voice growing muffled.

Laney drew her gun, pointed it forward, left hand supporting her wrist. She walked slowly toward the house.

"Is anyone there?" she yelled.

CHAPTER

47

ALFIE WAS COLD. The cold was inside his bones, inside his heart, inside his stomach, his throat, his head. He'd been cold before, sure. During the Boy Scout Iditarods, for example, when he had to sleep outdoors in January on a mountaintop. The night of last year's Iditarod, the mountain temperature fell to single digits, and one of the other Scouts got frostbite on his toes. But Alfie did okay on that camp-out. He had his subzero socks and boots, his snow pants and extra-thick thermal underwear. His mother had outfitted him well, and he spent the night burrowed into his sleeping bag, watching flakes flutter like tiny dust bunnies against the moonlit snow. Those evenings with the Scouts featured campfires and the company of others, hot food, chocolate bars. As usual, he didn't participate in any of the conversations, told no jokes. But he liked listening, and he liked watching, and he liked the smell of woodsmoke and pines and cold snow.

Now was different. Now he walked through calf-high drifts in nothing but his flannel shirt, jeans, and socks. His jacket was smoldering in the house he'd escaped hours ago. What else might be smoldering or burnt black was a question his mind gnawed for the past three or four miles. The basement where he'd been kept—burnt or salvaged? The crusty couch? And both deep under those thoughts and blindingly on top was Hopper—the sight of him, his shirt, hair, and part of his face on fire, a horribly yellow-black fire full of chemical smells and oily smoke; the sound of him, screaming, high-pitched, terror filled.

When Owen bent over him that morning, grimy wool blanket in his hands, ready to spread it over Alfie as if the boy really was his son, Alfie had been ready. He drew the can of WD-40 he'd found under the sink, pressed the nozzle with all his strength, and lit the spray with the lemon-yellow lighter.

The resulting flame wasn't spectacular, nothing like what a can of spray paint would have given him, but at a one-foot distance, it was enough. Oily, messy, hot, and sputtering, it hit Hopper in the upper chest, igniting his shirt, catching the side of his neck, then jumping to his hair.

Hopper reared back, emitting a terrible scream, and Alfie wondered in a shocked moment if the fire was right then flying into Hopper's lungs as he drew the blazing air into himself to yell. Hopper threw himself against a wall, trying to dampen the flames, then lurched toward the bathroom.

Alfie bounded off the couch and ran for the door. He heard Hopper turning the shower on, then a horrendous hiss, cursing, followed by a full-throated scream filled with pain and fury.

The front door was still padlocked. Alfie dashed for the nearest window as Owen stumbled out of the bathroom, drenched, red boils blooming on his neck and at his hairline. Half his hair was fried, as was one eyebrow. One eye swollen shut, he lunged for Alfie, and the boy ducked under his arms, bolted for the wood stove and lifted a thick branch from the pile. He swung, connected with the singed, blistered half of Owen's face, then ran around the man when he dropped to his knees, bellowing, hands blocking his head from further assault.

Incredibly, Alfie still had the lighter in his pocket, and as he ran past the armchair, he clicked it and held it to the fabric, forcing himself to count to ten while it caught. The room was dry and cold, and the elderly upholstery gave itself to fire willingly.

Owen was rising to his feet, muttering something that might or might not have been words. Alfie grabbed an old newspaper and held it to the burning chair. As it too caught and flamed, he tossed it at the man staggering toward him, singeing his own fingers. Running down the hallway toward the back door, he set fire to a roll of paper towels with the lighter, then used the roll as a torch, igniting a curtain, a stack of magazines piled on a stand, dropping it onto a rag rug when the fire reached his hands. The rooms began filling with smoke as the dry-rotted furnishings surrendered to flames.

A padlock on the back door.

Hopper's heavy hand clamped on Alfie's shoulder, and Alfie yelped, startled and scared, before elbowing the man just under the ribs. It wasn't a great hit, but it was enough for Hopper to let go, and Alfie skirted around him, dashed to the kitchen, and, to his surprise, saw a can of spray cooking oil. A flick of the lighter while depressing the nozzle and the room whoomphed bright and hot, flames squirming on the greasy linoleum, on the walls for ten seconds, twenty.

Alfie tugged on the window, but it wouldn't give, and the latch, when he tried it, broke his fingernails. He straightened and turned around.

Across the kitchen, Owen scowled in the doorway, one-eyed, two-faced, grim.

Alfie lifted the rusted toaster oven (thank God it was next to the window) and smashed it into the glass, shattering the single-glazed pane on the first try. The window was old, original to the house, brittle, and had broken easily, shards exploding outward, fragments littering the floor. He had to hit it a few more times to knock out enough glass. Flinging his body through the toothy opening as if performing a circus trick, he stretched his arms over his head, face tucked in, muscles stretched taut, and then collapsed into a ball when he hit the snow-covered branches and rocks underneath.

The random bits of fire in the house, given extra oxygen with the influx of fresh air, roared behind him. He ran, oblivious to the cuts in his arms, on the side of his cheek. Heedless of his shoeless feet, of his jacketless torso, hatless head.

He did not feel the cold for a while, fear and adrenaline keeping him alert and running for almost a mile before he stopped and bent over, hands on knees, spitting yellow bile onto the shadowed snow. After that he walked for another mile, his back to the house, not because he had the strength but because being stationary meant either Hopper finding and killing him or the cold doing the job.

Hypothermia was a serious concern, and he slowed to take stock of his body. The Boy Scouts had an entire brochure on cold-weather camping, and he'd read it and memorized it two years ago. He was shivering, so that was reassuring. It meant his body was in good enough shape to try to stay warm. He didn't think his mental acuity was affected. But he was in trouble—the lack of shoes the most serious of his problems. He scooped a handful of snow from a pine bough and put it in his mouth, letting his body melt it before swallowing. Dehydration was another worry.

His second concern was he didn't know his location. Not knowing his location meant he didn't know which way to go home. He had paid little attention to signage on the drive over, but he guessed Hopper's house was north of Sylvan, if only because south of Sylvan was New Jersey and higher population density.

So, he had to head south. He'd gotten his orienteering badge earlier in the fall, but that had been with a compass and a group and an adult to walk with him. Nevertheless, he remembered an exercise for when a compass was broken or missing. He chose a straight stick about two feet in length and stuck it into the ground. The sunlight, though dim and gloomy, was bright enough to cast a shadow. He placed a pebble at the end of the stick's shadow. Then he had to wait. He peed. He made a snowball and threw it against a tree. He did thirty jumping jacks to stay warm.

He wondered what his father was up to. He wondered if his father would mind if he died. This led him to speculate how his father would find out. As far as he knew, his mother did not have his father's contact details.

And this in turn led him to the question that confounded him the most—what was the point to relationships? Everywhere he turned, he was told that friendships were important, that love between two people was a wonderful, magnificent thing. Children needed parents, parents loved their children; BFFs, best buds, romances, and bromances filled his reading lists and the conversations of everyone around him.

But for what? He'd set out his freshman year with the intent to make a friend. He wasn't sure why, but he could no longer resist the pressure from his mother, his counselors, asking him didn't he want a buddy, a pal, a playmate.

And so he created the spreadsheet. First, he recorded the names of all the kids he came across during his day at school—classes, band, gym. Then he created columns—how often their paths crossed, what they talked about, whether they already belonged to a clique, what they wore, if they paid attention in class or fucked off.

He immediately crossed out all the girls. Girls were an effort he felt beyond him. He then crossed out everyone already in a clique, everyone who struck him as stupid, everyone who struck him as boring. At the end of two weeks of observation, he had circled two names on the list. For the week after that, he focused exclusively on those boys. He listened to their conversations and made notes. He documented the clothes they wore, the music they listened to, the social media they used.

He had settled on Jordan but been unsure how to begin when the talent show curtain fire fiasco solved the problem for him. Obviously, knowing Jordan had gotten him nothing but trouble, and here he was, freezing, starving, lost in the woods in the middle of winter. Although arguably his mother was the more accurate cause of this particular trouble. He concluded that every relationship in his life thus far either ended in misery or bred danger.

He looked at his stick and saw that the shadow had shifted. He placed another pebble at the end of the new shadow. According to the activity he'd learned with the Boy Scouts, as the sun moved, the direction of shadows made it possible to orient oneself. The first pebble was west, and the second pebble was east. He stood with the toe of his right foot touching the west pebble and the toe of his left touching the east one. He now faced south, and south he would go. If he heard cars, he'd head in that direction but stay out of sight until he could be sure it wasn't Hopper searching for him.

The path before him lay open and clear, and he peered at the trees, wondering if a blaze marked the trail. After another half hour of walking, he saw a glossy black something under a thicket and went to investigate.

What he found made him smile for the first time in days, and he did a little dance as he unfolded the plastic bag and shook out the camping detritus someone had left behind. The trash itself was of no use, but the heavy-duty plastic bag was priceless, and he perched on a log, feeling slightly less scared now. He peeled off his sopping cold socks and carefully tore the bag in half along the seams. It was a large trash bag (and he said an uncharacteristic prayer of thanks), enough for each half to wrap around one foot like a puttee. He tugged free a few of the dormant vines surrounding him and used them as ropes, securing the plastic around his skin. He then pulled the wet socks back on over each contraption and tied some more vines around the ankles to keep them from slipping off.

It wouldn't hold, but at least there was now a barrier between his skin and the cold, and soon enough his body temperature would heat the plastic. It wouldn't be like wearing hiking boots and dry wool socks (and he would never, ever take those two things for granted again), but it might keep his toes from frostbite.

This small find gave him a boost, and though the light had already begun to fade and flurries started swirling onto his bare head, his feet felt marginally warmer, he had a direction to follow, and he was no longer afraid.

He'd faced someone who meant to kill him, and he outwitted him. He found his bearings in the woods. He would find his way home.

The plastic bags around his feet squeaked as he walked, the vines cut into his skin, and he was thirsty again. He swept more snow into his mouth and kept walking.

Everyone always wanted him to be someone else. His father found him lacking. Kids laughed at him, teased him, called him oddball, weirdo, freak, asked him when he was going to bring his semiautomatic to school and shoot everyone. His mother cried in her room when she thought he'd gone to sleep, looked at him with eyes full of worry even as her mouth smiled. What did they want from him? Who did they want him to be?

More importantly, and this question occurred to him for the first time now as he hiked alone in the growing dark, what did he want? He'd never specifically asked himself. He knew for certain that he had, at one time, wanted his father back. He had wanted it so fiercely that he could not remember having any other thought or desire for months after his father left. After he understood his father was not returning, he didn't want anything, made himself not want anything, because wanting things he couldn't have was so painful he didn't think he could survive it.

This year, he'd thought he wanted a friend. Hence the list, and Jordan, and then Hopper and the pills and syringes and beer and porn and now this freezing, hateful day. He didn't care for any of it. The porn was interesting and had snagged itself into his memory to rise at inconvenient moments throughout his days. But he didn't need Jordan or Hopper for porn. He didn't need another person to talk to. He didn't need to share his thoughts. He didn't need someone to make him laugh. He didn't need a buddy, a friend, a soul mate.

With every step, he felt a hardness settle around him, a stiff shell that straightened his shoulders and lengthened his spine. He felt taller, stronger. His jaw set and his mouth thinned. If he walked out of this forest alive and with all his limbs and extremities whole and unharmed, he wouldn't need anyone ever again.

48

"THE FIRE TRUCK is coming," said Holly. She had dashed all the way to the road to get a signal, then ran back, and her voice was ragged, huffing as she stepped out from beneath the pine canopy.

Laney placed a tentative foot on the front steps, put her weight on the charred wood. They held.

"You shouldn't go in," Holly said, somewhere just behind her. "They said they'll be here soon."

Laney shook her head, her teeth clenched so tight she couldn't have spoken if she wanted to. She was at the top of the steps now, and the heat from the house was savage, its burnt exhalations bitter, oily, with an underwhiff of fitzing electricity.

"Laney, don't," Holly said, reached for Laney's shoulder. Laney shook her off. "This whole thing looks ready to collapse. Just wait, won't you?"

Laney toed open the door, and the house breathed an acrid smoke in her face. Something crashed within its depths. Something hissed. Something shifted under her feet, the floor rickety.

From inside the house, a scream, and she flinched, then rushed through the door. Light from the broken windows and partially collapsed roof illuminated a crushed, blackened living room.

Paradoxically, there was a wood-burning stove against one wall, cold and silent, nothing but a lump of gray ash visible through the gaping wrought-iron door.

Another scream, high-pitched and desolate. Laney bolted toward the sound, which was coming from under the caved-in ceiling to the right of the living room. Where a hallway once connected the front room to the back, plaster and drywall spewed coils of gray smoke, barred the way. The house creaked above her and that scream came again, scraping at her brain and reverberating in her guts.

"Alfie?" she yelled. "Alfie, are you here?"

A beam directly above her head popped, and a chunk of charred drywall fell to her feet. She squinted up into darkness, dust showering her face, grit in her eyes. Another piece of the ceiling plummeted, and the floor buckled under her.

Holly screamed from the doorway, and Laney's instincts took over, propelled her legs toward the exit. But what if Alfie was trapped somewhere in the hot ruins? She grunted and halted just outside the door.

Coward. She was nothing but a coward. A sob snarling in her throat, she stumbled back inside. A fresh gust of wind must have rekindled some of the fire and a portion of the roof blazed again, black and red, yellow and gray, spiraling and snapping toward that leaden sky.

The high-pitched keening came again, but now she recognized it was the wind driving through the smokestack. With the roof half-gone, the metal stack shook and rattled and bent, producing the sound she had mistaken for screaming. She holstered her gun and flicked on her flashlight, then climbed over the dust-covered rubble in the hallway and saw a doorway a few feet in.

Debris almost completely barricaded the opening, but she forced her way through by alternately shoving it to the side and stepping over it, then tripped halfway down a flight of cement steps. The steps themselves had remained whole but were covered in ash and bits and pieces of the house. Picking up her flashlight from where it fell, she scampered on her butt feetfirst, hands on the walls, until she found herself in a basement, dark, dank, smoky. The flashlight illuminated a plaid couch, an overturned chair, a lamp lying on its side.

And then, Alfie's jacket. She lunged for it as if it would run from her, grabbed it, held it to the light. It was his, she knew it was. She searched through the pockets and removed lint, a torn candy wrapper, a smooth gob of bubblegum. The inner pocket produced a folded and worn scrap of paper, and when she flattened it out, hands trembling, she saw Alfie's class schedule—his name clearly visible in the corner.

She pressed the paper to her cheek, as if trying to absorb whatever Alfie-ness had infused it during its residence in his pocket. She'd been right. This woman who owned the house, this Jane Hopper, was related to Owen. She had visited him in prison. And she had given him permission, explicitly or implicitly, to use her house when he got out.

The building creaked above her, and a distant crash reached her ears. She barely noticed, instead directing her light at every wall, the ceiling, the corners. Hopper had brought her son here. Had kept him against his will—she knew it was against his will; there was no other possibility at all.

Her light fell on the bucket her boy had been forced to use. Her fastidious child who liked everything just so. She cursed and touched the couch where he had slept. Itchy, filthy.

Another crash, closer. A footstep. Someone grabbed her arm, and Laney, years of training taking over, drew her gun, twisted her torso and elbowed the person in the chest, finishing with a follow-through of gun to chin. Too late to stop, she saw it was Holly, but the gun slipped upward, walloping her friend's jaw and cheek with a sickening crack.

Holly's eyes teared with surprise and pain. She pinwheeled her arms and stumbled backward toward the steps, one foot crashing through the frail wood of the upended chair and the rest of her falling awkwardly onto the stairway, her head smacking against the cement.

Laney gasped and crouched by her friend's twisted foot. Holly's eyes were pinched shut, her mouth already swollen and bleeding, her face blotchy. She mumbled something that sounded like, "Fuck, that hurts," and moaned in pain.

Holstering her gun again, Laney broke apart the rest of the chair. She carefully extracted Holly's foot, then scooted so she could cradle her friend's head and torso and drew her down onto the floor. Holly grunted, growing pale and clammy as Laney shifted her. Her foot remained slack and angled weird.

"I'm sorry," Laney said. "I'm sorry."

"She's got a gun!" someone yelled behind her. "Raise your hands where I can see them!" he roared, and she did, shouting, "Don't shoot, don't shoot, I'm a cop."

Then hands were on her, picking her up, rushing her out of the basement and out of the grumbling house.

They slammed her to the ground and handcuffed her, and someone removed the gun. An icy drizzle had started while she was inside and now soaked her hair and neck. "My son is in the house, he's in the house," she kept saying, even though she didn't know this for sure, but it was imperative they go in and look.

"She said she's on the job," someone said.

"Are you a cop?" a voice next to her asked.

She turned her head as far as she could, her cheek cold against the frozen mud, and said, "Retired. My ID is in my wallet. Inside jacket pocket."

A young cop helped her to her feet, still keeping the cuffs around her wrists, and rooted inside her jacket until he found her wallet.

They had brought Holly out and laid her on the ground. A fireman prodded her ankle gently with blue-gloved hands. He said, "Ma'am, the ambulance is almost here. Are you doing okay?"

Her pretty, delicate face was distorted, abraded along her chin and cheek, but she nodded politely anyway. She then said, "Motherfucker fucking fuck that's fucking painful."

Two firemen waited at the doorway, watching the gray hose between them snaking and moving inside the house.

Young cop placed his hands on his hips. "Is this your residence?" he asked Laney, and when she shook her head, he said, "What happened here?"

And so Laney gave them her name, and Holly's name, and Alfie's name, and Hopper's, and Jane Hopper's. She told them about her reasoning for driving two hours out of her way to visit a house she'd never been to, belonging to a woman she'd never met. And then she told them about her own search of the house and Holly's startling her, and her getting all cornered-cop-lashing-out on her friend. She felt close to crying by then. She'd been right, but too late. What if she had driven up the day before? Two days before?

Four firemen tumbled out of the house, grime roiling off their shoulders.

"House is empty," one of them yelled out. "We don't see anybody."

Laney took a step toward them. "Are you sure? Are you sure there's nobody under the rubble?"

The firemen paused, one of them removing his helmet. Soot streaked his cheeks and forehead. "Ma'am, are you confident your son is inside?"

She wasn't, of course. She was confident of nothing. She shook her head.

"We searched every part of the first floor and basement. We found signs of recent occupancy, but the building appears empty right now. The second floor is gone." The fireman looked back at the structure. "When was the last time you saw your son?"

"Five days ago," Laney said.

The six firemen stared at her in confusion.

The fireman leaning over Holly said something into a radio, then pressed her hand. "The ambulance is at the driveway entrance now."

Between the drizzling rain and the tanker truck pumping water onto the house, the fire had gone out, and the building sat blackened and hollowed in the gathering dark.

A second, older cop had called Ed Boswell and checked her story, then removed Laney's handcuffs just as Holly was being hoisted into the ambulance.

"I'm so sorry, Holly," Laney said, touching her friend's hand.

Holly said something, but it was hard to understand through her thickened, bruised lips.

"I'll call Oliver. I'll tell him which hospital you're in," Laney said to Holly's feet as the paramedic closed the door. "I'll come visit you!" she said louder. But how could she? She had tracked Alfie this far. She had to keep looking for him.

The cops and firemen had gone back into the house, treating it as a crime scene for the time being.

It was early evening and dark when she collapsed into her car, so tired her hands and feet shook. Her need to find her son, to touch him, to know he was alive and okay, was so overwhelming it drowned her. She had no thoughts, no wants; her hunger and thirst and weariness were nothing next to this primal need to hold her child in her arms.

She put her forehead down on the steering wheel and closed her eyes. "Alfie," she whispered. "Be okay. Just be okay. Just be okay."

CHAPTER

49

SOMETHING INSIDE ALFIE'S head disconnected. He saw the harsh, icy beauty around him—the frozen trees, stark and bare, the heaps of white on pine boughs, the black boulders and the mottled iron-gray sky. His body seemed removed from his senses, hands red and numb, a hollow belly, legs like pistons he couldn't feel.

At some point in the day he heard sirens and figured someone had discovered the house. He wondered how Hopper was doing. Surely he didn't die in the fire. If Alfie had been able to escape, Hopper would have as well. He'd been singed and hurt, but he was okay enough to pursue Alfie through the hallway. Certainly he was okay enough to save himself.

Alfie angled his steps toward the sirens and within a half hour was in view of the narrow, two-lane road, but stayed in the woods. Trudging slowly through the brambles, over the undergrowth, he was reluctant to be seen. What if Hopper didn't make it? Would that make Alfie a murderer? A manslaughterer? His mother occasionally explained her past cases to him, when a crime drama on television brought one to mind, for example. Murder in the first was when you really meant it and planned it; murder in the second was when feelings got the best of you and you just lost your mind for a minute and killed someone. Then there were degrees of manslaughter—voluntary, involuntary, vehicular. And let's not forget self-defense. That would definitely fit his situation if it came to a trial.

Alfie packed another handful of snow into his mouth, the coldness sobering, freshening. More to the point, how did he feel about what he'd done to Hopper? He couldn't tell. Just like he couldn't feel his feet or his hands. Just like he knew he should be ravenous, but he wasn't. He felt nothing. Tired, sure. Unwilling to be seen. He felt that. But guilty? Sorry? Anxious? He probed his mind, examined his body's reaction to his thoughts. Nothing. Blank.

Maybe he was still in shock. But then again, he rarely felt the things he knew people expected him to feel. And when he did feel them, he felt them so strongly the emotions nearly destroyed him.

He stumbled, his foot snagging on a nest of roots, and fell, scraping his palms. It was dark now, much too dark to keep walking through the woods. He could still see the road about forty feet to his right, and he made for it, stepping carefully over the brush and rocks and vines.

It was amazing how easy walking on the road was once he stepped on it. Nothing blocking his way, the surface smooth and even. He straightened, lifted his face to the sky. The moon had risen, full and warmly yellow, like a bowl of French-vanilla ice cream. Alfie sat down on the tarmac and slipped off his knotted, sopping, filthy socks. They were no use anymore. He retied the plastic bags even though they were barely more than raggedy strips by now, and continued walking.

He heard a car and hesitated. Should he face it and hold up his thumb, the way he'd seen people do in movies? Should he blend in with the shadows and wait it out? He was far from home still. Hours, if his memory was accurate about how long it took to drive up this way. In the end, just before the car crested the ridge behind him, he stepped partially in its way and held up both hands.

The driver swerved around him, the man's face clearly panicked, leaning on the horn as he flew past. He kept driving down the road a bit, then slowed, stopped. Backed up. Stared at Alfie.

Alfie continued holding both hands up, as if he were at gunpoint, waited for the man to roll down his window.

"What're you doing there, son?" the man asked. He was small and gray, with a woolen cap pulled snug over a neatly rounded head. He wore a beige-plaid scarf and a blue puffy coat.

"Sir, I'm lost," said Alfie. He'd try to stick to the truth as much as reasonable while avoiding confessing anything that might get him in trouble with the police.

The man leaned further out of his window and peered to the left of Alfie. Then to the right.

"Are you alone?" he asked.

"Yes, sir."

The man looked down. "Well, what in the world happened to your shoes?" he asked.

"They got caught in a snowdrift," Alfie answered after a moment's hesitation. He'd have to lie after all. He must. "I got lost," he said again. "I was with my troop and I got separated."

The man's features relaxed. "Well come on. Get in." He sat back and closed his window, clicked the latch so Alfie knew he could get inside.

The car smelled warm and homey and indescribably delicious. Alfie strapped himself in and turned toward the amazing smell. A large pizza box rested on the back seat. The man saw him look and put the car in gear.

"Where do you live, anyway?"

"Down in Sylvan," Alfie said. His feet, next to the heat vents, began to hurt, pins and needles for now. He was aware of his own smell in this close space—smoke and sweat and something greasy.

"Where's that? Is that around here?"

Alfie shook his head. "It's down in Rockland County," he said.

The man sighed. "And where's your troop camping? I can take you to the campground."

"They went home this morning," Alfie said. "I got lost early in the morning."

The man chewed on his lip. "Well, where's your phone?"

"I left it in my tent."

This lying thing was coming easier to him than he'd thought. He wondered if it was because he was so tired. He was half dreaming, and lying is kind of like talking about a dream—an alternate reality.

The man shifted his hip and rooted around for a phone, extracted it, punched in his passcode, and handed it to Alfie. "Do me a favor, will you? Call your parents? You can come home with me and have some dinner." He gestured at the pizza. "I feel for you, but I don't want to be making that drive tonight to get you home." He glanced at Alfie. "How old are you? Fourteen or something?"

Alfie nodded, "Almost."

"Yeah, thought so. I got three. But they're all gone now, off doing their own thing."

Alfie dialed his mother's number. It rang and rang, then went to voice mail. He started to leave a message, but hung up because he felt weird talking in front of the man and also because he didn't want to say the wrong thing and on top of that he felt his stutter like an ache in his jaw, waiting to pounce. He didn't know anybody else's numbers by heart, so he handed the phone back to the man.

"No answer, huh?" The man made a turn and went down an even darker road.

Alfie wondered briefly why his mother wasn't picking up. Was she asleep? Did she miss him at all? Suddenly he felt the alonest he'd ever been in his life, as if his body were an oversized walnut shell and his consciousness locked inside and him hurtling through space all on his own.

"Well, we'll try again from my house. The cell signal out here is terrible." He slowed and turned into a gravel driveway. "I swear sometimes they keep it this way to keep people from moving up into this area." He turned off the ignition. "You know, to keep the population down."

Alfie wasn't sure who the man was talking about and even less sure of his logic, but this was how he felt around most people, so he was almost comfortable. In fact, the talks with Owen, and the clarity of them, the way his words had resonated with Alfie, were the unusual ones. As he followed the little man into his tidy house, he reflected that in his life he'd met three people whose conversations did not confound him—his mother, his father, and Owen Hopper.

The man busied himself turning on lights, getting paper plates off a counter and onto an old, wooden kitchen table. He placed the pizza box on the table and looked uncomfortably at Alfie.

"You want to try calling your mom or dad again or something?" he asked, pointed at a fuchsia cordless phone half-buried under receipts, napkins, and take-out menus.

Alfie called, got no answer, and hung up again. "She's not picking up," he whispered, and looked down, noticing to his embarrassment the mud he had tracked in with his plastic foot-bags. He leaned against a wall and unwound the plastic from his feet, sheepishly balling it up. His feet looked terrible—bruised, scratched, filthy, and bloody. He wondered how he wasn't in more pain. Then he wondered if he'd gotten frostbite after all.

"Geez," the man said, and shook his head. "Come on, why don't you take a shower and wash all that off. I think I have some of my son's clothes in a box somewhere." He brightened. "Yes, good. Shower, put on some clean clothes, eat, and then if you still can't reach your parents, I'll take you to the police station. They'll be able to notify them." He coughed, looked away. "I just can't make that long of a drive anymore." He rubbed his hip. "Sciatica." A wince, and then he poured soda into a glass, took a sip. "You'll know when you get old."

Alfie followed the man to a narrow bathroom, hot-pink plush toilet seat cover and bathmats, black-and-white zebra-printed towels.

"My ex." The man shrugged. "She was really into pink." He laughed a short, uncomfortable laugh and closed the door.

The shower hurt. Whereas as long as his feet had been half-frozen and glued shut with mud and plastic, he'd barely felt the lacerations, now the skin softened and opened, the cruel cuts stinging. He climbed out of the tub to find a pair of old jeans, too short and loose in the waist, a gray sweatshirt with a purple falcon on it and the number *00*. Socks. Glorious, thick, calf-length, white gym socks. He opened one drawer after another until he found Band-Aids and did his best to tape his oozing skin back together. Then he folded his ruined clothes and opened the door.

He ate the pizza (just the one slice, unsure if it would be polite to ask for more, so he didn't) and drank the soda, and all the while the man told him about the town, and the men who ran it, and their backroom deals with the governor, who, the man said, wanted to keep this tiny town tiny and refused to add public transportation or extra garbage pickup days or even a stoplight at that intersection at the top of the mountain where three car crashes had killed nine people in as many years.

After he crumpled and threw away the paper plates and napkins, the man laughed his nervous little laugh and said, "Well, I guess I'll take you to the police station now. They'll get you home." He chewed his lower lip. "All I found were these dress shoes, though. Bobby took all his shoes with him, and I don't think I have anything else that will fit you." He pointed to a dusty and cracked pair of brown loafers that looked like they'd been in the back of a closet since before Alfie was born. Maybe before his parents were born. But they were shoes! With real soles!

Alfie shook his head. "That's okay, sir. I'm grateful for everything. My mom will return your things to you if you give me your address."

The man gave him a funny look as he ushered him back outside and into his now considerably colder car, where the lingering pizza smell had turned stale and garlicky. He packed Alfie's filthy clothes into a plastic bag and Alfie hugged the bag on his lap. The shoes were too big, and he had to shuffle to keep them from falling off, but he guessed that was better than too small, considering that the white socks were already turning brown with seeping blood.

He thought again about those sirens he'd heard earlier. Had they really been going to Hopper's house? He couldn't be sure. And if they were, and Hopper was alive and in some hospital (Alfie pictured him wrapped in bandages, suppurating and bleeding), was he telling the cops about Alfie's role in the fire? Arson and attempted murder. Alfie shifted uncomfortably. He wanted to go home more than anything he ever wanted in his life, but he did not want the police knowing about him.

And why wasn't his mother answering her phone?

Halfway up the mountain they came against a barricade and pink flares quivering on the road. A state trooper bent to the driver side window and said, "You need to turn around, sir. Bad accident up ahead."

The man clicked his teeth in annoyance and did a U-turn.

"Wasn't I just telling you they needed a stoplight up there? How many people have to die before someone comes to their senses?" He grimaced in a strange mix of pity and irritation. "We'll have to go down and around and up the other side. Adds twenty minutes to the drive!" Irritation was clearly winning out.

Alfie stared through the windshield, imagining the mangled cars and bodies at the top of the murderous mountain, wishing he knew why his mother wasn't picking up her phone.

They pulled into the small police station's parking lot around nine PM. Alfie climbed out of the car, reluctant, feet hurting, and stood leaning on the car door, watching the station's windows. He did not want to go in.

"Go on," said the man. "Go. They'll get you home. Go on." He had the falsely jovial, high-pitched voice people use to persuade little children or pets to do something. Alfie heard the frustration behind the words. The man was tired. The man wanted rid of him. The man had done a lot for him and didn't feel Alfie was his responsibility any longer. And of course he was right.

Alfie closed the car door and limped slowly toward the station. A few paces in, he turned back and said, "Thank you, sir. Thank you for helping me."

The man, relieved now, happy he could go home, smiled and waved and got into his car. Alfie took a few more steps toward the station and waved at the man. He waited until the man backed out of the parking spot, turned around, and drove away. He counted to one hundred.

Then he shuffled toward the road, looked at the night sky, found the Big Dipper, then the Little Dipper, then Polaris, and thus situating himself, began walking south.

Twenty minutes later, a trucker picked him up and agreed to drive him halfway toward Sylvan. During the hour-long drive, the trucker offered to suck Alfie's cock. When Alfie politely demurred, the trucker paradoxically relaxed and spent the rest of the time telling him about his nearly bald wife, who, he said, wouldn't give him the time of day, and his three children, who he was convinced were not his, and never once asked why Alfie was hitchhiking down a dark mountain road at night, in winter, without a coat or hat or gloves.

The trucker let Alfie out on Route 84 near Newburgh. It was now nearly eleven, and Alfie wondered if he'd have to spend the night under a bush by the side of the road. He decided to keep walking south on Route 9W, his thumb up, and around midnight a car full of teenagers pulled up.

They were coming from a rock show up by Poughkeepsie and they all stank of skunky weed, cigarettes, stale beer, and fruity cologne. They found his loafered, jacketless state hilarious. By then he was too tired to answer any questions save where he was going, and they, cheerful and pumped on the stimulation of the show, invited him in, enveloping him in their jokey, stinky exuberance. They were going to New Jersey, but Sylvan was on the way, or enough so, and they let him out five miles from home.

During the drive with them, Alfie marveled at the ease with which they laughed at and teased each other, at the names they called each other without taking offense, even for a second. As spent as his mind was, he still paid attention and cataloged the conversation and the wisecracks. He'd analyze them later.

The walk homeward was surreal. If he felt isolated before, lonely, unmoored, now he hobbled along the familiar road like a zombie, lurching and swaying, favoring first one foot, then the other. There is no quiet like the quiet of a country road in the dead of a winter night. No dogs bothered to bark at his passage, everyone and everything snug inside the dark houses, asleep under thick blankets. Even the deer who ventured into the backyards for the scant greenery they offered this time of year were absent.

He rounded the corner of his street two hours later, the familiar curve of the road soothing, welcoming. Slowly, his feet so sore he could barely put any weight on either, he staggered toward his driveway.

A car waited there.

Not his mother's car.

CHAPTER

50

L ANEY WATCHED THE policemen and the fire chief walk through the building, writing notes, taking pictures. She wanted to ask if they suspected arson but hesitated. In any case, if Alfie had started the fire, it was in self-defense. It must have been.

Once she pulled out of the driveway and away from the house's dead zone, she saw Ed had called numerous times.

"Are you sure it's Alfie's jacket?" he asked when she called him back.

"Yes," she said. "Absolutely."

"And whose house is it again?"

"A woman named Jane Hopper. I know she's related to Owen Hopper, but I don't know how yet."

"Did you know her?"

"No. No, of course not."

Silence.

"How did you know to go there?"

She sighed. "Accurint, CLEAR, FINDER. I still have contacts with access to the databases." No need to say the contacts weren't the ones doing the detective work.

More silence. "Okay. What else did you find out?"

She chewed her lip. "I missed him, Ed. By hours."

"I know," he said, his voice softer, less cop, more friend. "But he's alive. The sergeant I just spoke with said there's no sign of blood or violence. I mean, a lot would have been destroyed in the fire, but they're pretty sure nobody was killed in the house."

She stared at her phone in disbelief. "Wow, Ed. That's some bedside manner you got. I'm glad the sergeant is kinda, pretty, sorta sure my son wasn't murdered by a convicted felon in a secluded house in the woods."

"Laney, I'm coming up there now. We'll go through the whole place, and if there's anything their cops missed, we'll pick up on it."

"Okay, Ed." She hung up. Opened the glove compartment and dug around until she found the ancient granola bar she suspected was still hiding in the back. She had a habit of keeping a couple of them for Alfie at all times, since he was always starving lately. Choked it down. She had a long drive ahead of her, and no friend with whom to share the loneliness. She needed the calories to stay lucid.

She made the turn toward the rural route that would take her home. She was plumb out of ideas. She had been able to figure out where Owen Hopper had gone. She had been able to predict he had Alfie with him. But she was too slow. She'd arrived too late.

Her son was still missing. The vengeful murderer who'd kidnapped him was still roaming the world. Her best friend was in a hospital with a broken ankle and possibly broken jaw. And there was no way around this realization—everything that happened was her fault.

She rolled down one window for the cold air and sat up tall. There were more names on that spreadsheet of hers. There were more places where Owen Hopper could have gone. Hopper was not stupid. But his world was narrowing. She'd come home and she'd do more detective work, make phone calls, visit people. That's what she was good at. That's what she had always been good at—the work.

The route took her up a mountain. Her headlights, even with the high beams on, barely broke through the country dark. When

she saw the pink flares and barricade, she came to a stop, apprehension like a cold hand on the back of her neck. She pulled to
the side and checked her phone's GPS, then saw with horror she'd
lost the signal. She hadn't been listening to the GPS at all, her
mind churning through next steps, and so had not noticed when
it stopped talking to her.

She coasted back down the mountain, gripping the steering
wheel with rigid fingers. She had no idea where she was. And, as
she glanced at her dashboard with desperation, she was very low
on gas. She'd been planning to stop at the first gas station she
came across, assuming there'd be a few near the highway.

"Fuck," she said. Then she hit the steering wheel. Then hit
it again. "Fuck. Fuck this fucking road, and fuck this fucking
car, and fuck you, Owen fucking Hopper, and especially, fuck the
fuck Theo, you fucking loser fuck, leaving us, you're his fucking
father, what am I supposed to do, how am I supposed to do all
this alone!"

She heaved with suppressed sobs, emotion, exhaustion, fear,
and surprise. She hadn't expected Theo to come to the surface
like that. As far as she was concerned, she'd excised him from her
mind, from her heart, from her memories. She didn't depend on
him, she didn't want anything from him.

Yet there he was. Letting her down even in her own mind. She
coughed and peered at her gas gauge. It lit up, blinking, as if it
had waited for her attention. She had no choice but to keep going
onward, since behind her the road was closed and so far she hadn't
come across any intersections.

"Help me," she said, into the dark air, into the charcoal shadows. "Help me." If there were no people who could help, no one
she could call on, then she would ask the universe. And if the
universe was uncaring, then maybe there were forces within it she
could turn toward herself simply through the strength of her need.
"Help me."

CHAPTER

51

OWEN HOPPER'S CAR.

Alfie backed away, his breath coming quick now, loud; he couldn't get enough air inside, and the dark world around him spun. He tried to run, but his feet had their own knowledge, and they knew home, they wanted home, and they refused to carry him away from it.

He stumbled and grabbed onto the trunk of the old maple in his front yard.

If Hopper's car was in the driveway and his mother's car wasn't, where the hell was his mother?

He looked around, as if she might have gone visiting one of the neighbors and maybe had decided to park in another drive-way. He shut his eyes and waited for the world to stop spinning. Waited for his breath to normalize.

Was Hopper inside? A part of Alfie relaxed. If Hopper was in good enough shape to drive all the way here, then Alfie hadn't killed him. This was a good thing. Wasn't it? He tried to decipher whether he felt relief because this meant he couldn't go to jail for murder or because he was not a murderer. Thou shalt not and so on.

But all he could grab hold of was a feeling of reprieve. He didn't want to go to jail, and he didn't want to be a murderer.

What he wanted was to deal with whatever was in the house before his mother came home. Did Hopper come for him or for his mother? Either way, it was his problem now, even if his mother had put Hopper away in the first place. It had been his problem for months already. He just hadn't recognized it.

Alfie pushed away, released the tree trunk.

He took an unsteady step toward his house, then another. He crept, out of debility rather than by intent, toward the back door and turned the knob. It opened easily into the dark hall, three steps leading up into the silent kitchen.

Alfie entered his home. He had to use his hands to pull himself up the stairs, then leaned on the counter, the sink, the counter again, the fridge, the wall, and this way dragged himself into the hall and the living room beyond. The smell, faint when he was still in the kitchen, was stronger here—a mix of woodsmoke, blood, urine, alcohol—vile and frightening.

Owen's form was an absence of light, a black outline of a person against the tan couch. He was sitting, awake, alert—Alfie knew this by the angle of the man's neck, his tense, still shoulders, the faint, oh so faint, breath wheezing out of his burnt throat.

"You win," said Hopper, as if they had only stopped their discussion seconds ago, not hours. "You walking through this door proves my plan is the correct one. You are the one who needs to die. Not her." He stood. "Whichever one of you had walked through the door would have gotten it."

Hopper raised his arm, the gun catching a keen spark of moonlight from the window. "I wanted a different death for you." He took a step toward Alfie, gun pointing at the boy's chest. "But this will do the job."

Alfie had frozen in place. Whether it was the sleep deprivation, the exposure to extreme cold, or his swollen, bleeding feet, he couldn't move. He felt this was the only thing that could happen—him standing in place and this man shooting the heart out of him. And when Hopper pulled the trigger and the gun clicked, Alfie still didn't move, the sound and its meaning taking long, long seconds to reach his poorly firing synapses.

Hopper pulled again, and the gun fired this time, and Alfie fell to his knees. He fell because he thought he should—there had been a shot and the shot had been meant for him. Obligingly, exhaustedly, he dropped to all fours, then lay down on the rug. He liked this rug—it was soft and red, with intricate, small geometries that had kept him busy during long summer afternoons of nothing to do and nowhere to go.

He wondered if he was dying and decided it wasn't as scary as he imagined it might be.

Hopper knelt over him, his face veiled with shadow.

Alfie raised his hand automatically, a feeble protest, brushing and then snagging against an object sticking out of Hopper's pocket. What was it? It seemed significant. And familiar.

"What are you feeling?" Hopper asked, his voice a combination of solicitous and curious.

Alfie pulled the object out of the pocket, remembering now, and cupped it inside his hand. He thought about Hopper's question.

"I'm tired," he answered, the truth always being easier than a lie.

Hopper sat down next to him, cross-legged. "I'll stay with you until you die," he said. "I'll do that for you. Nobody did that for Otto, but I'll do that for you."

The object in Alfie's hand yanked him to a sharper consciousness, and to an understanding. "Do you miss Otto?" he asked. He made his voice slow, weak. He was operating on a plane both surreal and hyperreal.

"I miss him," Hopper said. "Like my heart was cut out and filled with dirt. Like that."

Alfie raised himself to a sitting position and stabbed the hypodermic needle into Hopper's neck, depressing the plunger with all of his remaining strength.

The man reared back, fell, and stumbled to his feet. Silently he ripped the needle out of his flesh, and even in the dark, Alfie saw a spray of blood follow the needle's progress, like a loosened spigot. Hopper kicked him in the legs, in his rump, his thighs, his legs again, then fell, overturning the lamp, its bulb crashing and shattering.

Alfie crawled away from him, pulled himself into the hallway and into the kitchen. He could hear sounds coming from Hopper—wet, gurgly, gaspy, choky sounds—and he crept under the kitchen table, curled around a table leg, and pressed his hands over his ears. He didn't notice blood pooling under him. He didn't feel any pain. All he wanted was sleep, and, astonishingly, within minutes, sleep was what he got.

CHAPTER

52

WHETHER DESPITE AN indifferent universe or because of helpful forces that aid lost mothers in need, Laney did eventually coast toward a gas station, its blue and red lights rippling in the night like a mirage at first, then solidifying into bright reality.

She filled the tank, bought candy bars and cans of soda, a stale, cellophaned cream-cheese bagel, a map. Apparently she was only twenty minutes from the route that would detour her around the accident (terrible, the clerk said, three-car pileup, two people dead, two alive, one alive but missing a leg) and deliver her to the highway. From there, an hour and a half and she'd be home. Her phone, after a restart, finally got a signal and showed two missed calls from an unknown ID followed by a call and terse message from Holly's husband.

The unknown calls panicked her, but no matter what she tried, she could get no further details. She might be able to get information on them from her carrier in the morning, or even from Ed, but until then she'd have to deal with the uncertainty.

She would shower and change, maybe lie down for an hour or two, then go see Ed, ask if he'd found anything new at the burnt house, show him the two calls. She wondered at the respite within her until she admitted it came from the conviction that Alfie had indeed started the fire and then tried to call her. And that meant he'd found a way to get on top of his situation. She had no way of knowing this for sure, of course. But it was what her soul chose to believe at that moment, and she went with it.

She drove carefully, eating her way through the bagel and the candy bars, drinking all the soda, so that by the time she turned into her street, she felt hyped-up and not a little ill.

She didn't recognize the car in her driveway, but its presence chased away whatever fogginess and stiffness still coated her mind. She got out warily, unstrapped her holster, and placed her hand on the handle of her gun.

Ice, blown down from the pines, pinpricked her face, flew into her eyes so she had to squint and hunch.

The front door was still locked, and for a second she thought maybe the car belonged to a cop, someone assigned to guard her. Except she hadn't been home in a day, so whose car was it? She decided against using her keys in the front. If someone was in the house, they'd hear the lock and she'd have no cover, her body an open target.

She went around to the back, and this time the door opened silently, swinging inward on well-oiled hinges.

Her body perceived the calamity before her mind did, adrenaline rushing to her heart, her eyes dilating, sweat breaking out on her forehead and upper lip despite the cold. She saw Alfie's feet under the kitchen table and yelped, sliding toward him, placing her hands on his legs and pulling. The blood beneath him was dark and rank, its spoiled-meat smell sending her into a frenzy of tugging and mewling because she couldn't scream, her voice box numb with horror. Finally, she hauled his bulk out from under the table and placed her hands on his face, his neck. He was alive, his pulse weak and uneven, his skin cool, clammy to the couch. But he breathed.

Her phone was dead, a quick rummage through his pockets (whose clothes were those?) failed to produce his phone, so she planted a kiss on his forehead and ran outside.

Her next-door neighbor, a young man in his twenties whose name she could never remember, answered the door in his underwear, sleep smeared and sour. A child wailed behind him, and his eyes narrowed in irritation. But he let her in and gave her his phone, and by the time she'd dialed 911 he was awake and solicitous, his baby slung over his shoulder like a towel.

The wife had ambled down the stairs as well and, hospitality being a big thing in Sylvan, offered Laney a cup of coffee.

But Laney didn't hear, had run toward her house after making the call, had nearly stopped breathing as she listened for the ambulance while the trees bowed and their branches crackled and snapped in the keening, ice-filled wind. She knelt by Alfie's side and raised his heavy head onto her lap, leaned toward his grimy ear.

"My baby," was all she could say to him. And it wasn't until Alfie's blue eyes slit open, glazed but alive, *alive*, that she heard another sound in the house.

CHAPTER

53

STILL KNEELING, HER hand on Alfie's head, she raised her eyes to the living room doorway. A gasping, raspy shuffling came from the other side, as if someone was limping or dragging themselves across the pine boards. She lowered her son carefully to the floor and pulled herself upright.

The rasping neared. A filthy, blood-stained hand gripped the doorframe, and Laney drew her gun out of her holster.

Owen Hopper coalesced out of the shadows and propped himself against the wall. His head was monstrous—red and blistered, bleeding, suppurating. One of his eyes was swelled shut, his shirt and jacket black with blood and dirt.

His good eye fixed on Laney with a triumphant malevolence, slid down to take in Alfie's fetal arrangement, then back up toward her. He had to lick his lips a few times before he could make any sound, and then he spoke. "Elaine Bird," he said.

"The police are on their way," Laney said, her arms raised, the gun pointing at Hopper's head.

"It doesn't matter," Hopper said. "Your son is dead. We're the same now. You and me. Childless. You killed mine and I killed yours. A fearful symmetry."

Where was the ambulance? It was taking ages. Her arms trembled, the gun's weight seemingly quadrupling every minute.

"What happened to you?" Laney asked.

His one eye blinked slowly. His tongue scraped along his lower lip. "You," he said. "You happened to me. You lied."

She waved at his bloody, pustuled head. "Who did that to you?"

He made a grinding noise it took her a few seconds to recognize as laughter.

"Your son," he said. "A chip off the old block." Wheeze. Rasp. Cough. "You should be proud." He coughed again and separated from the wall, spread his legs for greater balance, and leaned slightly forward. He looked as if he were on the deck of a listing ship, his knees bent to absorb the swells. He lifted his hand, and the gun he held glinted in the dim morning light.

"See?" he said. "Fearful symmetry. I kill yours, you kill mine."

She pulled her trigger.

He fell.

Someone shoved her from behind, grabbed her arms, twisted them, the gun falling from her numb fingers. Someone screamed at her to drop the gun, even though it was already skittering out of view along the floor. Someone's weight pressed her to the floor, and cold, sharp cuffs snapped over her wrists.

CHAPTER

54

ED BOSWELL SAT across from her in the hospital room, Alfie asleep between them.

Ed had brought her a sweater from her closet, a thick, green one with embroidered leaves along the edges and cuffs. He also brought a turkey sandwich, which she held on her lap, running a skinned-knuckled finger along the encasing plastic.

She was lucky—the hospital had an extra bed and had allowed her to sleep next to her son, though of course she hadn't slept, had instead spent the night watching him, helping him to the bathroom when he woke, giving him cups of water, rubbing his roughened hands.

Alfie's upper arm and both feet were bandaged. Owen's bullet had gone through his left biceps, and although he had bled and would need physical therapy, the bone had not been hit. The muscle would knit.

Frostbite on his toes was a serious concern, but the doctors thought it might be okay. The damage appeared to be superficial and would heal with time. He needed hydration and rest and warmth. His cheekbones were angular in sleep, not a child's roundness anymore, and his hair, stringy and matted, a dull dirty-blond against the blue pillow.

Ed Boswell studied the boy, pursed his lips, cocked his head, turned his steady gaze on Laney.

"Owen Hopper died this morning," he said.

Laney nodded. In ten years of being a cop and the following three years of carrying an off-duty weapon, she had fired her gun only the once (not including target practice every May to keep qualifying), when she was jumped by the chocolate heisters. And she had missed that time.

The shot she lobbed at Hopper hit him in the top left shoulder, shattering his clavicle, the bullet exiting from his shoulder blade and digging into the hallway wall behind him.

Boswell crossed his arms and sat back. "He had enough heroin coursing through his system to have produced three overdoses. It's safe to say he felt very little of his injuries." He looked back at Alfie's pale face with its blue shadows and hollows. "Interestingly enough, the overdose was apparently administered via a syringe to the neck."

Laney put the sandwich on the rolling table by the bed.

"The only reason he didn't die right away was because the heroin was injected into muscle and part of a tendon. That slowed absorption significantly and made him lucid enough to walk and talk when you arrived. Actually, we're still not sure how he managed it." He shrugged. "Hopper was a big guy with a lot of hate. Sometimes hate keeps people going." He held her stare. Repeated, "Laney, he was stabbed in the neck. By a syringe filled with heroin."

Alfie stirred and twisted in his sleep, his brows creasing with pain. Laney covered his hand with hers. He was feverish, dry skinned, but she reveled in the throb of his pulse, felt it through her fingertips.

"I'm not sorry he's dead," she said. Though she was sorry it had come to that. She was sorry about Otto and Harry. She was sorry her son had suffered and bled.

"No, I don't expect you are." Boswell stood and shrugged into his coat. "But I'll need to speak with your son. Soon."

CHAPTER

55

GARLIC AND MEAT, oil, butter, and cheese—the smells of a kitchen in high production. Laney removed a full tray of chicken parm from her oven, wrapped it in foil, and shoved a lasagna tray in to take its place. A third tray of baked macaroni and cheese (crusted with breadcrumbs, pricked with bacon) already waited on the kitchen table.

It was Sunday, and Holly had sworn to never miss another multitudinous family funday, not even during snow storms, not even with her foot in a cast.

Laney had an hour before she was to head over, so she poured two cups of coffee, added sugar and milk to both, set out two little plates with cookies. When she called Alfie to come to the kitchen, he came and sat down and ran a finger along the rim of his coffee mug.

He'd been quiet since coming home from the hospital. Not his usual shy, introverted quiet but something different. He was still thin, but his shoulders spread wider, his head no longer drooping on a lanky neck. The end of the hospital stay coincided with the beginning of the February break, and so they'd both been home, watching television, eating three or four meals a day, sleeping through the long, blustery afternoons.

He wouldn't discuss his experiences. She tried gentleness, concern, then insistence—even, once, threats. But her words darted at him and were absorbed, not so much hitting a wall as being taken in and diffused. He was still her considerate, obedient boy—he set the table (asked and unasked), kept his room neat, helped with laundry, limped to the end of the driveway with the garbage can on garbage day. He sat with her, a bowl of popcorn between them, and watched movies. But if she asked him about his time in the cabin, he simply continued doing whatever he'd been doing as if she hadn't asked, his expression as impassive as if he were alone.

The one time he did speak, little as it was, of Owen Hopper and his stay at the cabin was on the day he came home from the hospital. Ed Boswell came by, the visit strangely both a friendly stopover (he brought a fruit basket and a bag of cupcakes from the bakery) and an interrogation.

"How did you meet Owen Hopper?" Boswell asked, and Alfie answered in his new voice—a low and steady, unstuttered baritone. Alfie told of his and Jordan's meetings at Hopper's Mountain View apartment, and of the drinks and pills and videos.

"Anything else?" Boswell asked. "What did you talk about?"
Alfie shrugged.

"Did you go with Hopper voluntarily?"

Laney tensed. She hadn't asked Alfie this yet, had been afraid to. Probably needed a drink first. But there it was, and she leaned forward to hear the answer.

"Yes," Alfie said. "He offered me a ride because it was raining."

"Did you know that he would take you away?" Boswell asked.

Alfie paused. "I did not," he said. His blue eyes remained turned away from Laney. "I didn't think he would. He locked me in the basement."

Something in Boswell's posture weakened, and he looked down at his hands. "Alfie, you need to tell us what happened at that cabin."

Shrug.

"How did the house burn down?"

Shrug.

"We know you hitchhiked part of the way home. What happened to Hopper when the house burned?"

"I don't know."

"Did you think he was still in the house when you left?"

Shrug.

"What happened here, Alfie? When you got home? I need to know."

"He shot me."

"Hmm. Alfie, your fingerprints are all over the hypodermic needle."

Alfie closed his eyes. Laney couldn't tell if he was afraid, or if he didn't trust himself to explain properly. The detective's presence unnerved her as well, and she touched her son's hand lightly to show support. For the next half hour Boswell asked the same questions, different questions, calmly, forcefully. And Alfie did not answer.

Almost a week later, Laney had not gotten much closer to the truth. Or rather, the truth according to her son. She dipped a cookie into her coffee and nibbled a corner. The kitchen continued being steamy and garlicky. Her boy sat across from her and dipped his own cookie into his coffee and nibbled his cookie's corner.

And she said what she'd been thinking for this past week.

She said, "We're drawing a line. Today. I won't ask you again about it. I only ask that you take better care of your life. I see you are not a child anymore. You are your own person. Everything you did was exactly the right thing, because whatever it was brought you to this day, today. Alive. That's all that matters."

She touched his hand lightly, the way you would someone you knew from the office maybe, and pulled back.

He had started out listening with his eyes on her, calm, hooded, guarded. But at the touch his lip trembled, and he lowered his head. His chest, no longer the bony, hollow chest of a little boy, rose and fell in quick succession and he opened his mouth slightly because his nose had reddened, and he had to wipe at it with his sleeve.

They sat like that, the silence no longer cold, no longer cavernous, neither one of them touching their mugs or sweets. Garlic and tomato sauce and meat and cheese filled the steamy kitchen air. They sat until the oven beeped and the lasagna was done, and it was time to bring the trays two houses down where Holly and her outsized family were celebrating yet another Sunday on earth.

CHAPTER

56

E D CALLED HER the first week of March. Alfie was back in school, and she was home, getting ready to run a few errands (or skip them and go for a hike—the weather had warmed, grown foggy and almost balmy). She had gotten in touch with Janine about driving a school bus again, but Janine was evasive. The schedules were full. There were no openings yet.

"Laney," Ed said, "do you have time to meet for coffee?"

She hesitated. She knew her own shot was clean. Officer Ryan, the rookie, had seen Hopper point his gun at her, had seen her fire in what was clearly self-defense. Alfie's situation was more opaque. The fire in the cabin had been ruled arson, and since Alfie was a known firebug and Hopper would have had no reason to burn down his own residence, Alfie was the obvious culprit. More troublesome still was the needle to the neck.

But Alfie was only thirteen and wouldn't talk. His own injuries had been grave, arguably life threatening. He'd lost blood, almost lost one toe.

She didn't really believe either the Narrowsburg or the Sylvan police department would decide to arrest her son or pursue a criminal investigation against him, but seeing Ed Boswell was the absolute last thing she wanted. That never seemed to change.

"Today's not a good day," she said.

"Let's meet anyway," he said, in a tone she couldn't ignore.

A half hour later they sat across a table at the Majestic Diner, coffee and a bagel before each.

"I wanted to talk with you for a couple of reasons," Ed said, mixing sugar into his cup. "We're not going to pursue any charges against Alfie. Whatever he might have done, he did under extreme circumstances. He was held against his will, and a convicted felon tied to at least one murder tried to kill him."

He stirred, sipped, tore a chunk of bagel. "I wanted to tell you that."

Relief flooded her, sweet and light, and she hid it by downing half her coffee at once, scalding her mouth. "That's nice of you." She put her cup down, then chewed through a quarter of her bagel before asking, "What's the second reason?"

He sat back, his face both serious and shy. "Laney, you finding that cabin, that was good detective work. Some of the best I've seen." He stuck out his lower lip. "I'm not going to ask how you got access to the information you had."

She shook her head, but her cheeks warmed anyway.

He withdrew his wallet, flicked through it, and placed a business card on the table next to her plate.

"My family runs a private investigation business."

She looked up at him in surprise.

"I didn't want to spend my life working for my dad." His lip quirked. "But give them a call. I hear you're looking for a new job."

57

A COUPLE WEEKS after he came back, when his arm was still bandaged and sore, someone threw a half-eaten apple at his head in the cafeteria.

"Heard you killed your old boyfriend, fuckface," someone said.

"Heard you set him on fire."

A lump of something hard and sharp (a rock, selected from the school's driveway) wrapped in napkins hit him in the temple.

"Let me hear you squeal!" someone else said, and others laughed.

When Alfie looked around, he saw two girls smirking and filming the entire episode while a group of boys, juniors by the looks of them, snorted into their fists.

He remembered a story Owen Hopper told him one snowy afternoon in his Mountain View apartment, Jordan half dozing on the couch and cans of Bud on the floor by their feet.

Guys like throwing their dicks around, Owen had said. If you don't want one of those dicks to smack you in the face, you gotta throw some hot oil on it. Alfie always appreciated Hopper's way with metaphors. Once, Owen said, I had this big dude, like seven feet, three hundred fifty pounds, he was threatening me, see? Telling me he was going to beat me up, whatever. Now, no way can I take him in a fair fight. Not in an unfair one either. So I come up to him, real calm. And I look him in the eye. And I don't blink. Remember that. When you don't blink, you look crazy. Think Charles Manson. So I don't blink, and I say to him, you can kick my ass, sure. But one day, and you won't know when, and you won't know how, I'm going to cut your eyes out of your head. It's a promise. And then I counted to ten, and I *still* didn't blink. And you know what? The fucker walked away. Never bothered me again.

Alfie calculated his chances of getting away with doing just this to the fruit-and-rock-throwers. It was a quick calculation and involved weighing the probabilities of being reported to a counselor or the principal, being beaten to a pulp on the way home from school, and stuttering at the crucial moment in the speech, thus becoming even more of a laughingstock. In the end it was the girls with their phones who decided him. If he played this right, he'd be on video. And his reputation as someone you don't fuck with would be cemented. He didn't mind if everyone thought him crazy. They did so already. He just wanted them to leave him alone.

What was weird though, as he rose to his feet and hobbled to the table of his chortling, guffawing tormentors, he didn't feel himself. Owen Hopper's wiry, rangy ghost walked with him, and when he spoke, it was Hopper's Brooklyn cadence that came through.

The maneuver worked better than he might have hoped. Although the boys at the table whooped with glee when he finished, there was a panicked unease in their eyes, and one of the girls put her phone down, her face reddening furiously.

The video took about two hours to reach everyone who was anyone in the school hierarchy. After that, all he had to do was stare at someone without blinking to get them out of his way, and somehow, in a matter of weeks, they let him be.

Another unexpected but welcome side effect of having his feet so damaged and his arm in a sling was being excused from gym.

He could skip the boring team sports and the pointless racing around a stuffy court for the rest of the year. Instead, a young gym teacher-in-training with the unfortunate name of Mr. Flake had volunteered to work with Alfie on strengthening his upper body. Every day during eighth period, they met in the weights room, and Mr. Flake showed him how to use the machines, the dumb-bells, the benches. He started with the tiny one-pound weights, pink (of course they would be pink), and at first even those felt impossible to his mangled muscles.

But he improved. By the end of March, he had full range of motion in his hurt arm, and by the end of April he could do biceps curls with ten-pound dumbbells and squats with fifteen-pound kettle balls, lifting them over his head as he straightened.

He grew and lengthened, his shoulders widening. When he walked the hallways now, he kept his spine in the neutral position—pelvis, rib cage, and skull aligned—as Mr. Flake taught him, and his chin parallel to the ground. He started hanging out with Jordan again, tentatively at first, then with greater ease after Jordan asked him if he held him responsible for being kidnapped and Alfie said no, of course not, that's crazy.

His circle of friends expanded. He realized he'd always approached friendships from the wrong end, thinking he was the one who needed to be witty and clever, who needed to come up with ideas for things to do. In reality, all he had to do was stay quiet and look people in the eye. They would then carry the conversation along on wings or waves or gusts of words, depending on their personalities. He found comfort in their chatter and their presence.

Once in a while, when confronted with a new or unpleasant or confusing situation, he'd have the oddest thought. He'd think, what would Owen do? And then his would-be murderer's ghost might whisper in his ear or move his hand or work his tongue and mouth and speak for him.

He sometimes dreamed of Owen Hopper, but the dreams had nothing of the Mountain View townhouse or dank wood cabin in them. He dreamed they walked on a beach, hot sand beneath their bare feet, the smells of ocean and sunblock caressing their faces. Owen told him stories, outlandish stories, of all the places he traveled—England and Holland, Thailand, China, Iceland, and once Siberia with his wife, because that's where she was from. He told of how her family lived in a house with no running water, but they had a beautiful porcelain toilet propped over a hole in the floor, and how he once met a pirate through the pirate's girl-friend who worked the drawbridge in a tiny Florida town. In these dreams Owen called him Otto and Alfie thought nothing wrong with it.

On his fourteenth birthday, his mother bought him his own saxophone. His old rented one was gone irretrievably, stolen or lost when Owen's car had been taken as evidence. Next to the sax's solid black case, she placed a card, postmarked New Mexico.

"Your father sent you a card," she said.

He didn't realize he expected the signature inside to read *Owen* until he saw his dad's graceful script, and the sight of it was a gut punch, shocking and raw after all these years.

Alfie folded the card back into its envelope, and when his mother turned toward the cake, he threw it into the trash under the sink. He hadn't cried at all since what he and his mother had started calling "the incident"—not when the doctors told him he might lose toes, not when the pain kept him from sleeping, not even when Ed Boswell questioned him and he thought he might be going to prison.

But now he pressed his hand against his eyes and sobbed. And once he started sobbing, he couldn't stop, the tears pouring through his fingers, the ache in his throat and chest inescapable, obliterating, and in the end, purifying.

CHAPTER

58

ON THE FIRST hot day in June, Laney Bird dressed in a maid's smock, pinned a name tag onto her lapel, grabbed her handbag, and settled behind the wheel of her car. The name tag read *Magda*. The handbag contained a subpoena, and the man about to get served was sequestered in a Catskills motel.

She squinted into the bright sky, letting the sun warm her cheeks. Everything was in bloom—the untrimmed dog roses by her driveway, the azaleas flanking every door, columbines at the side of the road. She rolled down her windows, set the radio to the classic-rock station.

At the intersection where she should have turned left, she turned right instead, because it was only noon, and the day glowed with such a pretty light.

And she had to see Alfie. Only just see him. From afar. She'd developed this habit recently and she couldn't seem to break it. He had no clue she drove past the school every day, either during lunch or when he sat by the track when his gym class ran. She knew how to observe without being seen. Sometimes she used her phone in lieu of binoculars, pointing it at his slight frame and zooming in.

Was it really such unhinged behavior? She didn't think so. Not really. Anyway, not too unhinged.

She parked under an ancient oak and turned her attention toward the picnic tables and benches nestled within the school's glossy lawn.

Alfie perched on one of the benches in a group of four, listening to something another boy was saying. Propping his saxophone on his knee, he punctuated the boy's story with what appeared to be humorously timed honks.

Five minutes later she put her car in gear and rolled away, toward the highway and the motel and the business exec who would most certainly open his door to a maid in about an hour.

The detective agency for which she now worked was hosting a birthday party at a pub tonight, cake and drinks for one of the long-timers. She wouldn't stay long, but she was looking forward to it.

As she accelerated, she turned up the volume and made herself think of nothing but balmy heat, music, and the vivid green world spinning out behind her.

ACKNOWLEDGMENTS

THIS BOOK WOULD not exist were it not for Keith Allison, who had spent many years entertaining me with his undercover junkie stories, and then patiently answered my questions when I demanded details. Once I began writing this novel, he explained racketeering, buy and busts, and everything from the technical aspects of wiring and ghosting, to the more psychological facets of detective work. Thank you for believing in me before there was anything to believe in.

My deepest gratitude to my agent, Paula Munier, who is a guardian angel and is the best agent an author could want. Thank you for always knowing the right thing to say. Thank you to Terri Bischoff for taking a chance on a debut in the midst of a pandemic lockdown and to Matt Martz and Crooked Lane Books for saying yes. Thank you, Melissa Rechter for shepherding me through the publishing process with cheer and good will, and to Madeline Rathle for your professionalism and knowledge.

Thank you, Emily Beth Rapoport for such a sensitive and in-depth edit. Your suggestions made this story a much stronger one. Thank you, Kara Klontz for a perfectly sinister cover.

Writing might be a solitary occupation, but the writing universe is a warm and helpful place and I would have been lost without the sage and practical advice doled out by bloggers. Specifically, a huge thank you to Jillian Boehme, whose Authoress blog was a priceless source of wisdom and support. Thank you to Janet Reid and her Reiders who have enlightened me more than any other community on how to navigate the publishing waters.

An enormous thank you to Ben LeRoy, who somehow steadfastly supported this book when it was only one hundred pages old and who also happens to be a great human being. His comments and encouragement guided me to the finish line.

Huge thank you to the insightful and intelligent authors who took the time to read my early drafts: Nancy Bilyeau, Amy Creelman Purcell, Frimet Goldberger, Deb Rhodes, and Helen Custer.

River River Writers Circle at the Patisserie Didier Dumas was a place of magic, where Donna Miele and A. Anupama dispensed acceptance and cheer, and where I managed to write scene after scene despite noise, rain, snow, or a long day.

When I decided to become serious about writing, I took classes, and I must thank Russell Rowland who, after gently showing me I had no idea how to tag dialog, proceeded to teach me how to write a perfect sentence and then build to a perfect scene. Jordan Rosenfeld taught me to look deeper, read wider, and add tension.

Being a parent is the wildest adventure. Thank you to Ian, who is nothing like Alfie, except for his love of music and his great heart and his ability to accept everyone exactly as they are.